A GIRL CALLED ALABAMA

When Christmas plans go awry—Believe!

KAY CHANDLER
A multi-award-winning author

Cover Design by Chase Chandler

DEDICATION

A GIRL CALLED ALABAMA is dedicated to Enterprise Historian, *Dieon Patton*, owner of *CreativeXpression*, who graciously shared his amazing photos and a ton of fascinating information about his beloved hometown, Enterprise, Alabama. I have deep Enterprise roots and have always found it intriguing that the town chose to dedicate a monument to a pesky insect. It was fun to set this 1949 novel in a place with such an enchanting past.

A big thank you also goes out to The Pea River Historical & Genealogical Society who invited me to participate in an Author Signing Party to commemorate the 100th year celebration of the famous Boll Weevil monument, unaware that my soon-to-be-released novel was set in Enterprise. Amazing how God orchestrates things.

However, keep in mind this is a work of fiction, so don't ask about the lovely home at 4014 W. Lee Street . . . or the beautiful girl who once lived there. We'll pretend it all happened exactly the way it is written.

PROLOGUE

Hello. My name is Jericho. Jericho Johnson . . . uh. . . Rhoades. I Suwannee, I've had so many last names it's sometimes hard to remember who I really am.

I think it was about first grade that I became Jericho Brown. Mama gave birth to the twins, Myrtis and Mavis while Mr. Brown was living with us. He drank a lot but he was alright—as far as drunks go—and he didn't go far. My most vivid memory of Mr. Brown is of him sprawled out on the doorsteps, drunk as a coot.

Can't rightly remember if he was supposed to be coming or going. At least he didn't beat me the way that sorry ol' so-and-so, Butch Carpenter did, after he booted out Mr. Brown and moved in.

Mama told me my name was Jericho Carpenter and Butch was my real Pa. Not something I wanted to hear. Butch made me quit school to work in the fields. He was a runt of a man and I lost count of how long he stayed but I ain't never forgot why he left. I might've been thirteen, maybe fourteen, but I was big for my age and the last time he drew back that strap, I jerked it out of his hand and whooped the daylights out of him. Mama cried for weeks and never did forgive me for running him off.

Shortly after he left, Gus Johnson took up residence and things got better. Much better. Finally, I had a name I weren't 'shamed of. Besides, Jericho Johnson had a nice ring to it. Just before harvesting season, Mama had another young'un. But it didn't take long for Gus to find out Mama was seeing Butch on the sly. I had some bad days growing up but I reckon the saddest day in my life was the day I came in from the cotton field and saw Gus walking out the door with a packed bag and his baby, little Shug, under his arm. He put his bag on the floor and holding little Shug with one arm, he wrapped the other arm around me. I said, "Take me with you, Gus. I can't live here no longer."

Well, whether it was an excuse or the truth I won't never know, but it was clear as day he weren't gonna let me go with him. He said, "Son, if I was you, I'd think of joining the Navy. You take care of Uncle Sam and he'll take care of you."

The Navy? Me? But I never got through third grade. As soon as I could pick cotton, hold a plow or stay with the young'uns while mama cavorted, I was more useful at home. But the more I thought about it, the better it sounded. I couldn't read nor write worth a flip but I could sign my name, and before the sun went down, I was on my way to see the world. It wasn't until I signed up for the Navy and had to have my birth certificate that I discovered I was the offspring of a fellow by the name of Arthur Rhoades. I never heard Mama speak that name, but from her track record I can't help but believe he must've been a dirty rotten scoundrel and she felt I was better off not knowing.

I loved the Navy. Even after the accident in the Engine Room that landed two of us in the Naval Hospital, I never regretted my decision. Not even when Seaman 2nd Class Octavius J. Rockwell III blamed it on me, when he was the one who caused the whole thing. I had third degree burns across my chest and that's where Jericho Rhoades' story begins. Yeah. Jericho Rhoades, Navy fireman, 3rd class. That's me.

CHAPTER 1

Friday, September 23, 1949

Jericho Rhoades cringed with pain as the nurse tended the burns on his chest, but there was an even deeper hurt that went clear to the bone, piercing his fractured heart. It had to do with a girl called Alabama—a girl he'd never met, yet he'd know her anywhere.

The worse thing about being in the Naval Hospital was being in a cot next to Navy Seaman Octavius J. Rockwell III and forced to listen to his lying, foul mouth as he bragged about his exploits with women—some true, some nothing more than an overactive imagination.

Octavius reached over and grabbed the R.N. by her upper arm as she strode by his bed. Though Maggie pretended to be annoyed, it was plain to see she enjoyed the attention, the way she giggled and blushed.

"Turn me loose, Romeo. I'm your nurse, not your girlfriend."

"Aww, beautiful, you know you're the only one for me."

Jericho could only surmise it was the first time any male had ever called her beautiful since she was about the homeliest female he'd ever laid eyes on. For a fact, Maggie was as sweet as a Georgia peach—but about as unattractive as a poorly constructed outhouse.

She prized his fingers from her arm. "You crazy sailor, I said let go."

Octavius looked up into her eyes and whined like a sick puppy. "I'm feeling a little feverish. Maybe you should check my temperature." Feigning a series of deep-throated coughs, he said, "Can't you see I need your tender loving care?"

When she slapped at his hand, he reached down and jerked on her crisp, white skirt. "Come on doll face." He opened his mouth and stuck out his tongue. "Bend down and look in my throat. I feel like I'm coming down with something."

"Octavius Rockwell, the only thing you're coming down with is a case of enormous ego. There's nothing wrong with you other than the burns on your hands and they're healing just fine, so you can stop the pretense."

He started another coughing spell with even more intensity than the last, causing the nurse to giggle. "Stop it, Octavius."

"Can't help it. It's stifling in here. We've gotta have some air in this place. Why don't you bring me a cold one, then sit on the side of my bed and fan me, before I die from the heat?"

Maggie snickered. "I declare, you won't do, Octavius. You know perfectly well the only 'cold one' you'll get while you're here is in the water pitcher beside your bed."

She'd no sooner left the room before Octavius was bragging about how he'd have her wrapped around his little finger before he was discharged, and Jericho didn't doubt that he would. How a fellow could take advantage of someone as nice as Maggie was beyond his imagination.

A flattened voice drawled, "Octavius, you're pathetic." It was the first time Jericho had ever heard the kid say a word, other than to grunt a "yes sir" or "no sir" in answer to the doctor's or Maggie's questions. Thomas was a skinny twenty-one-year-old and none of the patients seemed to know why he was in the hospital and it was clear he had no plans to tell them.

Octavius's brow furrowed as he glared at the pale-faced sailor with hollow jaws. "You talking to me, bones?"

An awkward silence filled the room. Thomas picked up his book and continued to read as if he hadn't heard a word.

Octavius shot back. "I'll tell you who's pathetic, sailor. You're pathetic. You think we don't hear you squalling over there in the middle of the night? Poor baby wants his mama. Is that it? You miss your mama? If you were half a man, you'd be trying to woo our ugly ol' nurse. She's about your speed."

It was evident the kid wasn't going to stand up for himself. Octavius's boorish laughter caused the hairs on the back of Jericho's neck to bristle. Though he'd always been a man of few words, he felt he'd explode if he couldn't say what he'd longed to say to Octavius since the day of the accident in the Engine room. *Accident?* It was nothing more than stupid negligence on Octavius's part. Yet, he lied about how it happened, while pinning the blame on Jericho.

Perhaps it was hearing Octavius say those cruel things to Thomas that gave Jericho the nerve to finally speak up, or maybe it was hearing him poke fun at Maggie. For whatever reason, he couldn't keep it inside one minute longer. "Octavius, I agree with Thomas. You *are* pathetic."

Jericho braced for an explosive angry response, but Octavius just stared him down and smiled.

"Yeah? Pathetic, am I? You aren't just a little bit jealous, are you Buddy boy?" Jericho couldn't remember how he wound up with the nickname or who first called him Buddy, but it stuck.

As peculiar as it was, Octavius seemed to have taken a liking to Jericho from the beginning, for reasons unknown to anyone but Octavius.

Jericho's conscience wouldn't allow him to keep quiet any longer and the bottled-up words spilled out. "Octavius, I'll admit I ain't never had the women swarm around me like they do to you, but if I did, there ain't no way I could treat them in such a wicked way." His heart pounded. Now that he'd begun, he might as well finish. "Man, don't you ever feel bad, lying to girls the way you do? Making 'em think you're sweet on them, then turning around and poking fun behind their back because they believe you? That's just wrong. It's evil."

He laughed. Laughed like a hyena. Obnoxiously loud. "Jericho, admit it. You're jealous, but you really don't have to be. You're not a bad looking fellow but I'll tell you why you can't get a girl. You sound like a hick. Drop the hayseed lingo and see if you don't have women swarming all over you. Good granny, how did you ever get through school talking the way you do. No wonder they call you Country Rhoades."

"I ain't never had nobody calling me that but you, but I ain't ashamed of being country and I ain't ashamed of being a Rhoades." He shifted in the bed and sat straight up. Maybe if he knew the fellow who sired him, he wouldn't be able to make such a bold statement, but he figured the less he knew about the rascal, the better off he'd be.

Jericho could've admitted he didn't get through school, but he was pretty sure Octavious had already figured it out. He couldn't deny that for a split second—maybe even a little longer—he wondered if Octavius could be right about what he said—the part about having women swarm over him if he had more learning. But he didn't want a swarm. He longed to have just one to say the romantic things to him that a sweet young woman named Juliette

Jinright said in her letters to Octavius. Letters that Octavius poked fun at and read aloud in the Ward. Letters that made the other guys laugh. Not Jericho. The lump in his throat grew each time Octavius read the latest.

Juliette was just *one* of at least a half-dozen girls in three different states that Octavius found in the Pen Pal Section of the newspaper. He promised them all that as soon as he got out of the hospital, he'd be looking them up. Made out like each one was the one and only and even hinted at marriage to three who appeared to take the bait.

Jericho felt sorry for Mary Alice and Josie although he suspected they could possibly be playing Octavius just as he was playing them. But it was more than pity he felt for Juliette. She was the kind of girl that could make a fellow want to go home to. The kind of girl any man would feel privileged to marry. Well, any guy but a lying scoundrel like Octavius Rockwell.

"Octavius, do you really plan to go see all three of 'em when you get out of the hospital?"

"Jericho, if that's a serious question, then you're as big a sucker as they are. How could I possibly go to Tennessee, Pennsylvania and Alabama when I'm released from the hospital? I'll be back to riding the waves after I leave the infirmary. I won't have time to write all these letters once I'm out of here. You lucky stiff, your stint will be finished by the time you get out of this place and you can go home." Octavius clenched his teeth, causing

13

his temples to pulse. "I hate the Navy and can't wait to shed these bell bottoms. You don't seem to mind it. I wish we could switch places."

Home? It had a nice ring to it, alright. If only he had a real home to go back to. True, Jericho would be leaving the hospital in a couple of days, but he had no idea where he'd go. He hadn't heard from his Mama since enlisting and he had no desire to meet her latest live-in. Naturally, Octavius had no idea what he was saying, or he wouldn't be talking about wanting to switch places.

The thought of switching places made Jericho smile. Octavius's dad owned a successful steel mill and Octavius was forever talking about all the servants they had. Shucks, they had a different person for everything. There was a man who tended the garden, a woman who washed clothes, one who cooked and one who cleaned the house. They even had lights, running water and an inside toilet. Jericho loved listening to him tell about a kind of life he never knew existed.

Octavius's folks sent him to a couple of expensive colleges but when he flunked out of both, his daddy made him join the Navy—claimed it'd help him grow up. That hadn't worked for him so far, and Jericho couldn't see how ten more months was gonna be near 'bout enough time for that to happen.

A nurse's aide came into the room holding a stack of mail. Robert, a married fellow who'd lost a leg, reached up, confident one of those letters belonged to him. His wife wrote every day and sometimes he received three or four letters at the time. The aide thumbed through the stack. "Robert, I declare, I think you get more mail than anyone who has ever been in this hospital."

Octavius piped up. "What about me? I get more letters than he does."

"I meant real letters . . . you know . . . from home. Yours are from pen pals."

Though it didn't seem to register with Octavius, who was already tearing into an envelope, Jericho concluded she was right. Getting letters from half-a-dozen pen pals wasn't nearly as important as getting letters from the one person who really cared whether you were gonna live or die.

The fellows in the ward looked forward to what had become their daily dose of entertainment. Octavius would read each romantic letter and then poke fun at the gullible women for believing his lies.

"Hey fellows, you ready for this? It's from a dame who calls herself, Pennsylvania Party Girl." She writes, *"My darling Buddy, It's with eager anticipation I wait for each letter from you— I'm marking off the days on my calendar until you're in my arms."*

Jericho pushed up in the bed. "Wait just a cotton-picking minute. She called you Buddy."

"So? That's how I sign all my letters."

One of the new fellows in the ward yelled, "What difference does it make what he calls himself? Let him finish."

"Well, I don't appreciate him using my name."

Octavius laughed as if that were the funniest thing he'd ever heard. "*Your* name? Your name is Jericho, just like mine is Octavius. You have no claim to such a common nickname. I wager if I should stand on the deck and yell 'Buddy,' a half-dozen or more swabbies would come running."

"That may be true, but everybody calls you Octavius and nobody calls you Buddy. Nobody."

"I like you, Buddy boy, but I Suwannee, you really are a hayseed. It's not as if I'm hiding who I am. My name is on the envelope, for crying out loud." He picked up the envelope and pointed to the address. "There, see? What does it say?"

Jericho swallowed hard and pretended to read. "Says Octavius?"

"Of course, it does. Octavius J. Rockwell, III. But I never have liked my name—mainly because I don't get along with my old man who goes by the same moniker—so I always use Buddy, when signing letters to dames. Why does it bother you? You have a problem with what I write to my girls?"

He shrugged. "No. I just want to make sure you're not pretending to be somebody you ain't. Me, for example."

"Don't flatter yourself. If I was pretending to be you, I'd write, 'Hey, sugarfoot. I sho' do miss you.'" His laughter was interrupted by a coughing spell. Catching his breath in between hacks, he said, "If I wrote like you talk, I'd soon be begging

Thomas's mama and granny to write me, because I wouldn't be able to find a girl who'd write me back."

Jericho bristled. "Shut up, Octavious. You can poke fun at me all you want, but you ain't got no right to be so mean to Thomas. He ain't done nothing to you."

"Hey, lighten up before you have us all boo-hooing. You want me to apologize to Thomas? Okay, I will. 'Begging your pardon Thomas, if I've offended you.'" He grinned. "Alrighty, Buddy boy, how was that?"

The new fellow yelled, "For crying out loud, let the guy finish. This is more entertaining than waiting for the next serial at the picture show. Besides, Pennsylvania Party Girl is my favorite."

Octavious cleared his throat and picked up where he left off. *"Please don't be jealous, Buddy. I only go to the USO dances to try to bring a little cheer into the lives of the homesick, brave men who so valiantly serve our great country. It's actually very exhausting for me, since they all rush at me as soon as I walk through the door, wanting a chance to dance. I do my best to get around to as many as I possibly can. But once you and I are married, I'll save all my dances for you. You asked what I thought about a Christmas wedding on the boat. It's not exactly the wedding I dreamed of, but I'd marry you, anytime, anywhere, my darling. Let's do it."*

A sailor who answered to the name Cornwall let out a swear word, then said, "Octavius, isn't that the third woman you've promised to marry, come Christmas? I don't reckon you've heard the word bigamy before, but there are laws against having more than one wife at the time."

With an exaggerated eye-roll, Octavious grumbled. "You're as looney as they are if you think I plan to marry any of them. It's just easier to write 'em all the same thing to keep from getting confused over what I've said." He skimmed over the last lines on the stationary, but the volume in his voice dropped to a near whisper as he read: *"That reminds me, sugar. I need you to settle a bet for me. One of the girls here at the Diner said after you and I are married, Uncle Sam will send me a check every month. I said she was wrong. So, which one of us is right? Does Uncle Sam really send checks to military wives? Well, toodle-do for now. Yours forever, Ora Mae. Your Pennsylvania Party Girl."*

Cornwall slapped his hand against his thigh and hee-hawed. "Looks like she saved the best 'til last. She wants to marry you for your money. And you thought she was in love with you. That's hilarious."

Octavius's jaw jutted forward. He took a quick look at a picture included with the letter, then tore it up and tossed it in the trash. "Ugly old hag. Does she really think anyone would want to marry her?"

Jericho had a feeling his suspicions were right and the girls from Pennsylvania and Tennessee might be pulling the same scam as Octavius. Likely, they were saying the same sweet nothings to a dozen other servicemen. But it was that little gal from Alabama that worried Jericho. She was different. Sweet in an innocent sort of way. She never bragged about nothing, leading him to believe she was probably poor as a church mouse. She never talked about her looks, although Octavious had shown him a picture and she was about the prettiest little thing he'd ever laid eyes on. He could tell from her letters that she was sincere and had swallowed all of Octavius's obnoxious lies. How could he do that to such a sweet girl? *It ain't right. It just ain't.*

Jericho's heart sank when Octavius picked up the last letter and said, "I don't have to read the return address to know this is from the little gal in Alabama. She sprays it with perfume." He passed it over to Jericho in the next bed. "Here, smell."

Jericho felt his Adam's apple bob as he sniffed her perfume. He clamped his lips together and handed the envelope back to Octavius. He watched as Octavius unfolded the letter, then saw a wry smile creep across his face. "Listen to this, guys, but hold your laughter until I finish. Alabama is a looker for sure, but the girl's a real dingbat."

"My dearest Buddy,

I can hardly wait for the mailman every day, hoping there'll be another letter from you. It's hard to believe that I could've fallen in love with a man I've never met, although I feel as if I've known you forever. When you're released from the hospital I hope you'll send me a picture of you. Darling, I can't believe you suggested a Christmas wedding. There's no way for you to have known, but I've always dreamed of getting married at Christmas, my favorite time of year. I think that's just further confirmation that we were meant to be together.

Jericho's jaw tightened. What kind of low life would lead an innocent girl on by making her think he was gonna marry her? He held his tongue as Octavius continued to read.

"You are gentle, and kind and your deep faith has let me know that the Lord has led me to you. My faith is very important to me. I wouldn't want to fall in love with someone who didn't put the Lord first in everything. I'm sorry you can't attend church while in the hospital. I sense how much you miss it, but the Lord knows your heart. Just keep reading the Word and I'll continue praying for God to take away your pain."

Jericho had made up his mind not to let Octavius's shenanigans bother him, but this was too much. "Octavius, it's bad enough to lie about being in love with her, but that's just pure hypocrisy to pretend to love God. You ain't been to chapel or picked up one of them Bibles the Gideons left since we've been here. Ain't you afraid God will strike you dead for lying?"

Robert laughed. "I agree with Buddy. I advise you to stay inside during a storm. You just might get struck by lightning for those whoppers."

"Shut up, you guys and let me finish. It's a hoot. This chick has got it bad. She says, '*Buddy, darling, I can hardly wait for you to get here. Only a few more months until I'll be Mrs. Buddy Rockwell. I only wish your leave could be longer than a week, but I'm thrilled that we'll celebrate Christmas as husband and wife. I'll meet you at the bus station, Friday, December 23rd, then I'll take you to my house to introduce you to Mother. I haven't broken the news to her yet. I know she won't be too keen on hearing I plan to marry a sailor I've never met, but when she gets to know you, I'm sure she'll be okay with the idea. You can eat dinner with us and then you and I will go outside and sit in the swing on my front porch in the moonlight and talk until Mother makes me go inside. There's a nice hotel in town where you can stay the first night. Then, the next morning, we'll head to the Court House to tie the knot. I'm so excited I can hardly sleep at—"*

Jericho didn't hear the rest. He imagined himself sitting beside her in that swing with the scent of her perfume filling his nostrils. He envisioned her voice being sweet like the sound of birds singing. As they rocked gently back and forth, he'd point out the big dipper and tell her about the time he got a beating in second grade for drinking out of the teacher's big dipper. Not that it was such an interesting story, but it'd be an opportunity for him to let her know he did get a little schooling, even if he couldn't write a letter.

He was secretly falling in love with a girl he'd never met, and it burned him up to hear Octavius poking fun at such heartfelt romantic words that Jericho sensed were coming from a sweet, innocent heart. She was beautiful, compassionate and had an abiding faith in the Almighty. She was perfect. What was there not to love?

CHAPTER 2

Juliette Jinright didn't wait for the mailman to walk up to the door to put the mail in the box. She spotted him walking down the sidewalk and ran two blocks to meet him.

He smiled, reached in his bag and fumbled through several stacks until he pulled out the envelope she was waiting for. "I declare, Miss Juli, this must be a mighty special pen pal to get you so excited. A soldier, is he?"

"Sailor, sir."

"Why, of course. I don't know what I was thinking. Says so right up there in the corner. Octavius J. Rockwell III. That's a mighty fancy name. What does the 'J' stand for?"

She giggled. "I've never asked. He goes by Buddy because he doesn't like the name Octavius. I've hesitated to ask about his middle name. I figure if he wants me to know, he'll tell me."

"I hope that sailor knows how lucky he is to have such a sweet, beautiful pen pal."

Juliette felt a blush. "Thanks, Mr. Watkins, but I'm the lucky one. Buddy's humble and doesn't realize just how special he is."

"Well he sounds like a fine young man, and I'm glad. I'm sure those fellows serving our country look forward to getting letters. My pack has been much heavier, ever since the paper began publishing the Pen Pal Section with names of our servicemen."

"I've prayed for a Christian husband since I was fifteen, but I think the Lord has outdone himself. Buddy Rockwell is better than anything I could've hoped for."

"Husband? Goodness! I didn't realize you'd been corresponding long enough to be thinking of marriage."

"It doesn't take long when you meet the right one. I knew from the start Buddy was the man I've been praying for. We're planning to be married over the Christmas holidays, but I'd be obliged if you wouldn't mention it to anyone quite yet."

"Well, blow me down. From what your Mother was saying at church Sunday night, I thought you were still sweet on the State Attorney General's son . . . Ronald, I believe she called him?"

"Roland. His name is Roland, but he's Mother's pick, not mine."

"Christmas, you say?" Juliette had the distinct feeling Mr. Watkins didn't approve, but he was at least fifty. She was confident he didn't remember what it felt like to be young and in love.

"So, what did Henrietta say when you told her you'd be marrying this sailor you've never met?"

"Uh . . . Mother doesn't know it yet."

"Sugar, as a father myself, I wonder if you've given this enough thought. I hate to see you rush into something as serious as marriage to someone you've never even seen. Christmas is less than three months away."

"I appreciate your concern, Mr. Watkins, but trust me, I know what I'm doing."

"Well, I hope you're right. It's a shame your daddy didn't live long enough to stand up for ya'. I reckon you'll be asking Walter to do the honors?"

"To tell the truth, I haven't thought about it. I'll leave it up to Mother. Whatever she thinks is proper. Just a simple wedding with a few close friends at the Court House is fine with me."

Mr. Watkins laughed as if that were the silliest notion he'd ever heard of. "I'm sure it would be okay with you, but I don't see Henrietta Jinright settling for anything less than a huge blow out."

"You're probably right. Mother does like to do things up right. G'bye, Mr. Watkins."

"Bye, Sugar. I can see you're chomping at the bits to see what's in that letter."

Juliette could've opened it right there, but she wanted to wait until she was in the privacy of her bedroom, where she could linger on each sentence, absorbing every sweet, romantic word from the man of her dreams.

Greta was sweeping off the porch, when she ran up the steps. "Miss Juliette, is that another letter from that fellow of yours?"

"Shh!!" She glanced around, hoping her mother wasn't in earshot. "Sure is." She hurried toward the door before Greta had time to start a conversation. Running down the hall, she bounded up the stairs and almost ran over Jingles, her little Cocker Spaniel on the way to her room. Once inside, she slammed the door behind her and jumped up in the middle of the tall, canopy bed. Then, tearing into the envelope, her heart pounded as she unfolded the letter and read:

My darling Juliette,

The burns on my chest feel as if I'm swimming in a lake of fire. But I have no reason to complain, because I have the one thing every sailor in this ward desires, but few are as privileged as I. What could that be, you ask? Hope. Hope is what you've given me, my sweet. I live each day knowing there's something . . . someone worth living for. If not for your letters, I'm not sure I could've pulled through. The doctor says it's my will to live that has brought me this far. When the pain becomes too great to bear, I try to concentrate on what it will be like after we're married, and then I can withstand anything, just knowing we'll be together forever.

Thank you so much for the delicious divinity. I shared a piece with every sailor in my ward. I love these guys. A couple of them are very cold-hearted, but we don't always know what others are going through, so I just pray for them and leave it up to the Good Lord to meet their needs.

You asked what I plan to do when I'm out of the Navy. I have a yearning to become a minister and share the Gospel with others. I realize you've been accustomed to wealth, and you'd have to learn to live with less. Is that asking too much of you, my dear?

Oh, here comes the doctor to change the bandages on my chest, so I must close for now.

Longing to be with you, I remain,

Yours forever,

Buddy

****

Juliette stuffed the letter in a top drawer when Henrietta knocked on the door. "Coming, Mother."

"Were you busy, dear?"

"No ma'am. Do you need me?"

"The ladies from the Athenaeum Club will be here shortly and Greta has the refreshments ready. I wondered if you'd mind serving us when they arrive."

"Of course. But is Greta going somewhere?"

"Oh, no. She'll be here but I don't trust her to serve. Greta is a great cook and we're fortunate to have her, but I do declare that lady is as clumsy as an ox. I don't trust her to pour the Russian

Tea. I have no doubt she'd wind up spilling it on someone and I'd be embarrassed to tears."

"I'll be happy to serve the refreshments."

"Thank you, darling. First, I'd like for you to change clothes. Sweetheart, that calico dress you're wearing is so common looking. I don't know what possessed you to buy it. Put on the yellow organza. It looks so good on you."

"Yes, Mother. I'll be down as soon as I change." Juliette hated the yellow organza but arguing with her Mother would be a waste of time.

Her Mother was right. Greta was a fantastic cook. Her Lemon Meringue Pie had won a blue ribbon at the State Fair last year. But clumsy? No way. The real reason Henrietta didn't want Greta in the Parlor with her high-minded friends had nothing to do with clumsiness, and everything to do with Greta's poor language skills. Henrietta Jinright had little patience with anyone who couldn't speak proper English. Even so, Juliette didn't think of her Mother as a snob—just a bit persnickety.

Juliette stood at the punch bowl, acknowledging each lady with a compliment, just as Mother had instructed her to do. Sometimes it was an easier task than at other times.

"Good afternoon, Mrs. Watts. What a lovely Cameo. Is it an heirloom?" Mrs. Watts seemed quite pleased, but not nearly half as pleased as Juliette was that Mrs. Watts had chosen to wear it. If not for the small trinket, Juliette would've found herself at a total loss for words. Mother glanced over and smiled with approval.

Juliette carried a silver tray of Petit Fours around the room. Mrs. Thompkins said, "Precious, you are growing like a weed. I'll bet a young lady as pretty as you has lots of beaus. Am I right?"

Before she could answer, Henrietta interrupted. "You are definitely right. Juliette will have a difficult time choosing between her many suitors. I don't know if you're aware, but the State Attorney General's son met her at a Glee Club Competition and was smitten at first sight."

Mrs. Thompkins raised a brow. "You don't say. The State Attorney General's son. That's wonderful. Grover and I had the pleasure of meeting Mr. Harlan Roundtree and his wife at a fund-raiser and I must say, I've never met a lovelier couple. Henrietta, I'm sure you are pleased with your daughter's selection."

If Juliette hadn't been fully aware of the consequences, she would've blurted out the truth and announced that Roland was her Mother's choice, not hers.

Henrietta gushed, "I couldn't be more pleased. Ronald is a gentleman in every sense of the word."

Juliette said, "Roland, Mother. His name is Roland."

"I know, dear. That's what I said. Now, shouldn't you check with Greta and see if we don't have more finger sandwiches? The tray needs refilling."

"Yes ma'am."

Henrietta waited for Juliette to exit. "As I was saying, Roland has come down from Montgomery on several occasions to call on my daughter and he stays overnight at The Hotel Rawls."

"Well, it certainly sounds as if he's smitten."

"I agree, but it's not surprising. Juliette has always been very popular. She was Miss Cotton Queen, you know. Of course, she looks exactly as I did at her age."

After the last guest had left, Henrietta went into the kitchen to tell Greta it was time to clean up. Juliette sat quietly at the kitchen table.

Her mother patted her on the shoulder. "Why are you looking so gloomy, sweetheart? You should be feeling wonderful after hearing all the nice compliments the women lavished on you. I'm so proud of you."

"Mother, would you be just as proud of me if I told you that I won't be seeing Roland again?"

"Why, of course, I would, honey. But a young man doesn't drive that far to court a young lady if he isn't very interested. I can guarantee you he'll be back. Nothing could keep him away. I saw the way he looked at you."

"Mother, did you see the way I looked at him?"

"Honey, you take after me. We don't always reveal our feelings, but we both are very sensible when it comes to making decisions."

Juliette sucked in a deep breath. "Mother, I'm sure you'll change your mind when I tell you that Roland won't be calling on me again because I asked him not to."

For a split second, Juliette thought she saw fire shooting from her mother's eyes.

"You *what?* I can't believe my ears. Why in the world would you do such a thing, Juliette?"

"He was beginning to have thoughts of us having a life together."

Henrietta's eyes welled with tears. "Would that be so bad?"

"Yes ma'am. I think it would. I don't love him, Mother."

"Oh, Juliette, you read too many Romance novels. A good marriage isn't made up of kisses and hugs but of mutual respect and cooperation to achieve your joint goals. I learned to love your father, but honey, I was in love with another young man when your daddy and I married."

A lump formed in Juliette's throat. "I don't believe you."

"You might as well know, because it's the truth. I had to make a difficult decision, but I was mature enough to do the right thing."

"Did Daddy know you didn't love him?"

"I'm sure he did. But I have no doubt that he chose me for my looks, and I chose him because he was from a prominent family and I knew he'd be going places."

Juliette's lip quivered. "Mother, I think that is about the

saddest story I've ever heard."

"Grow up, Juliette. If I'd married the fellow I was in love with, you would never have been born and I might be taking in laundry today if I'd allowed my heart to rule over my good judgment. He was a dirt farmer and would probably still be a dirt farmer today if we had married. Fortunately for him, he was able to get out of his surroundings and make a decent living, but I'll always believe his drive to better himself came from his determination to prove me wrong."

When moisture filled Henrietta's eyes, she quickly turned away. Juliette couldn't discern if the tears were for a long-lost love or if her mother was grieving over Juliette's decision not to marry Roland.

"Juliette, why? Why didn't you discuss it with me before making such a monumental decision?"

"Mother, please don't cry. I'm sorry I've disappointed you, but we aren't as much alike as you'd like to believe. I'm in love with Buddy and I plan to marry him."

"You're *what?* You aren't talking about that pen pal in the Navy you've been writing to, I hope."

"That's exactly who I'm talking about, and I may be taking in laundry after we're married because Buddy plans to go into the ministry, and I'm okay with that."

Henrietta's jaw dropped. "Don't be ridiculous. You mean . . . like a preacher?"

"Not like a preacher. A preacher. Pastor of a church."

"Oh, child, grow up. Do you know how preacher's get paid? A bucket of syrup, a few dozen eggs and if they're lucky, maybe they'll get a ham around Christmas."

"Then, I'll learn to make-do with what we have. Mother, I love you very much and I hate to see you disappointed. But there's no way I would ever marry someone I didn't love. I understand now why Father never smiled. He knew."

"You're wrong. I never let on that I didn't love him."

"But you never let on that you did. How could you, Mother?"

Henrietta, gave a slight shrug. "You should thank your lucky stars that I made the decision that I did." Shaking her finger in Juliette's face, her voice rose. "Young lady, you'd better take my advice and think twice before jumping into a hopeless situation that could ruin your life."

"I love him, Mother. I wish you could be happy for me."

Henrietta threw up her hands. "I hope you don't think I'll be planning a big wedding if you're going to go against me this way."

"That's not a problem. Buddy and I will go to the Court House and we'll be just as married."

Henrietta's face scrunched up like a prune. "I'm feeling faint. Greta has dinner ready. You go ahead and eat. I won't be joining you. I couldn't eat a bite, the way I feel. You've always been so responsible, Juliette. I can't believe you'd want to throw your future away by marrying some sailor you've never even met."

She held the back of her hand to her forehead, the way she always did when pretending to feel a fainting spell coming on, then plodded into the kitchen with the corners of her mouth drooping. "Greta, I think I shall retire to my room. Bring me up a glass of water and a powder for this horrific headache."

Juliette felt terrible, knowing she'd hurt her mother, but she'd feel even worse if she agreed to marry a man she didn't love.

CHAPTER 3

The nurse's aide stepped over to Thomas's bed and pulled two letters from her satchel. "Sailor, here's a letter from your mama and—" She stopped. "What's this?" Holding up another envelope, she grinned. "Oh, my goodness, the return address on this one says it's from Annie Grouse. Have you been holding out on us? Is Annie a girlfriend?"

He shook his head as tears welled in his eyes.

She waved the envelope high in the air and teased. "Don't be shy. Tell me who she is or you don't get your mail."

His voice sounded coarse. "Granny."

"Who?"

"Granny Grouse." He reached up, his eyes pleading. "Please?"

Octavius laughed. "What d'ya know? Thomas's mama and grandma miss him as much as he misses them. How touching. I wonder if they bawl as much as he does."

The aide tossed seven letters on Octavius's bed. "Your pen pal list appears to be growing. When do you plan to stop this nonsense?"

"Stop? Why should I stop? This is the only fun I get to have in this place." Octavius said, "Listen to this one, you guys. Alabama swallows anything I say, hook, line and sinker."

As he began to read, he changed his voice, imitating a love-sick female. *"Buddy, honey, I can't believe you'd think it makes any difference to me that the burns will leave your chest bare.*

Octavious had never been called Buddy and he had no chest burns. Buddy's jaw tightened. His teeth made a grinding noise as he waited to hear the rest.

Just remember, I didn't fall for you because of a hairy chest since I've never seen you. I fell for you because of your love for the Lord and your unabashed honesty. It was the words pouring from a pure heart that lies beneath that chest that won my affection. So please, don't ever feel embarrassed. I love you for what's on the inside, not what's visible from the outside."

Jericho was pretty sure the veins on his neck were bulging, the way they always did when anything upset him and never had he been so upset. Unable to keep quiet any longer, blurted, "Wait just a cotton-picking minute. You're pretending to be me. Not only are you using the name I go by, but your burns are on your hands. I'm the one with chest burns and I don't cotton to you making light of something I find quite painful."

"Making light? Is that what you think I was doing. There's

nothing pitiful about burns on my hands, especially since I can still pen a letter with my right hand. But you have the makings of a serious problem. I thought if my plan worked, I'd let you know so you could use it to your advantage."

"I have no idea what you're talking about, but I do know you have no right to be lying to that girl. She obviously really cares for you."

"Dummy, don't you see how perfectly it worked? I'm pretty sure you won't ever have the hair to grow back on your chest, so I decided to go for the sympathy, although I was hoping it wouldn't backfire. You know—the image of a man with gruesome scars and no hair on his chest could possibly turn a girl off. But luckily it worked like a charm. I can almost see the tears streaming down that pretty little face."

"That ain't right, Octavius. You know it ain't."

"What's the big deal? I'll never see her. She's a looker for sure, but borrr-ing. I guess she seriously thinks I'm some kind of church-going saint who'd be content to sit in a swing and stare at a bunch of stars on a Saturday night, while a Bible-thumping prude sits on the other side of the swing. I'm a lover, not an astronomer. The only stars I care about are the stars in a pretty gal's eyes when I snuggle up close to her, feeling her breath on my neck."

"You're sick, man. Really sick."

"You got that right." Octavius coughed, then grabbed a metal bowl from the bedside table and spat in it. "Try telling that to

Maggie, will you? I feel like I've got bricks on my chest, but that ignorant nurse doesn't believe me."

"Octavius, the reason she doesn't believe you is because you lie when the truth would fit better. At least Maggie knows you're lying when you pretend you're crazy about her, but for you to make that girl from Alabama fall in love with you by feeding her a bunch of lies . . . well, it's cruel."

"You really haven't been around, have you, Buddy? Tell the truth. Have you ever been out with a woman?"

When he didn't answer, Octavius continued as if he knew the answer already. "When I get out of the Navy, I'll look you up and teach you the ropes. You haven't lived until you've been spooning with a real woman in a parked car on a lonely road, feeling her moist lips on yours and hearing her heart beat in rhythm with your own."

Jericho shook his head. "I don't think I could do that unless . . . well, you know . . . unless I really loved her and she loved me . . . and well, unless maybe I was engaged to her."

"Are you serious? No wonder you never get letters at mail call. You don't know how to woo a girl. You're not a bad-looking fellow and forgive me for being blunt, but you're so shy you're a bore. I like you, man. I really do. Let me see if I can say this to where you can understand. Juliette is like this lunch tray. I like it. But it's empty. It would be a lot more interesting if it had a plate of appetizing food on it."

"You don't make a dab of sense. She ain't no lunch tray."

"I'm saying there's nothing functionally wrong with her. Just like there's nothing wrong with this metal tray. It's built well and it has a function and from her picture, I'd say she's built well, also but I have a strong feeling she doesn't function." His reply brought snickers from some of the guys in the room. "But regardless of how nice this tray looks, I don't really have a use for it until the nurse sits a sumptuous plate of something that I crave on it. Then I pull it up close to me, like this... and my mouth waters and my heart beats as I prepare to devour the treat that's been set before me."

Jericho felt a blush on his face when several of the fellows in the ward laughed at the comparison.

Octavius said, "Now do you get my drift? Juliette is my tray, and although she's a mighty fancy tray, it didn't take me long to realize that this beautiful tray will never hold a mouth-watering treat to be devoured until some dumb cluck says the two words she's waiting to hear."

"What two words?"

"I do."

"You've lost me. You'll do what?" Jericho didn't care that the fellows laughed at him. This was Juliette they were discussing, and he wanted to know exactly what Octavius meant. Exactly what did he plan to do?

"I'm talking about the wedding vows. I'm saying there'll be

no goodies on that tray until she can get me to the altar and hears me say 'I do,' and I'll tell you right now, I don't. No siree, not this ol' boy. I won't be tied to any one girl until I've sowed all my oats, and the way I'm feeling, I've got a silo full of oats that are waiting to be sewn."

"You're wrong about her, Octavius."

His face scrunched into a frown. "Man, you talk like you know this broad. Have you been holding back on me?"

"Of course not, but I've listened as you've read her letters. She writes with feelings. A metal tray ain't got no feelings. You can't compare the two."

Octavius grimaced. "Ain't got no? I'm getting the feeling you're falling for this dame, and I don't have a problem with that. She's not my type and if you could get her, I'd say more power to you. But this little gal is from a highfalutin family. She's got class and as long as you continue to talk like a country-bumpkin, the only women you'll get are backroad hicks. Man, don't they have schools where you come from?"

"Sure, they have schools. My step-dad just didn't believe in them."

"Sorry about that, Buddy. Guess who this one's from?" Octavius held up a pale green envelope.

Jericho shrugged. "Ain't nothing to me. I don't care who it's from." His pulse raced. Recognizing the envelope, he knew exactly who it was from.

Octavius shook his head slightly. "I Suwannee, this chick from Alabama has got it bad. This is the third letter from her today." He stopped and grinned. "Here, Buddy boy. You want to read it?"

Jericho frowned. "Of course not. Like I said, don't mean nothing to me."

"Suit yourself. I don't want to read it either. She bores me." He ripped it in half, to the moans of the fellows in the ward, then tossed the envelope into the trash basket.

Jericho flinched when Octavius began another coughing episode. It seemed each one was worse than the one before.

"Buddy, I don't feel so good. Is it hot in here to you?"

"Hot? Not at all, but I hear the meal cart rolling down the hall. Maggie will be coming in soon. She'll get help for you."

Octavius reached over and spat in the metal tray. "I won't count on it. She doesn't believe me."

"She'll believe me. I don't know what's wrong, but I'm getting worried about you. I can tell you ain't fooling."

Maggie entered the Ward, pushing a cart with the dinner trays. She glanced over at the small metal dish near Octavius's bed and thrust her hand over her heart. "Oh, my goodness, Octavius. How long have you been coughing up blood?"

"I tried to tell you I was sick this morning."

Jericho said, "He's been coughing a lot."

She left the trays on the cart, took his temperature, then

41

hurried out of the room. Minutes later the doctor entered, asked Octavius a couple of questions, then two interns showed up and wheeled him out of the room.

Maggie came back in and handed out the supper trays. Jericho said, "What's wrong with Octavius?"

"Not sure if it's tuberculosis or pneumonia, but either way, I'm afraid he's a very sick man."

Rayford, a big man who had only been in the ward less than seventy-two hours raised up in the bed. "Holy Moly, TB? That means we're all gonna die, doesn't it?"

Maggie made an effort to calm the irate man, but he slung his feet off the bed and slapped at Maggie's arm when she tried to reason with him.

"I came in here with an ulcer. Painful, but at least I won't die with it. Get me my clothes, nurse. I'm outta here."

"Lieutenant Lassiter, you're not going anywhere, so lay back down and try to calm yourself."

"Calm myself? Calm myself! Easy for you to say. I'll bet you aren't married."

"You're right. I'm not."

"Well, I am, and I have four kids back in Jersey counting on their ol' man to come back home and I intend to do just that. Now are you gonna get me my clothes, or do you want me to walk down the hall and leave in this garb?"

"I wouldn't advise it, sir. I'm sure you know better than I, how long it will be before you can see those precious children if you should decide to leave this Naval Hospital without being discharged."

His gaze darted from bed to bed. He shouted, "What are you morons staring at?" Then pulling his legs back on the bed, he eased down under the sheet without another word.

Maggie said, "Believe me, I understand your concern, Lieutenant. I think we all do. Would you like for me to pray for you?"

He rolled over and glared. "Pray? No thanks. Save your breath. I'm gonna die. I just know it. I never should've agreed to come to this stinking infirmary."

Thomas' voice quivered. "At least you've had the opportunity to know the love of a woman and what it's like to hold a child in your arms that's a part of you."

An eerie silence filled the room. What was Thomas saying?

Thomas raised his hand, as if in school asking permission to be excused. "Maggie?"

"Yes, Thomas."

"If it's not asking too much, I'd very much appreciate it if you'd send up a prayer for me. I've tried to do it myself, but I'm not sure I'm getting through to God."

CHAPTER 4

Jericho had barely closed his eyes when the sun began to show through the window. Never had he spent such a long night. His thoughts weren't on himself, but on the sweet girl the guys in Ward B called Alabama. She was obviously very much in love with Octavius and would be devastated if anything should happen to him. Shouldn't she be told? He glanced down at the envelope and ripped letter in the trash basket and wished that he could read.

Maggie came in rolling the breakfast tray, although no one in the unit appeared to be very hungry. It wasn't what was being said, but rather what wasn't being said that cast the mood. After making the rounds, she said, "I know you fellows are concerned about Octavious and the doctor requested—"

Rayford blurted, "I don't give a hill o' beans about that creep nor do I care what the doctor requested. I want to know if I've been exposed to TB and if so, what's this hospital gonna do about it?"

"Sir, if you don't mind, I'd like to finish. As I was saying, the doctor requested that I let you all know that Seaman Rockwell does have pneumonia. The good news is that there is now a vaccine called Penicillin that has been very successful in treating bacterial diseases such as pneumonia. There is no reason to believe that anyone in this ward—including Octavius—will die, so please eat a good breakfast and stop worrying."

The only sound in the room was an occasional fork clanging against a metal plate, though some plates were left untouched. Maggie stood next to Jericho's bed. He whispered. "The truth, Maggie. Will he live?"

She bit her lip and nodded, though Jericho felt he knew no more after she answered than he did before. Was she simply trying to keep the morale up in the room? Was Rayford right? Did exposure mean a sure death or was there really a medicine called Pencil-something-or-other that could cure this deadly disease. They'd all been exposed, but no one more than Jericho, since there was less than two feet between his bed and Octavius's. But it wasn't for himself that he grieved. It was for beautiful, sweet Juliette Jinright who occupied his thoughts. Jericho was certain she'd be devastated if anything happened to the man she thought intended to marry her. He liked Octavius, even though he couldn't fathom why. It didn't change the fact that he was a louse. If Octavius died, Juliette would be grief-stricken, but if he lived and she learned he was simply stringing her along, it would not only be distressing, but humiliating. Either way, she was in for a heartbreak.

"Maggie, I know a lot of the fellows don't like Octavius, but we got along pretty good. I don't like to think about him dying."

"Then don't. As soon as the penicillin arrives, the doctor will begin his treatment."

"You mean he hasn't even started?"

"The hospital doesn't have it in stock, but we'll get it shortly after lunch. You fellows don't give the new nurse a hard time and make me out a liar. I've told her you're all a great group of guys."

Jericho's jaw dropped. "You're leaving? But why?"

"I'm getting married and I'll be moving to Virginia."

"Well, I wish you the best, Maggie. You deserve it. We'll miss you."

"Not you, Jericho."

"Sure, I will."

"I meant you won't be here to miss me. The doctor is coming by tonight to check you out and if all looks good—and I think it does—you'll be on your way home tomorrow."

Jericho chewed on his bottom lip.

"I thought you'd be happy. What's wrong?"

"I'm worried about Octavius. I'd really like to stick around and see how things turn out for him."

"Jericho, I won't pretend he's out of the woods, but there's nothing you can do for him here. Go home, sailor, and get on with your life."

What home? What life?

****

The news Jericho received from the doctor was not the news he'd hoped for. "Are you sure I don't need to stay at least another couple of days, doc? I'm still very sore."

The doctor smiled. "I'm accustomed to sailors pleading for a few more days in the infirmary when their other choice is swabbing a deck, but your discharge papers from the Navy were completed three days after you came in." He pulled a couple of sheets of paper from his clipboard. "And here's your discharge papers from the infirmary. Get a good night's rest, sign the papers and leave them in the office in the morning before you leave."

He nodded. "Yes sir."

The following morning, Jericho put on his only suit of clothes—his uniform—and waited for the new nurse to make her rounds. He quizzed her about Octavius's condition but with her chin in the air, she quipped, "I'm sorry, sailor, but a patient's status is confidential. I'm not at liberty to reveal that information. I'm sure you understand."

She was wrong. He didn't understand. All she had to say to put his mind at ease was that Octavius was recuperating . . . or that he was responding well to the medicine . . ." But if Octavius wasn't recuperating or responding, then that would mean—" No, he refused to think that way.

Jericho grabbed his discharge papers and headed to the office, where he sat for almost two hours, waiting to be cleared. Afterward, he returned to the ward to get his duffle bag. His heart thumped hard against his chest, seeing a stranger occupying Octavius's bed. Speaking to no one in particular, but to anyone who could ease his mind, he blurted, "What's going on? Octavius will likely be coming back to the ward soon. It ain't right to take his bed. He likes being near the window."

Lieutenant Lassiter said, "You were gone a long time. I figured you'd heard the news."

"What news?" Jericho's heart raced.

"That disease-infected scoundrel done killed over and we're all gonna do the same. It's just a matter of time."

"Are you saying Octavius . . . died? No. That can't be."

"You really didn't think he was gonna live, did you?"

His mouth was dry. "I don't know what I thought."

Thomas said, "I won't lie. I didn't like him, but I'm sorry to hear he died. When did it happen?"

The lieutenant said, "I reckon it was around two-o'clock this morning. That's about the time I woke up and heard the doctor talking to the nurse in the hall."

Jericho started toward the door, then turned around and dug a pale green envelope out of the trash can. He wasn't sure what he was going to do with it, but he had to do something.

The new nurse came in and rolled a wheelchair over to Thomas's bed. "Crawl aboard, sailor. You're needed in x-ray."

Jericho followed them down the hall to a waiting room. He waited for the nurse to walk away, then pulled a chair close to Thomas.

Thomas said, "Why are you in here? I thought you were on your way home."

"Truth is, Thomas, I ain't got no home, so I ain't in no big hurry to go nowhere. I didn't want to pry in front of the others in the ward—especially not in front of the lieutenant—but if I ain't being too personal, what's wrong with you?"

The tears welled in his eyes. "Cancer."

"Whoa, that's bad, ain't it? I'm really sorry, man. I wish I could do something for you, but I reckon ain't nothing nobody can do."

"Doc says I don't have more than six months to live, and the truth is, Jericho, I don't feel like I've ever lived. I want to fall in love, get married, have kids, build a home. Ya' know?"

Jericho laid his hand on the sailor's shoulder. "I do know."

"Thanks. Jericho . . . are you a praying man?"

Jericho cleared his throat. "I reckon I've tried it a couple of times in my life."

"You saying you don't believe it works?"

"No, not saying that. I'm just saying I don't rank up there with those folks that I 'spect the Good Lord lends an ear to. Like Maggie. That was a mighty fancy prayer she prayed for you. If God listens to anybody, I got a feeling he listens to Maggie."

"I liked Maggie. When she prayed, you could tell right off that she'd had plenty of practice. But I'd really like for you to pray for me. Would you do that for me?"

Jericho swallowed hard. How could he refuse, especially since he had a favor he wanted to ask of Thomas. A big favor. He sucked in a heavy breath, then let it out slowly. "Okay. I'll do it. Bow your head and close your eyes." Jericho wasn't as concerned that head-bowing was prayer-protocol as he was worried that Thomas might be watching him do something he hadn't had much practice at.

"Hey, God, it's me. Jericho. Jericho Rhoades. You might know me by another last name, but I was Arzetta's boy. I reckon there's only been one Arzetta in the whole world, so I 'spect you probably know who I'm talking about."

Thomas whispered, "God knows your name, Jericho. Get on with it. They'll be coming for me soon."

"You sure about that?"

"Of course, I'm sure. There are only two patients ahead of me."

"I mean are you sure God knows my name?"

"Says so in the Bible."

Jericho's jaw dropped. "I'm in the *Bible*?"

"No. I just meant it says God knows everybody. Now are you

gonna pray for me or not?"

"Yeah. Here goes." He cleared his throat. "God, I don't make no pretense of knowing why you do things like you do. I don't know why someone as good as Thomas is gonna die, when there are some dirty, rotten scoundrels that live to be old men. In fact, there's lots of things I just can't get under my cap." When he heard Thomas grunt, he peeked out of one eye. "Okay, I'll save that 'til later, Lord. But if I can have two wishes, I wish Thomas would get well and I wish that you'd comfort that little gal they call Alabama when she gets the news that Octavius won't be coming for her. Frankly, me and you both know he wadn't gonna marry her, no way. Well, that's my two wishes, and if you choose to let it happen, I'll be forever in your debt. Amen." He looked at Thomas. "How did I do?"

"Although God's not some kind of Genie who sits in Heaven granting wishes, I'm sure he'll make allowances for you not knowing that. You did just fine. Now, what can I pray for you?"

"We won't pester God, but there is sump'n you can do for me."

"I'll do what I can. But you need to understand that God isn't pestered by our prayers. He loves to hear from us. Buddy, I'm gonna pray that he'll place a Godly woman in your life—one who'll know from the moment she meets you that you've been sent straight from heaven. Now, what else can I do for you."

"Thomas, I know you can read and write, and I didn't want the other fellows knowing that I can't write nothing but my name. I need you to write a letter for me. I got a pencil and paper in my duffle bag." Jericho cringed. He should've thanked Thomas for wanting to pray for him, but he had no time to waste on small talk. His mind was on one thing and one only. "Thomas, will you do it? Will you write the letter for me?"

"Sure. Who's it to?"

"Juliette Jinright."

"Say, isn't that the name of the girl Octavius makes fun of? The one from Alabama?"

"Yeah, that's her."

"I get it. Now that Octavius's gone, you're hoping to move in on his girl."

"Don't be silly. First of all, she isn't Octavius's girl. She just thinks she is, but Octavius—may he rest in peace—never did give a plug nickel for nobody but hisself. I just think somebody oughta tell her why she won't be hearing from him no more. That's all."

"So, what shall I say?"

"Tell her that Octavius loved her very much but that he died and won't be coming for her."

"You're a good man, Jericho. Always thinking about the other fellow."

Jericho opened his bag and shoved a pad and pencil in Thomas's hand. He sheepishly glanced around the room, then whispered, "Her name is Juliette."

"You said that, already." Thomas squinted his eyes as he contemplated how he should word it. He put the pen to the paper:

"Dear Miss Juliette,

It is with true regrets that I must inform you that Navy Seaman 2nd Class Octavius J. Rockwell has succumbed to a fierce bout of a dreadful disease."

Jericho shot his palm in the air. "Hold it right there."

"What's the problem?"

"I don't think Octavius would've approved of you saying he sucked up to that disease."

Thomas' glanced back at the letter. "Succombed to . . . not sucked up to. It just means he died."

"Well, why didn't you just say that?"

"Do you want to hear the rest or not?"

"Go ahead."

"Octavius's thoughts were on you, and you only, as he fought hard to live so you two could carry out your plans for the future. He was constantly talking about you and how he couldn't wait to marry you. What a pity he had to die. He was crazy in love."

Thomas lifted the pen from the paper. "How's that sound?"

"Like a fairy tale. T'weren't a lick o' truth to it, except the part about he died."

"Wasn't that what you wanted?"

Jericho lifted a shoulder in a shrug. "I reckon."

"You want to sign your own name at the bottom?"

"No. Just sign it like this: 'Octavius's shipmate and devoted friend." He handed an envelope to Thomas, then pulled out the pale green one he dug from the trash basket. "Now, if you'll write her address on this here envelope, the way it is on the green one, I'll be much obliged."

Thomas nodded, signed the letter and was addressing the envelope when Jericho began rubbing his hands together. "Stop!"

"What do you mean, stop? I've finished. It's ready to be mailed."

"No. I've changed my mind. It was all a big fat lie and I had no right to ask you to be a part of it. Tear it up and forget I asked you to do something so stupid."

"I don't think it was stupid, at all, Jericho."

A nurse opened a nearby door and announced. "Thomas Tippins. We're ready for you."

Before the nurse wheeled him away, Thomas thrust his hand toward Jericho in a firm handshake. "Good luck, my friend. When you find a good woman to settle down with, think of those of us who never got the chance and choose to love her with your whole heart."

"Hey, don't give up. Who knows? Maybe God felt sorry for me not knowing what I was doing and will answer my wish for you, anyway."

Thomas smiled. "Prayer, Jericho."

"Huh?"

"Answer your prayer."

"Yeah, that."

Thomas wheeled toward the door, smiling. It was the first time Jericho had ever seen him smile.

CHAPTER 5

Jericho left the Jacksonville Naval Hospital, trekked over to the nearby park and bought a bag of parched peanuts from a kid pushing a wagon filled with penny sacks of nuts. After eating a few, he dumped the remainder on the ground for the squirrels. He felt empty inside. While in the Navy, he had a sense of belonging—being where he was needed.

Who needed him now? No one. They called him Buddy, but whose buddy? Nobody's buddy, that's who. Why didn't he re-enlist? If only Maggie hadn't left. She was chock full of advice. Good advice. She would've known what to tell him.

He jerked off his cap and ran his fingers through his hair. Why was he fooling himself, pretending he didn't know what to do? He knew what he wanted to do. He knew exactly. He wanted to go meet Juliette, let her know the man she was in love with was dead . . . and to offer comfort. A gnawing ache in his stomach felt as if he'd swallowed a pack of thumb tacks. Was offering comfort the real reason he wanted to see her, or was it because he was secretly in love with a girl he'd never met? The thought shamed him and he worked at convincing himself that his reason was noble. Surely, by now she would've assumed the reason the letters from Octavius had ceased was because he had fallen in love with someone else. A lump formed in Jericho's throat as he imagined her heartbreak over believing the man she loved enough to marry had jilted her. Wouldn't it better for her to know the truth—or at least the partial truth? Jericho would let Octavius's shameful actions go with him to his grave. Juliette would need someone to talk to. Someone who knew Octavius and could offer a sympathetic ear. He could do that and he would. For Octavius's sake. No. Octavius wouldn't care. It was for Juliette's sake.

Jericho bought a hot dog from a street vendor and walked back to the park bench. He hadn't intended to fall asleep, but lately it seemed all the things he intended to do, he didn't, and those things he didn't want to do, he did.

When he felt something poke him in the ribs at the break of day, he raised up to see a policeman glaring down at him. "Sailor, do you have somewhere you need to be?"

He supposed that was the cop's way of saying, no sleeping in the park.

The policeman sounded more than a mite disgruntled. "The

train depot is across the street on the corner and the bus station is two blocks over. I think you'd better make up your mind where it is you need to go and make haste. Loitering in the park is not allowed."

"Sure, officer." Grabbing his duffel bag he headed to the depot and stood in a long line waiting to buy a ticket.

"Where you headed, young fellow?" The ticket master asked without looking up.

"Don't rightly know, sir."

At that, the elderly gentleman raised his head and gazed into Jericho's eyes. "You do want to buy a ticket, don't you?"

He nodded. "I reckon I do."

"Then you have to tell me where you're going."

"Alabama, sir."

"Do you mind narrowing it down? Where exactly, in Alabama?"

"That's just the thing. As I said, I don't rightly know. Where would you recommend would be a good place to start?"

The old man rolled his eyes, then looked past Jericho at the disgruntled woman waiting her turn. He yelled, "Next!" The woman pushed past Jericho and made her way to the counter.

Jericho moved had dropped out of line when he heard the woman say, "Montgomery, Alabama." He hurried to the back of the line. When it was his turn, the old man said, "Did you figure out where you want to go?"

"Yessir. I'll take a ticket to ride that train to Montgomery."

He stamped a ticket and said, "Destination, Montgomery. Arrival five-twenty-five."

Jericho paid for his ticket and boarded the train with only minutes to spare, before it chugged down the tracks.

The trip was long, but he was rather enjoying the ride. It was nice seeing so much land for a change. A cute little fellow sitting in the seat in front of him turned around and giggled out loud when Jericho made a funny face. Unlike Thomas, he'd never thought much about having a family, but as he watched the scrawny little kid, he wondered what it would be like to be a daddy. Jericho hid his smile with his hand. *Me? A daddy?* What an absurd thought. To become a father, first, there must be a mother. He thought about the time Octavius asked him if he'd ever been with a woman. He didn't want the fellows to know, but he was pretty sure they all figured it out by the way he got all flustered, trying to think of how to answer. Truth was, he'd had plenty of girls making over him, but they were never the kind he wanted to go out with. Whenever he found a girl he took a liking to, he was too shy to ask her out.

Jericho had plenty of time to think on the trip. He thought about a lot of things. But mostly, he thought about the kind of men his mama brought home. Did he want to turn out like them? He shuddered at the thought. He wanted to make something of himself, so if he ever did have the privilege of having a little boy call him Daddy, he could make him proud.

He could always farm. He'd had plenty experience since dropping out of school the summer after third grade. He was pushing a plow when he was too little to see over it. If only he could read, there'd be a world of opportunities, but most every occupation he could think of required reading. There was one thing he was good at, and that was ciphering. As soon as he was big enough to drive the wagon to market, he was figuring in his head how much money he'd get in return. He didn't realize it was anything special until the swabbies on the ship kept giving him problems to figure. They seemed to think it was a bit peculiar that a fellow that couldn't read could work arithmetic in his head. Jericho never thought much about it, but if he was really as good as they said he was, maybe he could find work where ciphering was needed.

The train pulled up under a shed and a fellow came walking down the aisle, shouting, "All out for Montgomery, Alabama."

Jericho grabbed his duffel bag and stepped out of the train. Walking down the street, he spotted a sign in front of a rambling old two-story house. Although he couldn't read what it said, he was pretty sure it was a Rooming House.

He wandered inside and was met by a jolly woman in her late fifties, maybe early sixties. "Well, come in sailor boy. You looking for a room?"

He twisted his cap in his hands. "Not sure, ma'am. You rent by the night or by the month?"

"I rent by the week, but I give special consideration to our

"I had plans to leave tomorrow, but I reckon I might stay a mite longer. How much we talking about?"

"How's a dollar-fifty a night sound with breakfast and supper included?"

"Sounds fair, ma'am. I thank you." He reached in his pocket for his billfold. "Here's ten-fifty. I believe that would be right for seven days."

"Well, I'll be. That's right on the nose." She led him up the stairs and showed him his room. It was the kind of room he dreamed of living in when he was a child. Frilly white curtains on the windows, a pretty chenille bedspread on the bed, pictures on the wall and a lamp run by electricity. It was perfect.

"I suppose you're on furlough. When do you have to report back?"

"I've done served my tour of duty, ma'am. I was discharged a few days back, but I was in the Naval Hospital when the papers came through, and just got out yesterday."

"In the hospital? Oh, dear. I hope it was nothing serious."

"No ma'am." Jericho had no desire to talk about his burns.

"What will you be doing, now that you're out of the Navy?"

"Not exactly sure, ma'am. Folks say I'm right good at ciphering, so I was thinking maybe I could find something where I could use it."

"I'll say you're good. You hardly blinked an eye when I told you how much the room would be per day. Right off, you said ten-fifty. Just like that. That was very impressive."

"Shucks, ma'am. That weren't nothing. I just said three-dollars for two nights, six dollars for four nights, nine dollars for six nights and that leaves a dollar-fifty for Sunday making it ten-fifty for the week. That one was real easy."

"What are your plans?" She cupped her hands around her jaw. "Oh m'goodness, that must've sounded nosey. What I meant was, do you intend to look for work here in Montgomery, or will you be moving on in a week or so?"

"I ain't had time to give it much thought, to tell the truth. This seems like a right nice town, so I wouldn't have no objections to searching it out. I joined the Navy when I turned seventeen, so I ain't had no experience in job hunting."

"Well, the reason I asked was because I may know someone who could use a man like you for a least a week or two. Might give you a chance to make a little pocket change while you look for something more permanent. Would you mind if I called him?"

"I'd be most grateful, ma'am. You're very kind to want to help me."

"I'm going down the hall to make the call now. I'll be back shortly." She stopped and turned back around. "I forgot to ask. What's your name?"

"The name's, Jericho, ma'am, but most folks just call me Bud or Buddy."

"Nice to meet you, Bud. I'm Miz Lucy. Miz Lucy Matthews."

A few minutes later, Miz Lucy returned wearing a huge smile. "My son wants to know if you can start tomorrow."

"Pardon me, ma'am, but doing what?"

"My son, Donald, is a CPA and he said to send you over. He's been looking for someone who could help for a week or so. His partner was in an automobile accident and will be laid up for a while."

"You say he's a CPA fellow? Ain't that a new government agency, something like the FBI?"

"Oh, no I think you're referring to the Central Intelligence Agency. I've been reading about that. My son is a CPA, which stands for Certified Public Accountant. He deals with figures every day."

"Oh, I know what an accountant is."

"Would you be interested in helping him?"

"Ma'am, I'd be tickled to death to work for your son. Can I go see him now?"

She laughed as if it were the funniest thing she'd heard. Jericho didn't know whether she was poking fun at him or just amused that he'd be in such a hurry.

"Not tonight, son. It's late and he's left the office. But if you can be at his office in the morning at nine o'clock, I'm sure he'll be able to put you to work." She pointed toward the East and said, "His office is on Dexter, about three blocks from here, near the

Capitol."

"I'm much obliged ma'am. I'll be there. Only thing is, I ain't had a chance to buy me no clothes and I don't reckon the stores will be open by nine o'clock. Reckon he'd mind if I came in my uniform? It's the onliest thing I got to wear, but I have an extra pair of bell bottoms and a clean shirt."

"Well, you look mighty spiffy in that uniform, but I think I have a suit that might fit you nicely. It was my son's."

Jericho scratched his head. "You reckon he'd mind me wearing his clothes?"

Her lower jaw trembled. "I had two sons. The suit belonged to Willard and he was killed in the war. I think it would've pleased him to know that I gave his suit to a sailor."

"I'm sorry about your son, ma'am. I can't help wonder sometimes why God would allow a fellow who has a good home to go back to, to die . . . and then let somebody like me, who ain't got nobody waiting on him to return, to live."

"Son, I don't pretend to understand God's ways, but I do know he doesn't make mistakes. So, you can be assured he had a reason for allowing you to survive. Bring him glory by making the most of the life he's allowed you to live."

Jericho nodded his head and promised he would, although he had no clue what she meant.

CHAPTER 6

Jericho found it hard to believe that folks got paid good money, just to sit around and cipher all day. After working at The Matthews Agency for only three days, it was long enough to know this was something he'd like to do for the rest of his life.

He was paid Friday night, and Saturday he walked to town and bought him a brand-new seer-sucker suit and a pair of white loafers for seventy-five percent off. Funny how a suit and pair of shoes could make a man hold his head a little higher and his step a little faster.

Mr. Matthews had a new-fangled machine that you could put the numbers in, pull a lever, and get the total on a little roll of paper, but Jericho found it to be much quicker to do the ciphering in his head, the way he'd always done it.

Mr. Matthews stopped and watched as Jericho scanned over a long list of numbers, then quickly wrote down the total. "Well, I'm very impressed. It's easy to see you don't really need an adding machine, but I'd like for you to practice using it. Do you mind?"

"I don't mind at all. Might be kinda fun to see which one of us gets the right answer, me or the machine."

Mr. Matthews smiled. "My money's on you, Jericho. You're a math whiz, kid. Where did you learn to do that?"

"I went to the stockyards every Friday in the summers while I was growing up. I listened as the farmers bought and sold cattle and hogs by the pound. After a couple of summers, I learned how it worked, and I was figuring the price in my head. It came in handy when I began selling vegetables at market. Folks would sometimes try to cheat a country kid."

"You're amazing."

"It ain't nothing. Really. Numbers come easy. It's letters that give me trouble." The moment the words escaped, he wanted to retrieve them. Would his boss man fire him if he discovered he wasn't smart enough to read?

"Are you saying, you have difficulty reading?"

Jericho rubbed his hand across the back of his neck. "Ain't no need in trying to hide it, I don't reckon. Truth is, Mr. Matthews, I didn't get past third grade."

"Please, call me Donald."

Jericho let out a soft breath. "Yessir, Mr. Donald."

"Just Donald is fine." But it was what he said next that caught Jericho off guard. "Would you like for me to teach you to read?"

The thought of learning to read caused goosebumps on his arms. "I can already say my ABC's. I just don't know how to put 'em together to make words."

"Well, as smart as you are, learning to read should be a cinch. It's almost six o'clock, so let's lock up and we'll finish in the morning. My mama will get my goat if I keep you past suppertime. She's a stickler about having folks at the table on time."

****

Donald's words—'Would you like for me to teach you to read'—had managed to completely crowd out everything else in Jericho's thoughts. He lay awake until well past midnight, wondering what it would be like to read a newspaper, or road signs or cans in the grocery store. Was it possible Donald really could teach a grown man to read?

Jericho could hardly wait to get to work Tuesday morning. It was amazing how that adding contraption could get the right answer every time. The more he used it, the faster he became. By the end of the day, he'd completely stopped ciphering in his head and learned to trust the machine.

At twelve o'clock, Donald walked over to Jericho's desk with a paper sack and pulled out two fried ham sandwiches. He handed one to Jericho. "Compliments of my wife. I thought we could work on reading while we eat lunch."

Jericho's knees knocked under the desk. "You sure you want

to do this? I don't want to disappoint you. What if I can't catch on?"

"You'll catch on quick. You're already three steps ahead. You know your alphabet, so let's go through them and learn what each letter sounds like."

The hour went much faster than Jericho could've imagined. In less than an hour, he'd learned to recognize several words, like cat, dog, run and jump. Jump was the hardest, but he finally figured it out by himself.

Donald went back to his office and as Jericho's fingers knocked out the numbers on the adding machine, his mouth was forming sounds. "A is for Apple. B is for—"

At the end of the day, Donald handed Jericho a little book. "This is a book about a couple of kids called Dick and Jane. I want you to have it. If you set your mind to it, you'll be able to read it all the way through."

That was all he had to do? Set his mind to it? The little paperback book was dog-eared, and the cover was faded, but Jericho had never had a gift he treasured more. Someone had cared enough to want to teach him to read.

After supper he ran upstairs to his room, fell across his bed with his book and studied every letter sounding them out until they formed a word.

When there was a knock on his door, he quickly stuck the book under a pillow.

"It's me, Jericho. May I come in?"

"Miz Lucy?" He opened the door. "Sure. What can I do for you?"

"I was hoping I could do something for you."

"For me? I don't understand."

"Donald told me he was teaching you to read and asked me if I'd like to help."

Jericho's face burned with embarrassment. "I reckon you think that's kinda silly that a grown man don't know how to read."

"Hogwash. There are lots of men who can't read. I admire you for wanting to learn and I would be thrilled to have a part in helping you achieve your goal."

Jericho was amazed at how soon his embarrassment was replaced with an eagerness to learn. Miz Lucy was a good teacher. She was real good and never made him feel stupid when he missed a word. After only three nights, she said, "Jericho, you've learned the sounds. Just practice what you've learned and in no time, you'll be reading the newspaper with no trouble at all."

Miz Lucy left him another book about a boy and girl who lived in Vermont and got syrup from a tree. Anyone knows syrup comes from sugar cane, but he didn't care that the writer had never seen syrup made. All that mattered was that he could read.

After reading it for the third time, Jericho walked over to the closet to hang up his suit. He knocked his bell bottoms off the hanger and when he picked them up, a green envelope he thought was lost forever, fell from his pants pocket. His pulse raced. "Ju-lee-et." He read it over and over. "Ju-lee-et. Juliette. That's it."

Jericho had never put much faith in miracles, but if miracles were real, surely this was nothing less. Now, he had her address . . . the very town where she lived. He sounded out the last word on the envelope. "Al-a-bam-a." That one was easy. But what was the word before it? It began with an E. "En-ter-pris-see." He'd never heard of the place, but it was in Alabama. Did it really matter? It wasn't as if he'd actually go there.

He spent the night tossing and turning in bed, going over all the what-ifs. What if he'd allowed Thomas to mail the letter, instead of insisting he tear it up? By now, Juliette would've had time to adjust to the shock and he could let her know that he'd come as a friend of Octavius's, to do what he could to comfort her in her time of sorrow. She'd think him to be kind to have come such a long way to offer his sympathy. But how could he possibly guess how she'd react to him when he hit her with the dreadful news that Octavius—the man she loved—the man she planned to marry—was dead.

Why did he keep tormenting himself over a fantasy? A beautiful, refined girl like Juliette would have a dozen suitors waiting in the background. How foolish to think she'd ever fall for a hayseed like him?

Jericho felt a mite melancholy as he dressed for work

Wednesday morning. It was his last day to work for the Matthews Agency. He was thankful for all he'd learned in the past three weeks, and Miz Lucy and Donald had become his friends. He never remembered anyone taking such an interest in him. He couldn't remember because it had never happened. Ever.

At lunch, Donald said, "Jericho, you have been a life-saver. I couldn't have gotten through the annual budget without your help."

"Aw, shucks, Mr. Donald. You and Miz Lucy were the lifesavers. In three short weeks, you've taught me how to use an adding machine and how to read. This job has been the best thing that ever happened to me."

"You're smart, Jericho. I'm not sure you realize how smart. You really enjoy working with figures, don't you?"

"Yessir. It seems more like a game to me than work. I felt a mite guilty taking money for something I enjoyed so much."

"So, do you think this kind of work might be something you'd be interested in pursuing?"

"I can't think of anything I'd rather do, but to tell the truth, I ain't never known any CPA's, so it ain't likely I'll ever get the chance."

"I may can help. I have offices in Troy, Enterprise and Eufaula. We have a full staff at the Eufaula office, but the elderly gentleman, Gid Granger, who oversees the Troy and Enterprise offices needs another accountant in Enterprise and he could use two more in the Troy office."

71

Jericho's throat felt dry. Was he daydreaming or was Mr. Donald offering him the job?

"So, what d'ya say, Jericho? Would you be interested in filling one of those spots?"

The words stuck in his throat. "You really think I could do it?"

"No doubt in my mind. You're a math genius. I've never encountered anyone with such masterful skills. Which town would interest you?"

"Don't really matter, I don't reckon. I ain't never been to neither one of them places."

"I think you'd enjoy living in any one of our four locations. Eufaula is a beautiful old town. It was the second office we opened, Troy was third and now we're here. But Enterprise holds a special place in my heart. I met Gid, my business partner, when we were both stationed at Camp Rucker near Enterprise and worked in the same office. When we got out of the army, we decided to open an accounting office, there."

Jericho's brow furrowed. "Say that name again?"

"Gid. Gideon Granger."

"No. I mean the town."

"Camp Rucker? It's an army base."

"No. The place you opened the first office."

"Oh, Enterprise. Ever hear of it?"

"Maybe." Jericho pulled the envelope from his back pocket. He squinted as he studied the words on the paper, then shoved the envelope toward Donald. "I thought it said En-ter-pris-ee. Is this the same place?"

"Indeed it is. You did swell. Long and short vowels and silent letters can be tricky. But I'm proud how quickly you catch on." Donald raised a brow. "Is this Juliette a sweetheart, by any chance?"

"Yessir. She's a sweetheart, alright. She just ain't my sweetheart."

Donald took another glance at the envelope. "Oh, I see now that the letter isn't to you. Am I right to assume she's the addressee's sweetheart?"

"It's a long story." Jericho rubbed the back of his neck. "But if it makes no difference to you and you really think I can handle the job, I'd like to go to Enterprise."

"Enterprise, it is. Can you leave tomorrow?"

"I can do better than that. I can leave today."

"No problem. I'll call Gid . . . uh, Mr. Granger, and let him know you're coming. He'll be happy to know we've filled the position." Donald reached for the phone. "There's a nice hotel located a couple of doors from the office. I'll see if there's a bus leaving tonight and if there is, I'll get you a room at The Hotel Rawls."

Jericho barely had time to grab his clothes and get to the bus station before he found himself sitting in a bus on his way to

Enterprise, Alabama. Everything was happening so fast, he had trouble getting his thoughts together. He had a dream job waiting for him that should be occupying his thoughts, but instead, his mind was on a girl he didn't know and who didn't know him.

Would he have the nerve to look her up? What would he say if he did? Would it bring her comfort to talk with someone who knew the man she'd hoped to marry? Or would it cause more grief? Suddenly, he was sorry he didn't choose the Troy office.

But he didn't choose Troy. He chose Enterprise and he chose it for one reason and one reason only. After he got settled, he'd look her up, give her the sad news of Octavius's recent death and offer his sympathy.

Sympathy? Jericho felt a tinge of guilt. Sure, he was sorry Octavius had to die. But he was glad that Juliette would never have to know that Octavius had no plans to marry her, nor would she ever find out about the other girls he facetiously proposed to.

Jericho needed all the time he could get, to figure out what he'd say to Juliette once they came face-to-face. But there was one thing he knew for certain. She had to be told and there was no one else who would do it. He only hoped he could say something comforting that could help ease her pain. It didn't bother him that folks on the bus looked at him funny because he was talking to himself. It was necessary to practice out loud so he could see how it sounded. "Juliette—" No, he had no right to call her by her first name. He'd say, "Miss Jinright, I'm here as the bearer of some dreadfully sad news, but I felt it just wouldn't be right, if you didn't know that the man you planned to marry has—" Jericho stopped and started over. "Miss Jinright, I've come with some dreadful news, but somebody had to do it. It wouldn't be right if nobody told you the man you planned to marry has—"

He got stuck in the same place every time. He found it too difficult to say Octavius was dead, for fear she'd bust out crying and then what would he do? Why did he tell Thomas to tear up the letter? If only he had it now, it would be so much easier to say, "Miss Jinright, I brung you a letter," and then let her read it for herself instead of having a stranger blurt out the heartbreaking news?

But he didn't have the letter. It was up to him to find the right words. If she wanted to ask questions, he'd give her that chance, but if she didn't want to talk about it, then he'd leave her to grieve in her own way.

CHAPTER 7

A few weeks earlier . . .

After weeks with no mail from Octavius, Juliette's steps became slower and her hopes grew dimmer. She eventually stopped running to meet the Postman.

It was on a Tuesday morning, when she stood on the porch and saw Mr. Watkins waving a letter in the air. Juliette ran to meet him.

He yelled, "I suppose this is what you've been waiting for?"

The envelope had the Naval Hospital's return address in the left-hand corner. "Yessir, you bet it is. I knew there had to be a reason Buddy stopped writing. He must've had a set-back and couldn't write until now."

"Then I suppose the wedding is back on?"

"One way or the other, we'll be getting married Christmas. If he isn't able to come to me, I'll go to him. Excuse me, Mr. Watkins, but I've waited so long to hear from him, I can hardly wait to find out what's been going on."

Juliette ran past her mother and bounded up the stairs to her room. She tore into the letter and kept blotting her eyes as the tears blurred her vision.

Dear Miss Juliette,

It is with true regrets that I must inform you that Seaman 2nd Class Octavius J. Rockwell has succumbed to a fierce bout of a dreadful disease. Octavius's thoughts were on you, and you only, as he fought hard to live so you two could carry out your plans for the future. He was constantly talking about you and how he couldn't wait to marry you. What a pity he had to die. He was crazy in love.

Octavius's Shipmate and Devoted Friend

Juliette screamed, "No, no, no. It can't be true. He's not dead. I won't believe it. Lord, please, please don't let this be so. Please, God, please let this be a mistake."

Her mother knocked lightly on the bedroom door. "Juliette, sweetie, may I come in?"

When there was no answer, she pushed it open, went in and sat on the bed beside her daughter. "Honey, I won't deny that I was glad when that sailor stopped writing to you, but I hate to see your heart broken. I suppose in this letter he's officially broken off the relationship?"

"No, Mother. He didn't break it off."

"Then I don't understand. Why are you so upset?"

Juliette handed her the letter.

Henrietta bit her bottom lip as she read the brief letter. She lay down beside Juliette and wrapped her in her arms. "Oh, honey, I am so sorry. Bless your heart, I can't begin to understand what a shock this must've been. But at least you know now that the reason he hasn't been writing was because he was very sick. That must mean something."

"The only thing it means is that Buddy is gone and I'll never fall in love again."

"Oh, honey, please don't think that. You're very young and beautiful and one day, a young man is going to come into your life and sweep you off your feet."

Juliette sat up in bed with her legs crossed. "Mother, if that's your attempt to comfort me, it isn't working. You don't understand. How could you?"

****

The bus let Jericho out in front of the Rawls Hotel in Enterprise. Never had he seen such a swanky place. A short little elderly woman with blue hair stood behind the desk. She looked up over her spectacles.

"Welcome to the The Hotel Rawls."

He reached in his pocket and pulled out his billfold. "My name's Jericho Rhoades and my boss man, Mr. Donald Matthews called ahead and—"

"Ah, Mr. Rhoades. You can put your money back in your pocket. Mr. Matthews has paid your first week's lodging. He's instructed us to take real good care of you, so if there's anything we can do to make your stay more pleasant, please don't hesitate to let us know. My name is Lula Dawes. Just ring if I can be of service."

Jericho felt a little taller. Not because of the comparison with the four-foot short woman in front of him, but for the first time in his life, he felt like somebody. But why would someone as important as Donald Matthews lean over backwards to help somebody like him? It didn't make sense. "That's mighty kind of you, Mrs. Dawes."

"Miss. I'm Miss Dawes."

"Scuse, me, ma'am."

Her eyes squinted into tiny slits like she was trying to see something afar off. "Folks say God made a woman for every man, but I fear some woman got to my man before I had a chance to find him."

Jericho didn't know what to say. He bit his lip and tried to figure out if it was meant as a regret or a joke. Whatever her reason for adding that little personal detail, he didn't have to wonder for long how to respond. Miss Dawes hardly drew a breath before her next sentence.

"I understand you'll be working for Mr. Matthews. Do you know anyone in Enterprise?"

"The truth is, ma'am, I sorta know somebody, but I sorta don't. Shucks, I reckon that didn't make no sense a'tall."

A gold tooth sparkled like a fine jewel when she smiled. "No explanation necessary, young man. Sounds a bit mysterious and no one loves a mystery more than I do." She reached back of her and took a key from a small cubby hole. "Dinner is served in the dining room until eight-thirty. Country-fried steak, gravy and homemade biscuits is on the menu tonight, and I highly recommend it. It's the cook's specialty."

"Thank you, ma'am. Sounds real good."

Supper was even better than Miss Dawes had let on. Jericho went up to his room and sprawled out on the soft feather mattress. After sleeping on the thin cotton mattresses on the ship's bunks, it felt like lying on a fluffy cloud. Or at least how he imagined a fluffy cloud would feel.

A radio? He turned it on in time to get the Edgar Bergen show. Any other time, the skits would've made him laugh, but tonight it was going to take something funnier than a dummy to pull him out of the slump he was in.

Here he was in the same town with Juliette but unless he could find the nerve to look her up, he would've done better to choose another location to keep from being tormented. He pulled out the envelope. The address in the top corner was easy to read. W. Lee Street. Jericho was glad it was only three letters.

CHAPTER 8

Jericho arose early Thursday morning and after breakfast strolled down the street. It was too early for stores to open. He gazed at a large monument, situated smack kadab in the middle of the street. What a peculiar place for a stature.

He stopped in front of a men's store and imagined what he'd look like in the double-breasted suit on the mannequin in the window. Things in his life were happening so fast. But why? He thought about what Miz Lucy at the boarding house said to him the day he questioned why God allowed him to live but took her son. Still made no sense. He had nobody who cared if he lived or died, yet God let her son die, when he had a wonderful family who loved him. Her words were as plain as the day she spoke them.

Son, I don't pretend to understand God's ways, but I do know he doesn't make mistakes. So, you can be assured he had a reason for allowing you to survive. Bring him glory by making the most of the life he's allowed you to live.

Jericho didn't know what she meant then, nor did he understand now what she meant by bring glory to God.

At seven-forty-five, he crossed the street, straightened his bowtie and ran his fingers through his hair before walking into The Matthews Agency.

An elderly fellow hobbled over with an outstretched hand. "And you're Jericho, I presume."

He nodded. "Mr. Granger?"

"That's me. Donald has told me some wonderful things about you, young man. If you're half as good as he says, the agency is blessed to have you."

Jericho rubbed the back of his neck. "I don't know why Mr. Donald lets on about me the way he does. I ain't so smart. Did he tell you I couldn't read a lick until him and his mama learned me about how the letters sound? Not that I'm proud of it, but it's the truth."

The old man held his head back and hee-hawed, which made Jericho a mite uncomfortable. Was he poking fun at him?

"Jericho, trust me. Donald doesn't pin flowers on anyone who doesn't deserve them, so I'm confident you're as smart as he says you are. He's a good man and I've been reluctant to retire and leave him until he could find the right person. I feel like maybe he has."

Jericho took an immediate liking to Mr. Granger. He only

hoped the old fellow would decide to stick around for a good while.

After work, he walked over to Martin Drug Store, sat down at the counter and ordered a cherry coke. A distinguished looking gent sitting at a table nearby, picked up his chocolate malt, and took a seat on the stool next to Jericho.

"I haven't seen you around. You new here?"

"Yessir. This is the first time I ever been here. I just got outta the Navy."

The man's firm handshake made Jericho feel as if he'd met a true friend. "You don't say. I was a Navy man myself. Welcome to Enterprise. I'm Walt Wilkerson."

"Nice to make your acquaintance, Mr. Wilkerson. The name's Jericho, but some folks just call me Buddy."

The man's eyes widened. "Where's your home, Buddy?"

"I'm from Mississippi, sir, but I ain't been there for several years, so I don't consider it home."

Mr. Wilkerson stroked his chin. "I don't suppose you came to Enterprise because of a girl, did you?"

Jericho hesitated, not wanting to lie, yet not wanting to admit the truth. "Yessir, I reckon that's one of the reasons I'm here. I have something important I need to tell her."

The man stood, slapped him on the back and said, "Is she expecting you?"

He shook his head. "Oh, no. She don't even know I'm alive,

so she has no reason to be expecting me."

Mr. Wilkerson's face split into a wide grin. "Would you think me rude if I asked where this girl lives that you'd like to go see?"

"No sir, not rude a'tall. In fact, maybe you can tell me how to find Lee Street."

"Not only will I tell you, I'll take you there. My truck is parked out front."

"Don't want to put you out, sir. I don't mind walking if you'll point me in the right direction."

"Nonsense. It's my privilege."

Jericho went around to the passenger side of the blue truck parallel-parked in front of the drugstore. "The house number is 4014. That's 4014 West Lee Street."

"I know exactly where it is. I'm courting the widowed mother of the pretty young lady who lives there and she's going to be thrilled to see you. She's been quite melancholy lately and I think your coming will be just what she needs to cheer her up."

The lump in his throat was hard to swallow. "I wanted to come sooner."

"Well, you're here now, and I wouldn't miss this for the world. She'll be very happy to see you."

"I'd love to believe that, sir, but as I said, she don't even know I'm alive, so my visit may be a shock to her."

"Well, this is the kind of shock she needs. Juliette's wandered around in a fog lately, unable to eat or sleep. But having you here will do wonders for her. Say, it would be swell if you showed up in your uniform."

Surely, Mr. Wilkerson had his reasons. "I'm staying at the Rawls. If you really think it would help Juliette, I'll be happy to change."

"You sure you don't mind?"

"No sir." Before he could add anything further, Mr. Wilkerson was pulling up at The Rawls.

"I'll wait in the truck while you get into your uniform."

Jericho prayed all the way up the elevator and continued the prayer as he dressed. Maybe it was praying for Thomas that made him feel like there really was a God in heaven who knew him by name.

He'd carefully planned what he'd say to Juliette and now suddenly the words escaped him. Was he making a mistake? What if she started bawling? How should he react to try to comfort her? Would it be out of line to hug her?

His mind was still reeling as they drove to Lee Street and parked in front of a large, Victorian home, that looked like it belonged on a Christmas card.

Walking to the door, Mr. Wilkerson said, "Buddy, why don't you let me go in first and prepare her. Then, I'll open the door and invite you in."

That sounded like a swell idea. He was glad to know that Mr. Wilkerson was willing to go in and try to soften the blow of seeing a sailor standing at her front door.

"Stand back, Buddy, so Juliette or her mother won't see you when I open the door." Mr. Wilkerson stuck his head in and yelled, "Anybody home?"

A voice called back, "In the kitchen, Walt. Come on in."

Jericho paced the front porch as he waited. Why couldn't he remember what he had so carefully planned to say to her? Why was it taking so long?

Henrietta Jinright and her daughter Juliette looked up from the dinner table when Walter Wilkerson walked in. He tipped his hat and glanced at Juliette's damp cheeks. "I hope I haven't come at a bad time. I should've called first."

Henrietta brushed his comment off with a toss of her hand. "Nonsense. I wasn't expecting you, but I'm glad you came. Juliette and I could stand a little cheering up, couldn't we sweetheart?"

Juliette glanced up with bloodshot eyes and lifted a shoulder in a shrug.

"Well that's what I'm here for."

Henrietta said, "That's a sneaky look on your face. What have you got up your sleeve, Walt Wilkerson?"

"I've brought Juliette a gift, I think she'll be proud to receive."

"Oh? And where is this exciting gift?"

"Waiting on the front porch."

Though Juliette showed no interest, Henrietta said, "Well,

shall we go see, Juliette?"

Walter shook his head. "I think we should let her go alone."

Juliette said, "It's a kitten, isn't it? Thanks, Walt."

Henrietta said, "Well aren't you going to go look, sweetheart? Walt was nice enough to bring you a gift. I think you'd want to go see it."

When she made no effort to move, Walter said, "Please, go look, Juli. You'll be glad you did."

"Sure, Walt."

Juliette trudged out to the porch and looked down at her feet, expecting to see a kitten. She turned and her heart caught in her throat, seeing a tall, handsome sailor standing there with tears in his eyes.

His voice cracked. "Hello, Juliette."

"Buddy!" She screamed, then ran and leaped into his arms.

He tried to speak, but the words wouldn't come. All he could think about was Juliette Jinright was in his arms, kissing his neck. She loosened her grip, then grabbed him by the hand and pulled him. "Come inside and meet my mother."

"Mother, look who's here." Juliette wrapped her arm around Jericho's waist.

Her mother's brow met in the center. "You aren't saying this is—"

Juliette laughed through her tears. Yes ma'am, that's exactly what I'm saying. When I read in the Bible about poor, barren

Hannah praying for a baby and God sent her a little boy, I knew then that prayer was my only hope. When little Samuel was born, Hannah said, "For this child I prayed."

Juliette's gaze locked with Jericho's. "Now, God has seen my tears and heard my cry, and like Hannah, I can say, 'For this man I prayed.' Isn't that amazing, Mother? It's a miracle."

Jericho's brow raised. He'd heard enough about a miracle-working God to know that there was nothing He couldn't do. Not that he'd ever admitted it to anyone, and lately he'd done a little praying of his own, but he never in a thousand years would've expected God to do something this big for him.

Jericho held out his hand. "Mrs. Jinright, my name is . . ."

Juliette's mother tilted her head back and peered from beneath her glasses. "Sailor, you don't have to introduce yourself." She raised a skeptical brow. "I'll have to agree with my daughter. There's no other way to explain your presence . . . unless you're AWOL."

Mr. Wilkerson's brows meshed together "Henrietta!"

Jericho slowly withdrew his hand and holding his hat in the other, he clasped them both behind his back.

"Oh, Walt. I was kidding, of course. You take things too seriously. Young man, I'll admit I've not been in favor of this courtship, but if you are indeed the answer to Juliette's prayer, who am I to question God?"

Jericho glanced first at Juliette, then at Mr. Wilkerson. The woman might as well be speaking Greek, because he had no idea what she'd just said. He couldn't figure out if she liked him or not.

She said, "We haven't had a chance to get to know you, so I hope you will grant us the opportunity before you and Juliette jump into anything."

"Yes'm. Sounds fair enough, ma'am." Jericho felt he'd already jumped into something. It was as if he'd fallen out of a plane and landed in a foreign country. Either that, or the woman was nuts. What exactly did she think they were going to jump into?

Her eyes squinted as her gaze started at the top of his head and slowly made its way to his feet and then back up again. "How long will you be staying in Enterprise before returning to duty?"

Jericho twisted his cap in his hands. "Oh, I've been discharged, ma'am. I done got me a job at the Matthews Agency, so I'll be staying here in Enterprise."

"The Matthews Agency? Then you'll be working for Gid? Gid Granger is a close family friend. What exactly will you be doing there?"

"Ciphering, ma'am."

She covered her smile with a linen napkin. "Ciphering? Is that a fact? Well, I don't suppose Gid would've hired you if he hadn't properly checked your credentials."

She seemed to be warming up to him now that she'd learned he was working for the Matthews Agency. He thought it was a big deal, but he had no idea it would mean so much to other folks.

"You must've had to pull quite a few strings to wind up with a job here in Enterprise. It's plain to see you're a man who sets his mind on what he wants and goes after it."

"The truth is, ma'am, the reason I come here was because—"

"Fiddle-faddle. It's no secret why you're here. I gather your discharge was an honorable one?" She glanced at Walt's frown. "Oh, dear, that didn't come out right. What I meant was, Juliette told us about your accident, so I assume you received a medical discharge—which would be honorable, would it not, Buddy? Do you mind if I call you Buddy?"

"Buddy is just fine, ma'am. I went by the name Jericho until I joined the Navy, and that's when the fellows started calling me Buddy . . .and well, after a spell, it just took."

"Well, I do declare. Jericho, is it? A fine Biblical name. I wondered what the 'J' stood for."

Jericho recalled when Mr. Donald was teaching him the alphabet, he said "A" was for apple, "B" was for boy, but for the life of him he couldn't recall what he said "J" stood for. Never in a hundred years would he have guessed it stood for Jericho.

"Yes'm. 'J' is for Jericho, alright. J-E-R-I-C-H-O, Jericho." He was glad he could spell it.

"Well, I like it even better than your first name."

My first name? Jericho thought best not to correct her by telling her he only had one first name, but he wondered what she would've thought if she knew how many last names he had.

Juliette stood squeezing Jericho's hand. "Mama, you're asking a ton of questions. I think you're making him nervous."

"Heavenly days, Juliette, what a silly thing to say. He's not nervous at all. Are you, Jericho?"

Mr. Wilkerson said, "Henrietta, I'm sure these kids don't care about hanging out with us ol' folks. It's a beautiful night. Why don't you two go sit on the front porch in the swing. I'm sure you have lots to talk about."

Juliette giggled. "You bet we do." Still holding Jericho's hand, she pulled him down the hall toward the front door.

CHAPTER 9

For months, Jericho had dreamed of sitting on the porch swing with Juliette. If this was nothing more than another dream, he hoped he'd continue to have a repeat every night.

His pulse raced and his hands felt sweaty when they sat in the swing and she slid up and laid her head on his shoulder. It was wrong of him to think ill of the dead, but he couldn't help thinking how Octavius would've taken advantage of this situation. Not him. Juliette was too sweet . . .too innocent . . . too pure, to understand what she was doing. For what seemed like forever, they rocked slowly back and forth in the creaking swing. Jericho was sure she could hear the beating of his heart. He sucked in the aroma of her perfume . . . a scent he'd learned to recognize from Octavius's letters. *Octavius's letters . . .she thinks I'm . . . Octavius.* He licked his lips. "Uh . . . uh . . .Juliette . . . I'm not . . . I'm not— What I'm trying to say is that there's something you don't know about me and as hard as it is for me to get it out, it's only right that you should know."

She reached up and placed long slender fingers over his lips. "It's okay, sweetheart. I know all I want to know. The only thing that's important to me now is that you're sitting here beside me. Let's just bask in this wonderful moment of being together." The creaking swing appeared to get louder and louder.

He had to tell her. Didn't he? But why would she have insisted she knew all she wanted to know? Was that his cue to keep quiet? Octavius was gone, never coming back . . . and he was there. Juliette had never met Octavius. Who was to say that she wouldn't have picked him over Octavius, even if Octavius hadn't died? And with that thought, he chose to oblige her by keeping his mouth shut and enjoying the moment.

All the smart, brave, funny things he fantasized about saying to her as he listened to Octavius read her letters in the ward, began to come back to him.

He leaned his head back. "Look at all them stars, wouldja. Beautiful, ain't they? Sparkly like diamonds."

She giggled. "They are beautiful, but everything in my life is beautiful tonight, darling."

Darling? He jerked on the neck of his shirt, that seemed to grow tighter as he sat there. He cleared his throat. "Anybody ever showed you the Big Dipper?"

She pointed. "Yes, there it is."

He didn't know why he never considered she might be showing it to him instead of him pointing it out to her. "Yep. That's it, alright. I always remember something that happened to me when I was—" All those times he had practiced these lines, it went, "I always remember something that happened to me when I was in second grade." Now, he saw no need to mention the grade. The important thing was to let her know that he did get some schooling, in case at some point she might begin to wonder.

"When you were what, dear?"

"When I was going to school. We had two dippers hanging on a nail on the side of the school building. The biggest dipper b'longed to the teacher and all us young'uns were s'posed to drink from the littlest one. Well, one day—and to this day, I still don't know why I done it—but I reached for the wrong dipper and got the teacher's. She caught me and boy, did she tan my hide."

Jericho waited, expecting Juliette to giggle at his funny story. She didn't. Didn't laugh, didn't chuckle . . . heck, she didn't even smile. Now, that he thought about it, it was a stupid story. He felt a blush rising from his neck, heating his forehead. What was he thinking? The eerie silence made him nervous. He chewed on his bottom lip. Then, feeling the need for an explanation, he blurted, "To this day, when I'm outside gazing at the stars, I always think about that whooping I got the day I drunk from the big dipper. Dumb, ain't it? I don't even know why I told it." But he *did* know why. It was because he had practiced such a scenario every night

95

from the first time Octavius had read one of her letters in the hospital ward.

She reached up and kissed his cheek. "No, sweetheart. It isn't a dumb story."

His breath caught in his throat.

"It's a very sad story. Poor thing. You were just a child. I'm sure you meant no harm and couldn't understand why she'd be so upset."

"Nah, even as a little boy, I understood why she was mad. I figured she was afraid she'd catch some ferocious disease from a little throwed-away young'un like me. I never really blamed her and it wadn't like it was the worse whooping I ever got. But after I learned there was a big dipper in the sky, I wondered if the man in the moon got to drink out of it, or if that one was for Venus."

This time, she laughed. "Now, that's funny, Buddy. That's real funny." She reached for his hand and gave it a little squeeze. How could his mouth feel so dry while his hands felt so wet? If only he had taken the time to rub his hand across his pants leg first to wipe off the sweat. What good would it have done? By the time she touched him, he would've begun sweating all over again.

Their gaze met. Never in all his years had he seen anything more lovely. The guys on the ship had pin-ups of Betty Grable, but even Betty didn't hold a candle to Juliette Jinright.

She reached up and whispered in his ear, even though there was no one in hearing distance. "Buddy, sweetheart, I want to hear you say you love me. You do, don't you?"

He nodded, while trying to get the words in his heart to rise to his mouth. "Yes. I . . .I do . . . I really do." He stammered. "Love you, I mean. I really do, Juliette. Yes ma'am, I sure do love you, alright."

She snuggled close and looking up into his eyes, she whispered. "I love you, too darling. I've been thinking about the Christmas wedding. What do you think?"

"Uh . . . well, I like Christmas and I think weddings are swell, so I reckon a Christmas wedding would be pretty special."

"I'm glad you like the idea."

He felt her warm breath on his neck.

"Buddy? Don't you want to kiss me?"

Was she kidding? Never had he wanted to do something so bad in all his life. Shame swept over him as he recalled in vivid detail a conversation he'd had with Octavius, when Octavius said, "Buddy boy, you haven't lived until you've been spooning with a real woman in a parked car on a lonely road, feeling her moist lips on yours and hearing her heart beat in rhythm with your own."

Jericho remembered saying, "I don't think I could do that unless . . . well, you know . . . unless I really loved her and she loved me . . . and well, unless maybe I was engaged to her."

Well, here he was. He loved her and she just admitted to loving him. *Him.* He was here in flesh and blood and she just said it out loud. *She loves me. Not Octavius, but me . . . Jericho*

Rhoades.

She tilted her head back and closed her eyes. "Well?"

Jericho didn't have to think what to do, nor did he think what *not* to do. He just did it. With his arms wrapped around her, he pulled her close, and felt as if he were floating on air when his lips found hers. He kissed her lips, her forehead, her soft pink cheeks and her cute little chin. Then, suddenly, he pushed away. Was he no better than Octavius J Rockwell III?

His breathing had escalated to the point he could hardly speak. "I'm sorry, Juliette. I don't know what came over me."

"Jericho, you are so sweet. Please don't feel you need to apologize. I practically begged you to kiss me."

All the preparations Jericho made before arriving, had not included the possibility that he could be mistaken for Octavius. To tell Juliette the truth now, would be like having Octavius die twice. Wouldn't it? She had to know the truth—just not now.

"Buddy, the truth is, I've wanted you to kiss me from the moment you walked in the door."

"Seriously? From the moment I walked in the door? Are you saying it was me and not all the gushy letters that made you choose to kiss me?"

She giggled. "Well, I'll admit, the letters were very romantic but—" She stopped after the 'but,' indicating there was more.

And if there was more, Jericho wanted to hear it all. "But what? Please finish."

"I was just thinking how the letters didn't sound at all the way you talk. I'm not saying there's anything wrong with it . . . it just took me by surprise since I pictured you quite differently. I can't explain."

Jericho's face scrunched into a frown. "I think I can. I'm a hillbilly—a nobody. But then you didn't really fall in love with me. You fell for a bunch of letters filled with high class words. It's no mystery. I can explain."

Her eyes widened and Jericho was unprepared when she leaned over and planted a kiss right on his smackeroo.

She said, "Oh, my sweet Buddy. Don't ever refer to yourself as a nobody. You are the most important person in my life." She glanced down and her voice lowered. "It's true, you don't sound at all like the letters, but I know the reason for that."

"You do?" He felt chills run down his spine. *She knows!* All his fretting was for nothing. She knew and she loved him, anyway. Of course! The hospital must've returned her letters with a note on the front that the person she was writing had died. That was the only way she could've known. At least now, he could stop dreading having to deliver the news.

The moon had never looked as big or as bright as it did tonight. Jericho wanted to think of something to say but his tongue was tied in a knot. All he could think of was the feeling he had when her lips pressed against his.

She said, "Buddy, when did you first know that you loved

me?"

"That's easy. It was after that first letter that you wrote."

"Really? You knew that quickly? What was it I said that made you fall in love?"

"It wasn't so much what you said as what you didn't say. You didn't brag on yourself, although you had plenty to brag about. I could tell from your picture that you were the prettiest girl I'd ever seen. Not only that, but I liked that you're a God-fearing woman and your letters were sweet and genuine. Not like them others." He swallowed hard. He hadn't meant to bring up Octavius's other playthings. It just slipped. He could only hope she didn't pick up on it. He wouldn't hurt her for the world.

"What others?"

"Did I say anything about others?"

"You know you did."

"Well, what I meant was I listened to a braggart in the next bed read letters from all his lady friends but yours were the sincere kind any sailor would like to receive. Me, included. Sorry if I upset you."

"Oh." She laughed. "I will admit you gave me a scare. I was hoping you weren't saying that a lot of girls were writing to you."

Jericho laughed. "Shucks, you didn't really think that, did you?"

"I didn't want to, but to tell the truth, Mama and Walt had real reservations."

He jumped up. "I'm sorry. I reckon I come at a bad time. I didn't know they was going somewhere."

"No, I just mean, they were afraid you were like the sailors you hear about—you know—the kind who are said to have a girl in every port. They tried to warn me that you might be writing a dozen other girls the same thing you were writing to me, but I knew better."

When she reached for his hand, he eased back down in the swing. Suddenly, Jericho had rocks rolling around in his stomach. *I thought she knew. She said she knew.* "Uh . . . Juliette, maybe I should go."

She grabbed his arm. "Not yet, sweetheart. Please don't go."

"I don't feel so well."

"It's my fault, isn't it? I upset you when I said Mama and Walt didn't trust you. Well, it's obvious they don't feel that way now that they've met you. I can tell they're both crazy about you. And so am I. I don't think they wanted to believe you were like the others, but they felt the need to prepare me, in case they turned out to be right." She leaned her head on his shoulder. "But now that you're here, they can see that you're more than I even had a right to hope for. More handsome, more sincere, more of everything that's good and honorable. Oh, Buddy, I wanted to die when it appeared they were right and I began to believe that you might've been playing me for a fool. The humiliation was almost more than I could bear."

"No, Juliette. Don't say that. Don't ever say that." *Die?* His throat closed making it difficult to swallow. What if Juliette should discover it was true—that Octavius *was* one of the ones her Mother and Mr. Wilkerson warned her about? He could never allow that to happen. Jericho glanced through the window at the huge crystal chandelier over the dining room table and shuddered at the hideous thought of beautiful Juliette dangling from a rope. He had to tell her the truth and let her know he wasn't Octavious. But there was no way he'd do it until he was assured she wouldn't harbor such gruesome thoughts.

Juliette rubbed his hand between her two. "You're shivering. Are you cold, sweetheart? Perhaps we should go in."

Jericho placed his cap back on his head. "I really must go."

"I wish you could stay longer, but I understand. I'm sure you're tired. But you will come have dinner with us tomorrow night, won't you? Greta always serves it at six o'clock. Will that be too early for you?"

"Not too early, but I'm not sure if I should."

"Don't be silly. I'll see that Greta makes something special, since it will be a special occasion—our first meal together, with many more to come. See you at six?"

He nodded, though he couldn't look her in the eye. "Juliette, I want you to know that no matter what happens, I meant it when I said I love you. I love you so much I can't sleep at night."

Her brow creased. "I love you, too, sweetheart. But what did you mean by 'no matter what happens?' That sounded so ominous. Is there something you aren't telling me?"

How could he answer? Of course, there was something he wasn't telling her, but to blurt it out now could be the death of her. Literally. The death of her. His knees wobbled at the frightening thought. "Aw, shucks, I was just rambling. That's what happens when you get tired and I'm plumb wore out."

"Well, of course you are, darling. I'm afraid I was being selfish to want to keep you here. You will come over tomorrow night after work, won't you?"

"Yeah. I'll be here. We've got some things we need to talk about."

"Yes, we do. Christmas will be here in a couple of months and there's so much to do. I can't wait."

When Jericho hung his head, she lifted his chin with her thumb. "What's wrong, darling? You don't seem excited. You do want to marry me, don't you?"

His voice quaked. "Juliette, I ain't never wanted nothing so much in my whole life, and that's the Gospel truth. But there are things about me that you don't know and it ain't right to go on letting you believe a lie."

She caught him by surprise when her lips split into a big smile. Her eyes sparkled. "Oh, Buddy, if you're talking about all that foolishness you wrote about having a rich father and graduating from that prestigious school, think nothing of it. I'd already figured out that you were only trying to impress me."

"But, Juliette, that wasn't me."

"Of course, it wasn't you. It was that old devil who tempted you to lie, and now the Lord won't let you be at peace until you confess it for what it was. It's sinful to lie, but it's plain to see you're truly remorseful and I want you to know that I have forgiven you."

It shouldn't have surprised him that she caught on that he didn't have no fancy learning. This was getting more complicated by the minute. "Juliette, you're about the closest thing to an angel that I'll ever get to. I don't deserve your forgiveness."

"Buddy, how can I convince you that all your bragging wasn't what made me fall for you. I don't care about money. I grew up with a wealthy father who had more money than he knew what to do with. It's sad to say, but I don't think my daddy was ever happy a day in his life."

"If the talk of money and a fancy education didn't make you fall in love, would you mind telling me what it was?" Jericho had a personal reason for wanting her answer.

"Well, when you talked of going into the ministry, I knew then that money was not your God. Heaven knows, preachers barely make enough to survive on. That's when I figured all the braggadocios talk in your letters was coming from the devil. He was tempting you to lie. I'm not telling you anything you don't know when I remind you that Satan goes to and fro, seeking whom he may devour. That's what he does, but I won't let him devour you. If God is leading you into the ministry, we'll trust him to provide for our needs. We'll live on love and syrup and biscuits."

"I . . . I gotta go, Juliette. I shoulda left an hour ago." He meant it with all his heart. Not only did she think he was Octavius, she thought he was gonna be a preacher? He reckoned he could pull it off easier than Octavius, but neither one of 'em knew squat about the Bible. Octavius was a known liar. But was it worse to be a known liar, or an unknown liar?

CHAPTER 10

After Jericho left, Juliette went into the house and was sneaking up the stairs before her mother and Walter noticed her.

"Juliette, sweetheart, come into the living room. I'd like to talk to you."

She paused on the fourth stair and held to the banister. "I'm really tired, Mother. Could it wait until tomorrow?"

"What I have to say won't take long. Come in here and have a seat."

Juliette slowly made her way down the steps, then stood in the doorway and mumbled. "What do you want, Mother?"

"For goodness sake, don't act as if I'm sending you to the slaughterhouse." She pointed to a nearby chair, which Juliette took as her cue to sit down. "I merely wanted to ask you how you feel about that sailor, now that you've had an opportunity to see him. And hear him."

The slur didn't go past Juliette. She knew exactly why her mother tacked on the last three words. "You sound as if he's just another sailor, Mother. Please call him Buddy, and it's not as if I don't know him. I fell in love with him through his sweet letters. Why is that so hard for you to understand?"

"Honey, people can be anyone they want to be on paper, I'm merely wondering if he met your expectations."

"It's late, Mother, and I'd like to go to bed. Why don't you stop beating around the bush and get it all out at once instead of hem-hawing around the subject?"

"Juliette! That's no way for you to talk to me."

"Sorry, Mother, but I have a feeling you have something on your mind and for both our sakes, I think it would be wise if you let me know what you're getting at, instead of making me guess."

"Well, I did hope you'd be the one to bring it up, but now that you've forced my hand, I'll go ahead and say what I'm sure we're both thinking. That young man's English is worse than Greta's, and she didn't come to this country until eight years ago."

Walt, who had been quiet until now, laid the newspaper down and blurted, "For crying out loud, Henrietta. If it doesn't bother her, why should it bother you?"

She shot an icy glare in his direction. "Walt Wilkerson, it bothers me because she's my daughter and I'll thank you not to interfere."

He picked up his paper and continued to read.

Henrietta took on a more sympathetic tone. "Juliette, honey, I know you're infatuated, and I'll admit, he's awfully handsome so I don't blame you for having a crush on him, but—"

"It's not a crush, Mother. I love, Buddy, and we're going to be married in seven weeks and five days and I hope it will be with your blessings, but if you can't bring yourself to accept him, then it'll be a loss for all of us." She stood and planted her hands on her hips. "I love him and I plan to marry him, so I hope you'll learn to accept him."

Henrietta thrust her hand over her heart. "Oh, my sweet naïve child. You have no idea what you are saying."

Walter mumbled something under his breath.

Henrietta's brow lifted. "What did you say, Walt?"

"I said, your daughter's in love, Henrietta. She's eighteen years old, and if I remember correctly, you were only seventeen when you married."

"Yes, but I was much more mature at seventeen than she is at eighteen."

"Henrietta, you've always boasted about how mature Juli is, and now that she's about to make a decision that doesn't meet your expectations, all of a sudden she's immature? I don't think you even believe that."

"Walter Wilkerson, how dare you defy me in front of my daughter. I'd like it if you'd leave right now."

"I'm sorry I upset you, Henrietta, but I think you'll be making a big mistake if you try to come between these two kids."

"Ah ha! There. You've admitted it. Kids! That's exactly what they are. Kids with outlandish notions about love and I'd appreciate it if you'd not interfere in something that is of no concern of yours."

"That's where you're wrong, Henrietta. Juli is my concern. I promised Steve before he died that I'd look after her. I love her as if she were my own daughter, but you know that, don't you?"

"Well, Steve Jinright is dead, and I hereby relieve you of any perceived obligation you may feel toward *my* child. She's neither your responsibility nor Steve's and I will not allow Juliette to ruin her life by getting involved with that . . that—"

"Nobody? Is that the word you're searching for, Mother?"

"Juliette, that isn't what I was going to say, but you'll have to admit, he's not our kind."

"Our kind?"

Walt stood, laid the paper down and glared at Henrietta. He picked up a box of matches from the sofa table, then reached in his shirt pocket and pulled out a pack of cigarettes. He lit it, blew out a puff of smoke, then placed the matches back on the table. It was his ritual when he needed time to think before speaking.

"Henrietta, I'm going, but if you insist on controlling Juli's life, I fear you'll live to regret it."

"Get out, Walter Wilkerson. Get out!"

His boots made a clomping sound as he stomped down the

hall. The front door slammed with a bang.

Henrietta's bottom lip trembled.

"Mother, go after him. You know you want to."

"No. He's becoming way too possessive of you and I'll not have him telling me how I should raise you."

"Raise me? Mother, I'm eighteen. You've already raised me. In case you haven't noticed, I'm grown."

"Ha! You *think* you're grown, but you're still acting like a thirteen-year-old schoolgirl. Sweetheart, I know what's best for you so you might as well put these foolish notions of marrying that ignorant sailor out of your mind. I'll not stand by and watch you ruin your life. I simply won't allow it."

****

Walter drove straight to the Rawls and walked up to the desk. "Would you ring Buddy Rockwell's room, please?"

The elderly lady's eyes squinted as she searched the records book. "Buddy, did you say? I don't recall anyone by that name, but perhaps he checked in before my shift."

"I'm sorry, I believe his name is Jericho. Perhaps that's the name he used."

Her eyes lit up. "Jericho! Why, of course. Such a nice young man." She snickered. "Handsome, too. If I was twenty-five years younger, I'd be setting my cap for that one."

"Would you mind ringing his room?"

"No need to do that."

"I beg your pardon?"

"He isn't in."

"Are you sure?"

"Of course, I'm sure. I don't make up things about our guests."

"Sorry, I didn't mean to imply—" Walt let out a heavy sigh and turned to walk out.

The little old lady chuckled. "But I know where he is."

Walt turned on his heels and waited.

"He walked down to the drugstore. He asked me if there was anything I needed from there. As I said, he's just the nicest young fellow. I did say that already, didn't I?"

Walt nodded. "Thank you, ma'am."

CHAPTER 11

Jericho was sitting alone at a round table in the back of the room, sipping on something from a metal tumbler when Walt approached him.

Jericho jumped up. "Mr. Wilkerson, we meet again. You must enjoy these chocolate malts as much as I do. I'd be pleased if you'd join me."

"Thanks, Buddy, but that's not what I'm here for." Walt pulled out a chair and straddled it backwards.

A waitress yelled out, "Walt, you want your usual?"

"No, thanks, Doris. I just came in to see Buddy, here."

Jericho's brow shot up. "To see me, sir? Is something wrong? It's not Juliette, is it? Please tell me she's okay."

"Stop worrying, Juli is fine. She's not the problem."

"Problem, sir?" Jericho hung his head and ran his fingers

through his hair. "She knows, doesn't she? I reckon she hates me. I was gonna tell her. I promise, I was. I just had to have time to think how to say it."

Walter chewed on the corner of his bottom lip. "You low-down scumbag."

"Call me what you will, but I promise, this isn't the way I planned it."

"You had me believing that you loved her as much as she loves you, but Henrietta was right. She had you pegged from the beginning as just another sailor with a girl in every port." He glared into Jericho's eyes. "I want to punch you in the face and I just may not be able to restrain from doing it. Not only have you lied to sweet Juli and made her fall in love with you, but you've made a fool out of me and may have caused me to lose the woman I've been in love with for twenty years."

Jericho closed his eyes and reared back in his chair. "This ain't the way it was s'posed to go down. I've made such a mess of things, so go ahead. Hit me if it'll help make things better."

Walt's chin quivered. "How about you telling me exactly how you expected it to go down? I suppose you wanted to see her face when you broke the news to her that it was all a big joke. You never intended to marry her, did you?"

"Me? No sir. I never had any such intentions."

"My lands, Buddy. Have you no heart? How could you be so cruel?"

Jericho rubbed the back of his neck. "I don't get it. Are you saying you want me to marry her?"

"Of course not. I don't want her to marry someone who doesn't love her. She deserves better."

"But I do love her."

Walt leaned back in his chair. His gaze locked with Jericho's. "I'm confused. You *do* love her?"

"More'n I ever thought it was possible to love anybody."

"Then how did we get into this conversation?"

Jericho scratched his head. "I think it was when you sat down here and called me a low-down scumbag. I ain't saying you was wrong. I've called myself worse, plenty of times."

"Maybe we should start over. I'll say this slow and I expect an honest answer. Buddy, are you in love with Juli?"

"Yes sir. I think we've done got that far. To tell the truth, I think I knew I was in love with her the first time I heard one of her letters being read in the hospital ward."

"Are you saying you passed her letters around for everyone to read?"

"Not me, sir. Octavius. He always read 'em out loud and most of the fellows got a big laugh out of 'em." He sucked on his straw, until it was obvious from the slurping sound that the tumbler was empty. "I didn't laugh at the letters. Not one bit. I just wished she was saying those sweet romantic things to me instead of to Octavius."

Walt's gaze locked with Jericho's. "Instead of Octavius? Are you trying to say you are not Octavius?"

"Me? No sir. My name is Jericho."

"But that's what the J stands for, isn't it?"

"Yes sir. I believe that's right."

"Then you are Octavius Jericho Rockwell III. Am I right?"

"No sir."

Walt pulled in a deep breath, which made a whistling noise when he slowly exhaled. "Then who are you and what are you doing here?"

"I'm Jericho Rhoades, sir, and my reason for coming was to tell Juliette the man she thought was gonna marry her—Octavius Rockwell—well, he died, and I thought it just fitting since I knew him, that I should come tell her he was dead—you know, to comfort her in her deep sorrow."

Walt scratched his head. "Buddy, is that the truth?"

"No sir."

With his hands clasped back of his head, he glared at the floor. "Excuse me? Did you say no?"

"Yes sir."

Slowly raising his head, he said, "Would it be too much to ask of you to tell me the truth?"

"Ain't no imposition a'tall. Truth is, I sorta lied . . . not just to you, but to myself, also, when I said my reason for wanting to see her was to offer comfort. It was an excuse. I came here because I couldn't stay away. I had to see her. Not that I wouldn't have tried to comfort her, but the real reason I wanted to see her was because I'm madly in love with Juliette Jinright, sir. I reckon that don't make a dab of sense, being as how I just met her in the flesh last night, and she ain't never writ me a lick, but I love her and that's the honest truth."

"Sailor, it's beginning to make more sense than I thought possible a few seconds ago. So, you're telling me, the letters Juli wrote were not to you?"

"To me? I wish! Shucks, I didn't even know how to read nor write 'til after I left the hospital. Mr. Donald Matthews and his mama taught me what all the letters sounds like."

"The pieces are beginning to fit."

"Sir, as God is my witness, I had no intention of fooling Juliette, you or anyone else into thinking I was Octavius. I didn't catch on until it had gone so far I couldn't find my way back. When I went with you to her house, and she looked up at me that first time and sailed into my arms, I Suwannee, it took me by such surprise, I didn't know what was going on. I didn't realize she mistook me for Octavius. Not at first, nohow. Then when she kissed me out on the—" He lowered his head. "Begging your pardon, sir. That slipped and I'd be grateful if you'd forget I said it. I ain't one to kiss and tell. In fact, until tonight I ain't never been one to kiss, but I'm getting off track. The point I was trying to make was that things were moving so fast, I didn't have time to figure out what was going on."

"Not only you, Buddy, but neither could I. After Juli received the letter from the hospital, saying Octavius was dead, she was so despondent, I was truly worried about her. But Henrietta—that's her mother—well, she wasn't too concerned. In fact, it sounds heartless, I know, but just between the two of us, I think she was glad he was dead. She held to the opinion that all sailors have girls in every port and that Juli was making a big mistake by thinking he was serious about wanting to marry her."

Jericho swallowed hard. "Hold on, there. I'm confused. You say she received a letter from the hospital saying Octavius died?"

"Yeah."

"Are you sure?"

"Of course, I'm sure."

"So, she already knows he's dead."

Mr. Wilkerson, chuckled. "Well, not anymore, since she's convinced you're him."

"Well, I'll be—I wonder if the hospital sent letters to all the girls who thought Octavius was gonna marry 'em. If so, they had a slew of letters to write."

Mr. Wilkerson's jaw jutted forward, like a bulldog's when he's about to attack. "So, Henrietta's hunch was right. He had no intention of marrying Juli, did he?"

"He didn't plan to marry none of 'em. It was a game with him.

Octavius told four girls he was gonna marry 'em, come Christmas, when he had no thoughts of marrying nary one of 'em. I never considered that the hospital might write to tell her of Octavius's passing, being as how they weren't married."

"Oh, the letter wasn't sent by the hospital, but by a friend. I simply meant it was mailed from there on hospital stationary."

"A friend of Octavious's? Are you sure? Cause as far as I could tell, I was about the only friend he had—and not meaning no disrespect to the dead, but I wadn't too crazy about him, myself. I don't 'spect you'd know who signed it, wouldja?"

"You might say it was anonymous. Henrietta showed it to me, and if I remember correctly, it said it was from 'Octavius's shipmate and devoted friend.' Well, that might not be the exact words, but it's close enough."

Jericho popped his palm to his forehead. "I think you got it word for word."

"Then, you know who wrote it?"

"Sure do." He poked his thumb at his chest. "Me!" Seeing he needed to explain, he said, "What I mean is, sir, I told my friend Thomas what to write and how to sign it."

Mr. Wilkerson's nose crinkled. "You? But then why did you—" He ran his fingers through his thinning hair. "Never mind. This is too complicated for my brain."

"I think I can explain. After Thomas read it back to me, it suddenly seemed cruel to give sweet Juliette the news in a letter and that's when I decided I'd come deliver the message personally. I told him to tear up the letter. I wonder why he didn't. However, the longer I waited, the harder it got to get up the nerve to come see her. But I have a question for you."

"Not sure I can answer but ask away."

" If Juliette had a letter saying Octavius was dead—and you've said you read it yourself—then who did you think I was when you drove me to her house? You couldn't have thought I was the guy who'd been writing to her, if you knew he was dead."

"That's an easy one to answer. Juliette didn't want to accept the news that Buddy was dead." Mr Wilkerson chuckled. Not a ha-ha chuckle, but a sort of mournful-sounding chuckle. Then he got all moody when he said, "That little lady has a direct line to Heaven, and it was no secret she pleaded with the Lord to turn things around."

"Are you saying she thought if she prayed, then God would bring a dead man back to life? For her? And you believed it?"

"Well, according to the Bible, Jesus brought Lazarus back from the dead, and if he ever intended to do it again, I had no doubt he'd do it for sweet Juli."

Jericho chuckled. "So, you thought I was Octavius, 're-incarcerated', or whatever they call it?"

"No, reincarnation didn't cross my mind. But when you told me your name was Buddy and you'd been in the Navy, had never been to Enterprise before, but was looking for a girl, I assumed there was a big mistake and Juli's beloved Buddy wasn't dead after all. I couldn't wait to see her face when she learned that you—or at least the you I thought you to be—was still alive."

CHAPTER 12

Octavius J. Rockwell III sat on the side of the hospital bed, reading his mail aloud, while Thomas paced back and forth across the room with his duffel bag, waiting for his discharge papers.

A sailor shouted from the other side of the ward, "Hey, Octavious, those letters are boring. Whatever happened to that girl called Alabama? Did she find out what a clod you are and stop writing?"

Octavious shrugged. "I don't know and I don't care. When I got out of ICU, I had a slew of mail, but nothing from her. Makes no difference to me. I don't chase after any woman."

"Is it true that when you get out of here, Uncle Sam is giving you a comfy job with dirt under your feet?"

"Yep. I'm on my way to the Naval Air Station in Pensacola."

"Lucky bloke. How did you manage that?"

"Wasn't my doings, although I'm not complaining."

"I guess it pays to have a daddy who holds the strings. So how many of those

pen pals are you planning to look up after you leave here?"

"None of them. The only good-looking one in the bunch was Alabama and since I promised to marry her Christmas, I might be in trouble if I showed up."

Cornwall said, "I don't think you have to worry. I'm sure she's over you, since she's no longer writing to you."

Thomas walked to the door and looked down the hall, then strode over to the window. "I know why she stopped writing."

Octavius groaned. "Sure, you do."

"I do."

Robert laughed, "Tell the rest of us, Thomas. Why do you think she stopped?"

"I don't *think*—I know."

Octavius rolled his eyes. "Pay him no mind. Mama's Boy has no idea what he's talking about. Whatever disease he's got has reached his brain."

Thomas said, "You're wrong on both counts, but what's new? First of all, I no longer have cancer. The surgeon assured me he removed all traces, and secondly, I happened to know for a fact that Alabama stopped writing you when she found out you were dead." He lumbered back over to the door. "Where is that nurse? I'm ready to get out of this place."

"Dead?" Octavius hee-hawed. "I was right. Mama's Boy is loco."

Cornwall nodded. "I think he's telling the truth. I believe that's about the time the letters stopped."

Octavius's jaw dropped. "Dead? You're both delusional. It must be catching."

"You didn't know? We all thought you were dead. That lieutenant—I think his name was Lassiter, who was here when they took you to ICU swore he heard the doctor telling a nurse in the hall that you died. We all believed him and didn't learn until days later that it was another fellow from across the hall. Naturally, upon learning it wasn't you, the whole hospital went into mourning and even the nurses came to work dressed in black."

When the guys all laughed, Octavious shrugged it off. "Makes no difference to me why she stopped writing. She was a goody-two-shoes, anyway. It was fun at first, with me trying to pull off being a saint, but that got boring after a while." He rolled his eyes. "She actually believed I was gonna become a preacher . . . like that would ever happen. I just wish I could've been a fly on the wall when she got the message that I was dead. She's probably still boo-hooing."

Thomas raised a brow. "I doubt it. She's probably already planning to make a preacher out of Buddy."

Octavious stiffened. "Buddy? What's he got to do with me being dead?"

"He told me what to write, but then told me not to mail the letter. But after we found out you weren't dead, the guys all dared

123

me to send it. So, I thought why not?"

"I don't care about her, but what was that crack about Buddy?"

"I think after I read the letter back to him, he felt she deserved to have the news delivered in person. He was crazy about her."

Octavious grinned. "Yeah, he looked like a little sick puppy every time I read one of her letters. I got a kick out of watching him suffer."

Thomas sat his duffel bag on the foot of his bed. "I'm guessing his suffering days are over. I wouldn't be surprised if he wasn't with her at this very moment. They're probably giving one another hugs of comfort, during their deepest hour of grief, over the demise of their mutual friend, poor, dead Octavious." His statement brought laughter from the other sailors in the ward.

Octavious face scrunched into a frown. "Buddy and Alabama? Nah, you're crazy if you think she'd give him the time of day. That little gal is out of his league."

Thomas pursed his lips. "I have a gut feeling you may be wrong. Dead wrong." His comment brought chuckles from the guys in the ward.

"You're crazy, man. Poor, ignorant Buddy was dreaming if he actually thought a girl like Alabama would take a second look at a hayseed like him. I showed y'all a picture of her house, didn't I? It's even bigger than ours, and although she never said, I have a feeling her family is rolling in dough."

Cornwall said, "I think it would be funny if you showed up on her doorsteps, since she thinks you're dead."

Octavious shook his head. "I would, but I'm afraid her old lady would sue me for breach of promise when she finds out I don't intend to marry her daughter. My old man has already had to pay out one time and I'm afraid he'd cut off my allowance if he had to settle another breach of promise suit. I think it's best to let dead sailors lie, if you know what I mean."

A nurse came in with a wheelchair and a folder full of papers that she handed to Thomas. "We're ready to get you out of here, sailor. Hop aboard."

Thomas took a taxi from the hospital to the train depot. He approached the ticket window, pulled a slip of paper from his billfold, then said, "Enterprise, Alabama."

****

The drugstore was closing, and Mr. Wilkerson and Buddy walked out to Mr. Wilkerson's truck, lowered the tailgate and sat on the edge. Their conversation was far from finished. They shared a common bond. Both loved Juliette and didn't want to see her hurt.

Buddy said, "I told her I'd go see her tomorrow night. It'll be a chance for me to let her know how things got so twisted, and I'll set her straight."

Mr. Wilkerson shook his head. "No, no, no. You can't."

Buddy didn't feel right arguing with his elders and although Mr. Walt didn't act all that old, he was definitely an elder. Yet, everything inside of Jericho told him the truth was always better than a lie. Besides, she had to know the truth sooner or later, and the way he saw it, the sooner, the better

"Don't you see, Buddy? It would be like having him die all over again."

Buddy sucked on the inside of his jaw, a habit he often did when something was weighing heavily on his mind. He was glad Mr. Wilkerson wasn't pushing him to respond. Then, smacking his fist on the table, he said, "No sir. I'm sure you're a lot smarter than me and it pains me to go against you, but I just can't do it. It ain't right, sir. I'd be living a lie." He leaned in and lowered his voice when the soda jerk appeared to be staring in their direction. "I'm obliged that you want to protect sweet Juliette, but this ain't the way to do it. The truth is always best."

Mr. Wilkerson clasped his hand on Buddy's forearm in a friendly manner. "You have a good heart, Buddy, and I admire you, but frankly, my concern is for Juliette. I know her better than you do. And I saw you two together. There were sparks there."

"Yeah, but them sparks in her eyes were not meant for me. As far as she knew, she was kissing Octavious."

"You're wrong. She was kissing you. I've known Juli since she was born and she's had plenty of suitors coming around, but she's never looked at any fellow the way she looked at you. She's got a thing for you, sailor. No doubt in my mind, those sparks were meant for the man she saw standing in her doorway, and not for some pretentious guy who wrote a bunch of mushy letters."

As much as Jericho wanted to believe it, it didn't make sense. "Really? You really believe that?"

"With all my soul. Don't you see? If you should blurt out that you aren't Octavious, she'll be terribly embarrassed that she kissed a stranger. But if you wait until she doesn't think of you as a stranger, she'll be glad you're you and not Octavious. By then, it won't matter."

He needed time to think. "Mr. Walt, all this talk is whirling around in my head like a haystack in a cyclone. I ain't got no way of knowing which direction it might blow—whether things gonna stay the same or if everything is gonna be turned upside down."

"Trust me, Buddy. Play it my way, and you'll both thank me in time to come."

"But when do I tell her I ain't him?"

"What's the hurry? I'll tell you when it's time."

Buddy crossed his arms behind his head. "I don't know, Mr. Wilkerson. This don't seem right to me. Don't seem right a'tall, but you're a smart man and I know you have Juliette's interest at heart."

"Buddy, it's the only way, unless you want to break her heart."

"You know I don't want to do that."

127

"The letters were all from 'Buddy,' and you're Buddy. Right? So, you just be yourself. You don't have to lie."

"But what if she asks about my last name?"

"Why would she? She thinks she knows. Leave it like that. There'll come a time when you can tell her how this all happened, but now is not the right time."

"Yessir, I just hope you know what's best." He hopped off the back of the truck and held out his hand. "Thank you, Mr. Wilkerson, for wanting to help me do the right thing."

"Sure, kid. I'll see you tomorrow night." He jumped off the bed of the truck and slapped Buddy on the back. "And stop worrying. I have."

"You? But why should you worry?"

"Because Juli is like my own daughter. Her father was my best friend, and to be perfectly frank, I didn't like anything Juliette told me about that other Buddy. He was a braggart and I had him pegged from the get-go. Just do as I tell you and lay low and when the truth does eventually come out, Juliette will be so in love with you, she'll be thrilled that the other cat didn't show up."

CHAPTER 13

Having too much on his mind to even think of sleeping, Jericho walked down Main Street, looking in all the store windows. He'd never cared to window shop before, but he never had a reason for wanting to look nice for a girl. He had his seer-sucker suit, but he didn't want to wear it every day. He recalled how the kids made fun of him in the second grade for wearing the same muslin shirt to school every day. That was the good thing about being in the Navy. Everybody had the same suit of clothes.

He started to cross the street and stopped to admire a beautiful monument of a woman wearing one of those tunics like the Greeks in pictures wore long ago. Her hands were high above her head and in her hands was a— he squinted his eyes and drew closer. Surely it wasn't what it looked like.

Pondering why a town would have such a strange monument, especially in the middle of the street, he heard footsteps behind him and turned. A soft voice said, "You aren't from around here, are you?"

She was almost as pretty as Juliette. Almost. Her long dark hair was tousled in a nice sort of way, kind of like a sudden wind had swept by and left a few twirly strands falling around her eyes. Dressed in a white uniform and white shoes, he assumed she was a nurse. He felt his face grow warm when he realized he was still staring and had failed to answer. Stuttering, he said, "No, I'm . . .I'm . . . I just got me a job working with an accountant." He threw his shoulders back. "I do ciphering."

"Well, I declare. Work for an accountant, you say?"

Jericho's first thought was that she didn't believe him, but why would she? It was hard for him to believe, too. "His name is Gideon Granger and he's my boss. I work at the Matthews Agency." He pointed down the street. "That's it down yonder."

She gave a little chuckle, and he jerked at the neck of his shirt that seemed to tighten around his throat, at the thought she might be laughing at him.

"Well, what a nice surprise. I was wondering what you'd look like and now I know. I pictured you to be a scrawny old geezer with a patch of hair combed over an otherwise bald head . . . and thick glasses." She batted her eyelids and twirled a lock of hair around her finger. "Boy, oh boy, was I ever wrong. You're young, and you ain't bad looking."

Jericho glanced away, unable to look her in the eyes for fear she could read his mind. As crazy as it seemed, he felt she could see straight through him.

She put her hands behind her and lifted herself up on the ledge of the wall surrounding the monument. "If anything is out of place on your desk tomorrow, or the tile isn't as shiny as you prefer, then you can blame me."

If she was trying to confuse him, she was doing a bang-up good job. "Why would I want to blame you?"

"Because I'm the cleaning woman for the Matthews Agency. I just got through cleaning the building, but I heard talk that you'd be coming." She thrust out her hand. "My name is Shelby Sellers."

Jericho felt his shoulders relax and he swiped his hand across his pants leg to dry the sweat, then grasped her hand in his. Surprised that it didn't feel as soft and delicate as he assumed it would. It shouldn't have been surprising, since she had her hands in cleaning liquids day after day. "Nice to meet you, Miss Shelby Sellers. My name is . . . my name is Buddy."

"Buddy who?"

"Just Buddy." Not answering her question made him feel snobbish, but there was no way he could reveal his real last name to a stranger before he had a chance to explain to Juliette. In such a small town, he could only imagine how quickly something like the new guy in town's name could get back to her. He couldn't help wondering if Mr. Wilkerson's plan was the right way to go. Being upfront from the get-go seemed like a far better plan, yet he couldn't deny Mr. Wilkerson did know Juliette better than he did.

"Well, Just Buddy, welcome to Enterprise."

When Shelby laughed, it sounded beautiful, like those little crystal bells he saw in the gift shop at the drugstore.

"Thanks. I was just pondering over this peculiar monument and wondering why the woman is holding up a roachy bug. Folks in Enterprise must think mighty highly of roaches." He shook his head slightly. "Me, not so much."

"It's not a roach. It's a boll weevil."

"Well, I ain't never had no occasion to consider boll weevils. You saying they're a good thing?"

"The farmers around here think so."

"Why is that?"

"It's a funny story, really. Years ago, cotton was the only cash crop in Alabama. Then a swarm of boll weevils swept through Coffee County and destroyed all the cotton."

"Don't sound like a good thing to me."

"Well, it was, because it forced them to find another way to put food on the table, so they planted peanuts and as it it turned out, it was more profitable than the cotton. A scientist who studied agriculture, Dr. George Washington Carver had been telling farmers that diversifying was the way to go—you know, switching crops around—but it was hard to get them to change their way of doing things, until the boll weevil destroyed the cotton. So, Dr. Carver was right, and in 1919, considering the boll weevil a blessing in disguise, they dedicated a monument to the pesky insect."

Jericho looked up at the ugly metal boll weevil and shook his head. "That's some story."

"I just wish you could've heard Granpa tell it."

"Shucks, I don't think nobody could tell it no better'n you did."

"Thanks, but it was a lot better watching his eyes light up when he told it. Grandpa said the situation appeared to be disastrous in the beginning, but God turned it around for good."

"You really believe he does that? God, I mean. You honestly think he can turn bad things into good?"

"I do, don't you?"

"Kinda."

She snickered. "How can you kinda believe. You either believe it or you don't."

"I didn't believe until I met a friend in the Navy, named Thomas. He got me to thinking about such things that I never really took time to consider before. Now, you might say, I'm still in the pondering stage."

"Well, it's getting late and I've got to wash out my uniform after I get home, so I best be on my way. It was nice meeting you, Buddy."

"Yeah, same here."

She held out her arms for him to help her off the ledge,

although he was pretty sure it would be easier to get down than it was to get up there.

She turned to walk away, and Jericho yelled, "Wait. Where do you live?"

Pointing, she said, "Out on the edge of town, that away. It's about a mile or so from here."

"Then I reckon I oughta walk you home. It's not safe for a young woman to be out this late at night, walking all alone in the dark."

She laughed. "It's plain to see you're new here. I don't know where you're from, but I'm as safe walking in Enterprise at midnight as I'd be in the middle of the day. Folks around here all know one another. No reason for me to be scared, but I'd love the company."

He shrugged. "Fine. I ain't got nowhere I need to be. Might as well."

"Swell. Thanks."

His pulse raced when she reached for his hand. It was the shortest mile-and-a-half that Jericho had ever walked. The time flew by. It was the longest span of time he'd ever spent alone with a girl, and he felt he'd made a real good friend, when she let go of his hand.

"Well, this is it."

Jericho tried to hide his surprise. Somehow, he expected a girl as pretty as Shelby would live on a farm in a big, nice house. He thought the house he grew up in was a shack, but this little shanty wasn't much bigger than their outhouse. "This is your house?"

She shook her head. "Nope."

"Then why are we stopping?"

"This is my home."

"That's what I asked."

"No. You asked if it was my house. The house belongs to Mr. Holloway, the farmer my daddy works for, but the home belongs to us."

Jericho scratched his head.

"A home is made up of a loving family who resides in the house. My mama taught me that when I was a little girl. She says a home is where love grows. We might not have a house, but we have a beautiful home. You're looking at the outside. Our home is on the inside." She reached for his hand and smiled. "You don't get it, do you?"

Oh, he got it alright. Jericho's mama owned their house. It was the house she grew up in. It had a leaky roof, a fireplace that was falling apart and a porch that was so rotten, it was dangerous to walk on, but it was theirs. But he'd much rather have a home. "I get it. I do. You're a lucky girl."

"Yes, I am. Thank you for walking me home. Goodnight, Buddy"

"Goodnight." He turned to walk away and stopped when he heard her call his name.

"Buddy, do you think I'm pretty?"

"What makes you ask?"

"Just curious. Do you?"

"Well, yeah, you're very pretty, but I don't reckon you needed me to tell you that."

Her smile lit up her face. "Yes, I did. Thank you." She turned and ran up the steps and into the tiny cottage.

The walk back to the Rawls seemed much further than it had when he walked with Shelby.

That night as he lay in bed at the hotel, his mind switched back and forth from Juliette's big fine white house, to Shelby's tiny shanty, and for the first time in his life he realized he really did get it. It wasn't what was on the outside, but what was on the inside that really mattered, and that didn't just go for houses. It was true for people, too.

But would Juliette see it that way? Would she realize that although he might look and sound like a hick, that there was more to him on the inside than was visible, to the naked eye? Would she be able to see his heart and know how much he loved her? Would it even matter?

CHAPTER 14

Jericho could hardly wait to get to work Friday morning. Mr. Granger had even given him his own key. So, when he arrived early, he was surprised to find Mr. Granger had beat him there.

"Buddy, do you know what time it is? Where have you been? I thought you wanted this job, but if you think you can walk in here at lunch time and work for me, you're badly mistaken."

Jericho felt his muscles tighten as he pointed to the clock on the wall over Mr. Granger's desk. "Sir, it was my understanding that I was to be here at eight o'clock."

"Then why are you just now dragging in?"

"Mr. Granger, look." He pointed to the clock. "It's a quarter 'til. I won't be late for fifteen more minutes. Are you okay, sir?"

"Of course, I'm okay."

Jericho noticed the old fellow began to breathe faster. And heavier. Mr. Granger lumbered over to his desk, fell into his chair and dropped his head. "I'm . . . I'm sorry, Buddy. I wasn't thinking straight. You're not late."

"I'll call the doctor."

"No! I'm fine, now."

"Are you sure, sir? You don't look so good."

"I said I'm fine. Forget it. I didn't sleep well last night so I came down to the office around midnight and I guess it caused me to lose track of the time. Now, would you mind looking in the safe and get the bag with the money out and take it to the bank for me? The bank closes in the afternoons before we do, so I always make the deposits the following morning, but I have a slight headache, so I'd appreciate it if you'd take care of it for me."

"A headache?"

Mr. Granger waved it off. "Stop fretting over me. It's from a lack of sleep. Now, please get the money and deposit it."

Jericho felt as if he were in the midst of a bad dream. *What just happened?* He strode across the room to the office safe, then realized he didn't have the combination.

"Mr. Granger, the safe is locked. Maybe you should open it."

"The combination is two turns to the left, stop on fifty, then thirty-seven to the right, then . . . no that's not it. Turn to 50 to the right, then turn . . ." He closed his eyes tightly. He opened his wallet and pulled out a slip of paper. "Here. This is the combination. Now, please, get the deposit and take it to the bank."

Jericho reached for the paper, read it, then handed it back.

"Why are you giving it back to me? I asked you to open the safe."

"I will sir. I read the combination. I can open it now."

"You're saying you can remember it?"

"Yessir." Jericho walked over to the safe, opened it and took out the money bag.

Mr. Granger rubbed his hand across his chin. "The deposit slip should be in there with the money. Look to make sure I put it in there last night."

Jericho pulled the drawstring, then nodded. "It's in here, sir."

"Good."

"Mr. Granger, are you sure you feel okay?"

"I wish you'd stop asking. I've already explained that if I seemed a little disoriented this morning, it's because I didn't sleep well last night. Sorry if I snapped at you, son. Can we just forget that it happened?"

Jericho nodded. He'd try to forget, but it wouldn't be easy.

Mr. Granger returned from the bank and placed the empty bag back into the safe. Whatever went on earlier was apparently nothing serious because he seemed to be in fine spirits, now. He dealt with five different clients throughout the day, without as much as a hiccup.

Mr. Granger handed Jericho a huge ledger and asked him to add the figures on pages 125-187. As he added each line of numbers, he couldn't get his mind off the way the morning had begun. The more he thought about it, the more he began to question his own thoughts. Had he built the scenario up to be much more than it was? Mr. Granger had admitted he didn't sleep well the night before. He came to work several hours early to get things done, and it only seemed as if it should be time for lunch when Jericho walked in. But was that really all there was to it? He gnawed on his fist. If that was all that happened, maybe he could buy it. But then there was the combination to the safe. Jericho was quite sure the old fellow had used the same combination for years. How did he forget? Was it because he was already flustered from being confused about the time? Or embarrassed that he'd lost his temper over something that wasn't Jericho's fault? Jericho relaxed, realizing the bizarre episode could've been due to a dozen different factors or a combination of all them. The important thing was that it was over, whatever the reason.

****

Jericho watched the clock all day, halfway dreading six o'clock and halfway looking forward to it. What if Mr. Granger decided to keep him past five?

The tight muscles in his shoulders loosened when at exactly five o'clock, Mr. Granger opened his desk drawer, took the money bag out, went over to the safe and turned the lock.

Jericho anxiously waited until he heard the click and saw the safe door open. He let out a soft sigh. All his worrying was apparently in vain.

"Buddy, I think I'll call it a day. After you put things away, you can go, but make sure you lock the door as you leave."

"Yessir. Goodnight, Mr. Granger."

As soon as the door closed, Jericho snatched up the ledger and stuck it in the desk. He turned out the lights and was ready to walk out when the door opened. His heart sank. Was the old man coming back in to give him extra duties?

"Hey, sailor."

"Shelby? I'm surprised to see you. I reckon I was thinking you worked later at night." Truth was, he hadn't really thought about it. Not until now.

"Normally, I clean the Bank building first and don't get here until around nine o'clock, but I came here first tonight, hoping I could see you. I've been waiting outside the front door, hoping you wouldn't walk out with Mr. Granger. I wanted to tell you how sweet it was of you to walk me home last night."

Jericho hadn't noticed until now how dark it was in the room. "Not a problem." He reached up by the door and switched on the light.

Shelby giggled and switched it back off. "You afraid of the dark, sailor?"

She edged up close to him. Too close.

"Don't be silly. Why would I be afraid?"

"I could tell last night you were feeling what I was feeling and you're all I've thought about all day."

"Shelby, maybe we can talk later, but I have an appointment and I'm running late. Are you staying in here to clean or are you leaving, too?"

"Oh! This didn't work the way I'd hoped, but I don't want to make you late for your appointment. I'll go ahead and clean this building since I'm already here and do the bank when I finish." She pressed closer. "Wanna kiss me bye? I don't mind if you want to."

Jericho rubbed his hand over his mouth. How do you tell a woman you don't want to kiss her? "Sure." He leaned down and pecked her on the lips, then hurried out the door, his heart pounding. Shelby was a sweet girl, pretty, and a hard worker. If he wasn't already in love with Juliette, he could see himself falling for her. Had he given her reason to think he cared for her in a romantic sort of way, because if he had, he had to find a kind way to let her know there was nothing further from the truth.

He ran all the way to his hotel and took the stairs instead of waiting for the elevator. Since he wore the suit Miz Lucie gave him yesterday, he put on his new seer-sucker suit. He wanted to look nice for Juliette. He passed by the florist, just as the lady was about to lock the door. "Ma'am, I don't mean to hold you up, but is there anyway you could sell me one of them bouquets before you close for the night?"

"I'd be happy to. What did you have in mind?"

"I don't reckon I know. Whatever you think would be proper for a fellow to give a young lady he's hoping to woo?"

She smiled, then ducked into the back room and came out holding a half-dozen of the prettiest flowers Jericho had ever seen. She stuck a few ferns in with the bunch, then wrapped it all in green paper.

CHAPTER 15

Jericho rang Juliette's doorbell at exactly six o'clock and she came to the door looking like a model out of a magazine. Her beauty took his breath away. "You sure look pretty, Miss Juliette."

"Silly, don't call me Miss Juliette. Makes it sound as if you're my butler instead of my beau." She glanced at his hands. "Are the flowers for me?"

"Uh. . . sorry. They are. I don't know what they're called. The lady at the flower shop picked them out."

"They're daisies and they're perfect. I love daisies. Come on in, Greta is putting the food on the table."

They entered the dining room and Mrs. Jinright was already seated at the long banquet table. "Have a seat, young man. I like to eat while the food is still hot."

"Sorry, if I held you up, ma'am."

Juliette giggled. "You didn't hold us up, did he Mother?"

Before Henrietta could answer, the doorbell rang. "Juliette, please answer the door."

She walked back into the dining room. "It's Walt, Mother. I told him we're about to eat but to come on in and have dinner with us."

Henrietta's face turned red. "I'm sure the invitation didn't take him by surprise, since he knows we eat at six o'clock every evening."

Mr. Wilkerson stepped into the room and turned to the maid. "Greta, I hope it won't put you out to add one more plate. Juliette has so graciously invited me to dine with her this evening."

The tension in the room was so noticeable Buddy sensed he could be the reason and nervously squirmed in his chair. He picked up his napkin and tucked it into his shirt collar. After seeing Mr. Wilkerson flap his napkin in the air and stick it in his lap, Buddy tugged on the corner of his napkin and eased it down to his lap.

Juliette said, "Mother, did I tell you Buddy has a good job at the Matthews Agency?"

"Juliette, I believe we covered that subject last night."

"Oh, yes, I suppose we did. Well, did he tell you about the explosion that took place on the boat he was on? It must have been dreadful."

"Juliette, please! I am aware of the accident, but I don't think that's proper table conversation. Now, would you stop the chatter and eat your dinner."

Mr. Wilkerson passed Buddy a platter of fresh pork, then handed him a bowl of something that looked a mite like the meatballs they served on the ship. "No thank you," He tried to pass it off on Juliette.

She forked a generous helping on her plate, then said, "Have you ever eaten Raspeball, Buddy?"

He shook his head. "Never heard of it."

"Then you must try it. It's Greta's specialty. She pushed the bowl back toward him."

"Is it rude to ask what kind of animal it comes from?"

Herietta rolled her eyes. "For Goodness sake, just try it. It's potatoes, for crying out loud."

He winced. It wasn't hard to tell he'd offended Juliette's mother. "Sorry, ma'am. I'll be happy to try it. I'm crazy about potatoes." He made sure to lick his lips and rave about how delicious the whatchamacallit was in hopes that he could edge into Mrs. Jinright's good graces.

When they'd finished their meal, Greta brought in bread pudding with raisin sauce and it was easy to brag on that. Buddy couldn't remember ever having anything that tasted better, or even as good. Bragging on the dessert came easy.

Juliette slid her chair back and reached for his hand. "Shall we go out on the porch and swing?"

He glanced at Mr. Wilkerson, who gave him a slight nod and a wink. Buddy took that as his cue to keep up the act until he received further instructions.

****

Greta cleared the table and Henrietta and Walt went into the Parlor. Henrietta said, "Walt, I can't believe you had the nerve to show up here after the impertinent way you acted last night. If you're here to apologize, it's way too soon. I'm not ready to forgive you."

"I don't recall asking your forgiveness. Frankly, I came to give you an opportunity to apologize, but I see you aren't ready, yet. That's okay. I can wait."

Her lip curled slightly, then stretched into a wide smile, and soon they were both laughing. "Walt Wilkerson, you are the most unreasonable person to deal with that I have ever known. You turn everything into a joke. Now, if you'll please get serious, I want to know what we're going to do about these two kids."

"We? Why do you think they need our interference?"

"You know perfectly well what I'm talking about. His English is atrocious, but even if he never opened his mouth, it's plain to see he's had no proper upbringing."

"You can see all that, can you, Henri? If Uncle Sam could gain access to your amazing vision, we'd have no need for periscopes."

"You're being facetious, but if you'd be honest, you'd admit that you see it, too. I couldn't believe he'd come calling on my daughter wearing a seer-sucker suit, which I'm sure he bought on sale after Labor Day. And white shoes, in October. I'd be embarrassed for poor Juliette to be seen walking down the street with him."

"My stars, Henri, I never knew you to be such a snob."

"There's nothing snobbish about me. It's called being aware of proper etiquette. That nice young man from Montgomery—the State Attorney General's son—is crazy about my daughter, and I won't sit idly by and watch her throw her life away. She listens to you, Walt. Won't you talk to her and make her understand?"

He hung his head. "Henrietta, I'm afraid she understands a lot more than you and I did, twenty years ago."

"You're bringing that up again? I know you've never forgiven me for choosing Steve over you. Is that what this is all about?"

"I can see a parallel. Frankly, at the time you made your decision, I did think you should've picked me, but I soon changed my mind. You needed Steve and all that he could give you. I could never have made you happy. He had family clout and I was just a body man at the Chevrolet Place. You think I didn't know why I got the short straw?"

"That's just not true."

"No? Then tell me, Henrietta. Why did you choose him over me?"

She gnawed on her lip, then said, "What difference does it make. It's water over the bridge."

"Under." He grinned.

"What?"

"It's water under the bridge."

"Over, under. My point is that it's in the past and who I chose to marry makes little difference at this point, but the man she chooses could make a lot of difference in Juliette's future."

"Steve really loved you and he tried hard to make you a good husband."

"And he did."

"Then why didn't you let him know?"

"What makes you think I didn't?"

"He was my best friend from first grade until the day he died. My daddy was a tenant farmer for his dad, and Steve and I grew up hunting and fishing together. He was a lot of fun, but I saw the air go out of him those last few years. He stopped smiling."

"Air? I have no idea what you're talking about."

"I think you do. He found out too late that you never loved him. You loved having the Jinright name, but not the Jinright man. Funny thing about love. I knew it, yet I loved you still."

"Walt, I made the decision that was right for me and if I had it to do over again, I'd still choose Steve. I was mature enough to understand what was important, but I'm afraid Juliette has stars in her eyes and can't see what a mistake she'll be making if she allows that sailor to keep hanging around. I won't stand by and watch her ruin her life."

"The way you ruined Steve's?"

"I resent that. Steve and I gave up things to get what we wanted, but we both were well aware of what we were doing."

"Henrietta, I've always wondered . . . have you ever told Juliette about us . . . our past, I mean?"

"Why should I? She knows I admired Steve, but I never loved him and I don't think she can forgive me for that. She thought Steve Jinright hung the moon, but she's also very fond of you. I'm not sure she'd feel the same if she knew we were in love when Steve and I married."

"Nor would I ever want her to."

CHAPTER 16

Juliette and Buddy sat in the porch swing, gently swaying back and forth. She eased her hand over, touching his, yet careful not to reach for it. Her heart thumped when she felt his hand sliding into hers, their fingers intertwining.

Neither spoke for at least five minutes. Then, Buddy said, "Juliette, what if you discovered I'm not who you think I am?"

She giggled. "You mean like if I found out you were an international spy, trying to pry U.S. secrets from me?" She leaned her head on his shoulders. "In that case, I'm afraid our country might need to line up a firing squad and shoot me on the spot, because I've been hypnotized by your charms. You could get anything out of me with very little opposition."

"I'm serious. Would it matter to you if I wasn't Octavious J. Rockwell? What if I was a nobody? Say, if you found out my name was Joe Smith. Would it make a difference to you?"

"Of course, it would. I didn't fall in love with Joe Smith, I fell in love with you, sweetheart. I could ask the same question. Did you fall in love with me, or fall in love with someone else by a different name?"

He gave up. There was no way to make her understand without coming out and being completely honest, which he thought the best idea, yet he was inclined to trust Walt and wait.

"Buddy, there are some things we haven't discussed, which I don't think would've been appropriate to put in a letter, but now that we're together, I think it's something we should talk about."

He eased his arm over her shoulder. "Okay. Like what?"

"Well, for one thing, where would you like to live, now that you're out of the Navy. Do you plan on moving back to where you grew up in Kentucky or—"

He pulled her close. "Why would I to do that? I like it here in Enterprise and I love my job."

"Is that all that you love in Enterprise?"

He chuckled. "Of course not. I love you, Juliette, more than any town or job. I'm just saying, I'd be happy to live here the rest of my life. I've never been this happy." He kissed the top of her head. "Any more questions?"

"Have you ever thought about what kind of family you'd want?"

He paused, then answered, "I have. I'd like the mother of my children to be a sweet, beautiful woman like . . . hmmm. . . let me try to think if I've ever met a woman who fits that description."

She giggled and playfully swatted him across his broad chest. When he instinctively grimaced, her eyes widened, quickly filling with tears. "Oh, my poor darling, I'm so sorry. I forgot about your burns. How could I have been so careless?"

"Hey, stop worrying. I'm fine. I'm grateful it weren't no worse than it was. I could've easily been burned on my face, too, but at least I can hide the scars on my chest."

"Buddy, I meant what I said in my letters when I told you that after we're married, I don't want you to ever feel you have to hide your scars from me. You do remember, don't you?"

He felt his Adam's apple bob when he attempted to swallow. "Yes." He mumbled, "I remember every word you wrote."

"Good. I have another question. How many children would you like to have?"

Buddy couldn't think straight. "A lot?"

She laughed. "I'm serious. How many do you think would be perfect?"

"I reckon one would be perfect and any after that would be more perfect."

"I think so, too. I love you, Octavious Jericho Rockwell III."

He winced.

****

Henrietta walked Walt out on the porch and Buddy slid his hand away from Juliette's. He jerked straight up in the swing when her mother gave them an icy stare. She said, "Juliette, it's late. I think it's time for you to go inside and for your visitor to leave."

Buddy jumped up. "Yes ma'am. I'm sorry if I overstayed my welcome, Mrs. Jinright. And I want to thank you for inviting me for supper, tonight. It was all mighty good. I really like them taters . . .potatoes."

She glanced at Walt and rolled her eyes. "Goodnight, Jericho."

"Goodnight. And goodnight to you too, Mr. Wilkerson."

Walt said, "Would you like a ride back to the Rawls, Buddy?"

"Don't wanna put you out, sir."

"No trouble at all. I'll be going that way."

Jericho looked at Juliette. "Nite, nite." Her smile melted his heart. How did he get so lucky?

****

When Jericho went upstairs to his room, he found Shelby in the hall. "What are you doing here at the hotel?"

"Waiting for you. Where have you been?"

"What do you mean, 'Where have I been? Shelby, I don't cotton to you following me around."

"I thought you liked me, Buddy."

"Is she prettier than me?"

"Don't matter which one is the prettiest. I love her and that's the difference."

She smiled. "So, you're saying she's not prettier than me."

"I didn't say that."

"You didn't have to. I could tell you thought it. Besides, I know you're teasing. You haven't had time to meet anyone."

He opened the door and she pushed her way in. Glancing down both sides of the hall, he whispered, "Shelby, what are you doing? You can't come in my room."

She giggled. "Oh yeah? I just did."

"What I mean is, it ain't right. Somebody could find out and get the wrong idea about why you done it."

Her lips tightened into a long white line. "So, what if they're right. I wouldn't care. Would you?"

"Well, yeah. Actually, I would."

"Why?"

"Well, for one reason, it could ruin your reputation."

"I don't care. I'm tired of folks judging me. Let 'em talk."

"You need to leave, Shelby."

"I don't think you really want me to."

"You're wrong. I told you I have a girl and I don't want nothing to ruin it for me."

She started to cry. "I thought you were teasing."

"Why?"

"You didn't act like there was anyone else when you walked me home the other night. And you sure didn't act that way when you kissed me in your office."

155

"You asked me to kiss you. What was I to say? Besides, it wasn't a passionate sort of kiss, it was simply a peck on the lips."

"Maybe you didn't feel the passion, but I did. You led me to believe you had feelings for me. I feel like such a dunce."

"Aww, Shelby, don't cry. I do have feelings for you, but as a friend. To be honest, I was glad to have you as a friend and I thought you understood."

"Well, I didn't. Don't laugh, but I think I'm in love with you, Buddy. I understand you don't feel the same way about me, but can we at least remain friends?"

Love? She didn't know what she was saying. She barely knew him. How could she say she was in love with him? His throat tightened. Was it any weirder than him falling in love with someone he'd never met? He wrapped his arm around her shoulder. "Sure, we can be friends. I can't think of a better friend to have."

He couldn't let her leave crying. "It's a nice night for a walk, Shelby. How about it?"

She smiled through the tears. "Seriously? I'd love it."

"Then meet me at the monument when you're finished cleaning."

"Why don't you wait with me?" When he didn't answer, her lip trembled. "I get it. You're ashamed to be seen with me."

"Don't be ridiculous. It's for your own good that we aren't seen coming out of the elevator together."

Jericho and Shelby strolled down Lee Street and the walk appeared to be just the thing to lift her spirits. She pointed to a large brick house. "That's where the Carrington's live. Mr. Carrington works for the railroad. Nicest folks you'd care to meet, even if they are rich. The Carringtons are a good example of rich folks who won't have a problem getting a ticket to heaven. Just saying they're the exception, not the rule." A little further down the street, she pointed to a large Victorian home—Juliette's house. "Take the folks who live there, for example. Snooty as all get out. That's where Mrs. Jinright and her spoiled daughter, Juliette live. Folks say Mrs. Jinright only married Mr. Jinright because he was rich and she was upset because her daddy had just lost their fortune in the stock market."

"Sounds to me like this town has a lot of gossips with a lot of idle time on their hands."

"It's not gossip. It's the truth."

"Shelby, you act like you think just because somebody happens to be rich, they can't be good, decent folks and it just ain't so."

She shrugged. "Well, you know what the Bible says about it being easier for a camel to go through the eye of a needle than it is for a rich person to get into heaven. And judging from the ones I've met, I figure it'll be even harder than that for most of 'em."

"But it ain't impossible."

"Not saying it's impossible. Just near 'bout impossible. Why are you getting mad at me, just because I'm telling you what the Bible says?"

"I ain't mad. Just saying things ain't always as they seem."

At the end of the pavement, the big houses with beautiful landscaped yards ended and sitting about a hundred feet away from the dirt road was a tiny log cabin with a tin roof. It was almost hidden by all the reeds growing up around it. The old outhouse in back was overrun by vines. Jericho thought it odd to go from one extreme to the other in such a short distance. "Looks like that old house might be abandoned."

"Yep. Nobody's lived there for as long as I can remember."

"I wonder why. It ain't fancy, but it's solid."

"They say the man who owns it keeps it to remember where he came from."

"What's that supposed to mean?"

"He grew up poor but when he was in school, the peanut farmer his father worked for let him keep all the peanuts he could find lying on the ground, after they were dug. He started selling nickel bags of boiled peanuts downtown on Saturdays. I hear folks liked him so much, they often paid extra. After he finished high school, somebody—though no one seems to know who—helped to finance him and he opened a grocery store. Now, he owns a whole slew of grocery stores and he keeps this little cabin to remember when he didn't have it so good."

"That's a real fine story. If I ever got rich, though, I think I'd want to forget about being poor. Let's go and take a look inside."

"Not me. I'm sure there are all sorts of varmints living in there."

Jericho didn't insist. He walked Shelby home, and they sat on a stump in front of her house. "Shelby, I reckon I shoulda told you earlier, but Juliette's my girl." His knees knocked. What made him say she was his girl? If he had taken time to think about it, maybe he wouldn't have blurted it out, but what was done was done. Besides, the way he figured it, when she kissed him, that gave him a right to claim her as his girl.

Her mouth gaped open. Then slowly, the look of shock faded, and she laughed out loud. "You and Juliette?"

Jericho didn't often let things get under his skin, but her laughter made him bristle. "I'm not funning. It's true. and I'm gonna marry her, you wait and see. You don't have to believe me, but it's the honest truth." Feeling a little foolish for trying to convince Shelby that Juliette would pick him over some rich dude—even though it was the truth—he jumped off the stump. "Goodnight, Shelby."

"You're mad at me, aren't you?"

"Mad? Of course, not. Why would I be?"

"The way you swelled up like a toady frog when I laughed at the silly notion of you with Juliette, it looked like you were mad."

Shelby held out her arms for him to lift her off the stump.

When he did, she kissed him on the side of his face. "Goodnight, good-looking."

"Nite-nite, Shelby."

Headed back, he stopped in front of the log cabin and decided to go in and look around. When a bat whizzed by his head and he saw three others clinging to a ratty old curtain, he'd seen enough.

CHAPTER 17

Octavious found his desk job at the Naval Air Station in Pensacola, Florida to be tolerable, although he couldn't stand the fellows he was forced to work with. It was evident they were jealous of him, but why should he care? He didn't need their friendship. It would be a little less lonely, though, if he could find at least one friend like good ol' Buddy Rhoades. He missed the kid. Octavious couldn't put his finger on it, but there was something different about Buddy that seemed to draw people to him.

The guys in the office made a point to demonstrate their resentment toward him by never including him in their off-duty activities. However, he couldn't deny that living near the beach made up for some of the negatives. Although his father was insistent that he follow in his footsteps and make the Navy a career, it wasn't going to happen. No way. Octavious was counting the months when he'd be free from the Navy to go and do as he pleased—and he'd soon have the moolah to do it with.

In a matter of weeks, he'd turn twenty-five and would have access to the trust fund his grandfather set up for him. He'd already spent that money a hundred different ways as he lay awake at night, planning what he'd do first.

He'd look up his old pal, Buddy. It might be fun to see if he could turn a turnip root into a juicy hunk of meat the girls might go for. The challenge made him smile. He thought about what Thomas said and wondered if the kid really did go to Alabama to search out that little gal. She seemed naively sweet, so maybe she'd let him down easy. Octavious chuckled that he'd have such a sympathetic thought. Could it be there might actually be a hint of compassion hidden inside him somewhere?

****

Saturday morning, Jericho awoke when someone knocked on the door to his hotel room. Afraid to answer, for fear he'd find Shelby standing there, he lay still. Then the knocks became louder.

What was wrong with the girl that she'd be so brazen? Didn't he make it clear she couldn't be coming to his hotel room? Juliette was a reasonable girl. He was certain she wouldn't object to him having a casual friend who happened to be female but entertaining that female friend in his hotel room could cause him to lose the only girl he'd ever loved.

If it meant ending the friendship with Shelby, so be it. He hated to hurt her feelings, but he knew no other way to make her understand the trouble she could cause. The knocks grew louder. Afraid someone in a neighboring room would look to see her waiting to enter his hotel room before daylight and get the wrong idea, he jerked on his pants as quickly as he could. "Hold on, I'm coming," he grumbled as he snatched open the door.

"Juliette!" His eyes widened. Then he glanced down at his bare torso. "I'm so sorry. I . . . I need to grab a shirt. I wasn't thinking when I opened the door." He quickly slammed it in her face, grabbed a shirt from off a chair, then cracked the door open and peeked out, "Sorry, I suppose I should've invited you in."

She giggled. "I'll wait in the hall for you to finish dressing. I can only imagine the gossip in this little town if I went into a man's hotel room, especially a man who was only half-dressed."

"Yeah. Of course. You're right. I'll be right out."

While buttoning his shirt, Jericho glanced down at the gruesome scars on his chest and grimaced. What was he thinking? She didn't appear to be sickened by the ugly sight, but she was too nice to let it show. He tucked his shirt in his pants and hurried out. "What are you doing here? What's wrong? It's not even daylight."

"Nothing's wrong. My favorite part of the day is sunrise, so I had Greta pack us some ham and biscuits with her homemade fig preserves. I thought we'd have a picnic breakfast on the lake and watch the sunrise. How does that sound?"

"It sounds great. Thanks. And where is this lake?"

"On our farm on the edge of town. I have my car."

Juliette spread a checkered cloth on the ground and pulled six of the largest, fluffiest biscuits he'd ever seen, from her picnic basket. There was only one thing more beautiful than the sun shining on the still waters, and that was the girl sitting beside him with her full skirt spread out on the ground. Her blouse had an elastic neckline and was pulled down slightly below her shoulders, though her long, wavy hair covered the bare skin. The sun made her hair look as if it had glitter sprinkled over her head. He wondered what it would feel like to run his fingers through those beautiful locks.

"Juliette, you're about the prettiest thing I've ever seen."

"About?"

He felt his face burn. "No, that's not what I meant."

"I was just teasing you, Buddy. I knew what you meant, and I thank you. I want to be pretty for you."

He rubbed his hand across his mouth. What if Shelby should ever run into Juliette and tell her he said she was pretty. Juliette would be terribly hurt and rightfully so. How would he ever explain? Would it matter to Juliette that Shelby put him on the spot and he felt compelled to give her an answer? There was no denying Shelby was pretty, but seeing Juliette here now, he could say without a doubt there was no comparison.

After downing four cathead biscuits, two with ham and two with preserves and drinking a thermos flask full of coffee, Jericho stretched out on the ground. "Look!" He pointed to the clouds. "What do you see?"

Juliette lay down beside him. "I see a bird?"

He laughed. "Not in the tree. I mean what do you see in the clouds?"

"Oh." Her mouth gaped open. "Oh m'goodness, I see an angel. See? She has two wings and there's a little halo over her head. Do you see it?"

He turned his head to the side, and with his gaze fixed on her, he said, "Plain as day. It's an angel, all right."

Her laughter was infectious. "Silly. I was talking about the angel in the clouds, but she's breaking up." Her lip turned down. "She just lost a wing." She sat up. "Buddy, I need to get back home before Mother misses me."

His brow meshed together. "You slipped off? She doesn't like me, does she?"

"It's not that. She doesn't know you, but once she gets to know you, she'll be crazy about you, just like I am. She's been very protective of me since my father died."

"I don't want to stop seeing you, Juliette. What should I do?"

"Oh, I'm not suggesting we not see each other. I'm just saying she wouldn't approve of me initiating this picnic. You'll still come calling on me next Saturday night as we planned, won't you?"

"I'd like to, Juliette. I'd very much like to if it won't cause problems for you."

"It's no big thing, honest. Mother knows I love you and that we plan to get married."

Married? There's was nothing he wanted more than to come home from work to find Juliette waiting for him every evening. But how would she take it when she discovered he not only didn't write the letters, he wasn't the one who proposed, and he let her believe his name was Octavious Jericho Rockwell III? Mrs. Jinright had already made up her mind that she didn't like him. He could only imagine how she'd feel about him when she learned the truth.

He helped Juliette put the things away in the basket and she drove him back to the hotel. He slid across the seat and kissed her, before getting out. "See you Saturday night. Seven o'clock?"

"You're welcome to come earlier if you'd like to have dinner with us at six."

"Thanks, but I think I'll skip dinner and show up around seven. Thanks for the breakfast picnic. That was a first for me, and I enjoyed it."

"So did I. See ya' Saturday night."

He watched her drive away. There so much about this relationship that worried him, but sweet, Juliette Jinright was worth worrying over.

CHAPTER 18

"Henrietta, it's wrong and you know it."

"Walt, she's my daughter and I'll do whatever I think is in her best interest, so I'd appreciate it if you'd keep your thoughts on the matter to yourself."

"Fine. I'm just saying you're risking turning her away from you."

"I'm turning her away from me? I'm turning her away from that hick she thinks she's going to marry. Walt, there's no way I can allow her to ruin her life. She's a child. She doesn't know what a terrible mistake she'd be making."

Juliette opened the front door and was surprised to see her mother and Walt in the Parlor.

Henrietta said, "Juliette, I thought you were still in bed. Where have you been, and what are you doing with the picnic basket?"

"Well, Mother, I was counting on you being in your room. I thought I'd be able to avoid this conflict, but since you're here, I might as well confess. Buddy and I have been having a picnic."

"At this time of morning?"

"It was a beautiful time of day. We picnicked at the lake and it was so romantic. The sun was still rising, the birds were singing, and we had a nice breeze. It was perfect."

Walt stood. "I think I should go."

Henrietta shot a glare his way. "That's not necessary. Why don't you stay? I have some exciting news to tell Juliette."

Juliette sat on the sofa beside her mother and clasped her hands together. "Exciting news? What?"

"Darling, I have booked a cruise for the two of us. We'll have so much fun. I know you've always wanted to go on a South Sea Island Cruise, and you'll finally get your chance."

"But Mother, I believe that was your dream, not mine."

Henrietta's lip quivered. "Oh, I am so disappointed. I'm sure you told me you'd love to take a cruise, and I've already bought the tickets, which didn't come cheap, I must add. That's gratitude for you." She pulled a handkerchief from her pocket and blotted her eyes, before ringing for Greta to bring her a glass of water and a powder for her head.

"I'm sorry, Mother. I didn't mean to disappoint you. I'm sure it'll be fun. It's just that I've waited so long to see Buddy, and he's finally here. You can understand that I hate to leave him, can't you?"

Sounding whiney, she said, "Of course, I understand, darling. But it's not as if we'll be gone forever. We'll be back before he hardly has time to miss you."

"When do we leave?"

Juliette's show of interest appeared to be the antidote needed for Henrietta's aching head. "That's the exciting part. Walt is driving us to Mobile after lunch. We have reservations at the Battle House Hotel there and will set sail in the morning. I'm so excited I can hardly stand it."

"We're leaving today?"

"Yes. I was lucky that I could get the tickets in time." Henrietta grunted. "But I must say, I'm very disappointed. I was expecting you to show a little more enthusiasm."

"I'm sure it'll be fun, Mother, but I need to let Buddy know. We have a date for Saturday night. I'll drive over to the Rawls and let him know."

"You'll do no such thing. I won't have people in this town seeing you traipsing around in the hotel looking for a man. It isn't proper. You can write him a letter and we'll mail it on the way. He'll get it in plenty of time to know you won't be here Saturday. I've packed your bags, already."

Juliette trudged up the stairs. She understood this was a trip of a lifetime, but if only it had come at another time in her lifetime. Walking into her room, she almost stumbled over the trunk her mother packed for her.

She ran back downstairs. "Mother, why the trunk? I can get everything I need in the new Samsonite luggage and train case you gave me for my birthday. I'll never need that many clothes."

"Oh, honey, there'll be so much to do on the ship and so many events to attend, I want to make sure you have an outfit for every occasion for the next two weeks. I've already checked and there's no need to skimp. I went shopping and I even have a few surprises packed for you. We're going to have the time of our lives. I can hardly wait. Your dad and I went on a cruise for our honeymoon and it was the most exciting thing I've ever done. You're gonna love it."

After Juliette left the room, Walt said, "Henrietta, you know what you're doing is wrong. Tell her."

"I have no idea what you're talking about." She stood and picked up his cup from the coffee table. "Would you like another cup of coffee?"

"No, and I think you know exactly what I'm talking about. You told her she'd be gone two weeks."

"You're mistaken. I merely said I made sure she had enough outfits to wear for two weeks. I don't suppose it will be so terrible if she wears the same outfit a second time. That's all I meant."

"Tell her the truth, Henrietta. Tell her she won't be back for a month." He picked up the newspaper beside his chair and opened it. Pointing to an article, he said, "and tell her the only reason you booked this cruise was because Roland Rountree will be on it and you're doing everything you can do to get them together."

"Walt, keep your voice down before she hears you. How many times do I need to remind you that Juliette is my daughter and I'll raise her as I deem appropriate? I don't need nor appreciate your meddlesome interference."

"Henrietta, I'm beginning to believe I'm nothing more to you than a handy chauffeur you can engage at a moment's notice to get you where you want to go."

"That's ridiculous and you know it."

"Maybe. But it's how it seems to me. I'll take you to Mobile, since I agreed, but then I think we should put space between us for a while until we can figure out how things stand between us."

"Gracious me, Walt Wilkerson, who put that burr in your britches? I'm sorry if you think I've taken advantage of your good nature. I suppose maybe I do take you for granted sometimes, but you're such a sweetheart. You'll find my bags in the hallway and Juliette's trunk is in her room."

Juliette took stationary and a fountain pen from her desk drawer.

Dear Buddy,

It is with deep regrets that I find it necessary to cancel our date for Saturday night. My mother has just surprised me by announcing she has booked us on a South Sea Island cruise, and we'll be setting sail tomorrow. Yes, dear, tomorrow. I suppose she wanted it to be a big surprise, and it certainly was. I know I should be excited, and I'm sure it will be a wonderful trip, but I'd much rather stay here and be with you. Naturally, I can't tell her because I know she was doing it for me. She said we'll be gone for a couple of weeks, which I'm sure will seem more like a couple of months, since I'll be wanting to get back home to you, my darling Buddy.

I love you, so much,

Juliette

She sprayed it with perfume, folded it and wrote Mr. Jericho Rockwell, Room 212, The Rawls Hotel, Enterprise, Alabama on the envelope. Placing a stamp upside down to indicate her love for Buddy, she deposited the letter in the mailbox for Mr. Watkins to pick up.

CHAPTER 19

Monday morning, Jericho was transferring figures to the ledger when Mr. Granger hobbled in.

"Good Morning, Buddy. You're here early."

"Yessir." Jericho still was baffled by what happened to the old man on Friday, but he seemed in good spirits this morning. "I decided to come on in and get started on the books."

Mr. Granger lumbered over and patted him on the back. "Good for you, son. You're a hard worker and I'm fortunate that Donald saw fit to send you here. I'll be seventy years old in fourteen months and I feel like it'll be time for me to move on and let someone younger run the agency. The way you work, I can believe it could possibly be you. You catch on quickly and will be well-trained for the position by the time I retire. I assure you I'll be ready to give you my endorsement."

"Thank you, sir. That makes me feel real good to know you

think so highly of me. I'll sure do my best to live up to them kind words."

Jericho felt his ego swell at the thought of running such a prestigious agency. Did Mr. Granger really feel he'd be qualified in little more than a year? He glanced over at the door that had Gideon Granger's name in bold white letters and imagined Jericho Rhoades written in its place. That should even impress Mrs. Jinright.

The remainder of the day went smoothly, and at five o'clock sharp, Mr. Granger pointed to the clock. "Looks like it's time to call it a day. In case I haven't told you enough, Jericho, I want you to know I'm glad to have you working for me. I couldn't have handled this load by myself, and I trust you. That's very important when we have as much cash coming into the office as we have." He pulled a cash box from his desk drawer, took the money out and placed it into the bank bag.

Jericho didn't want to appear that he was watching, but he couldn't help wondering if Mr. Granger would be able to remember the combination tonight.

When he heard the clicking sound, and the safe door open, he breathed easier. So, the old man forgot the numbers Friday. It could happen to anybody. It was just easier to blame it on age when it happened to someone as old as Mr. Granger.

"Jericho, why don't you put the books away and let me take you out for a good hot meal at the Wildcat Barbecue."

"Wildcat?" He grimaced. "I don't know about that, sir. I ain't never eat no wildcat."

Mr. Granger held his head back and guffawed. "It's called the Wildcat after the Enterprise mascot. The barbecue is the best pork you've ever put in your mouth."

The café was small, but every table was filled, and Buddy and Mr. Granger took their plate to one of the tables outside.

Never had Buddy had anything that compared to the smoked barbecue, corn on the cob, slaw and cornbread. "You're right, sir. This is about the best barbecue I've ever had."

"About the best?"

Jericho realized he needed to stop using that word. It almost got him in trouble the last time he said, 'about.' "What I meant to say is it is definitely the best."

He laughed. "That's better."

Mr. Granger drove him to the hotel and thanked him once again for what he called, "good work ethics." Jericho had never heard the phrase before, but he could tell from the way Mr. Granger was smiling, that it was a good thing to have.

****

Standing on the deck of the ship, seeing all the people below waving and wishing them a farewell, the excitement began to build, and Juliette realized how silly she'd been to want to give up such a wonderful experience. "Mother, I'm sorry if I acted as if I didn't appreciate this fantastic trip, but I had no idea what to expect. Thank you."

"Didn't I tell you, you'd love it? Would you like to stay out here, or are you ready to go to our cabin and unpack?"

"I think I'll go get a wrap, then come back and sit on the deck. It's a little chilly out here."

"That's fine, dear. We'll both head back and I'll stay in and read until I fall asleep, if you don't mind being alone. I'm afraid I didn't sleep well in the hotel last night."

They headed back to their cabin and Juliette found a wool lap blanket on a chair. "Great. This is just what I need."

Henrietta said, "I'm glad you're enjoying yourself, darling. I was so in hopes that you would."

"I miss Buddy, already, but I'll have lots of experiences to share with him when we return, and by then we'll have lots to do to get ready for the wedding."

"Honey, let's just bask in the here and now. We'll deal with other mundane things after the trip is over."

"I'll try, Mother, although I don't consider my wedding to be mundane."

Juliette lay back in a deck chair and wrapped the lap blanket around her. A sweet-looking elderly couple passed by holding hands, and she smiled, imagining her and Buddy in forty years. They'd still be holding hands, too. She was sure of it. She closed her eyes and tried to remember her mother and father holding hands, but there was no such recollection. The lump that settled in her throat the day her mother admitted she didn't love Juliette's dad, returned. *Poor daddy.* A tear tried to seep from her closed eyes.

"Juliette. What a nice surprise!"

Her eyes popped open, and Roland Roundtree and two other fellows, all wearing Yale jackets were standing at the foot of her deck chair.

"Roland? I didn't expect to see you."

"Strange coincidence, isn't it? Are you traveling alone?"

Juliette sat up. "No, I'm with mother. And you?" She blushed. "Oh, I can see you aren't alone. Are your parents on the ship?"

"Are you kidding? What fun would that be? This trip is to celebrate my graduation from Yale. I was supposed to leave in June but came down with a bad case of mono. Almost died. Sickest I've ever been, so Pop rescheduled."

"Mono? Never heard of it."

"Really? I thought I told you about it. I spent six weeks in Johns Hopkins Hospital, where I had to take my finals in order to finish with my classmates. I'd just gotten home when I met you."

"I had no idea. Well, you certainly look fit and fine, now, so I'm assuming there are no aftereffects."

"I wish. I was on the Tennis Team but had to give it up. Too easily fatigued."

The big guy said, "Don't believe him. He was on a losing

team and blaming the mono is a convenient way to save face."

Roland punched him on the arm with his fist. "Shut up, man. Are you trying to make me look bad so you can move in on my girl?"

"How can I move in on someone I've never met. You haven't introduced us, gourd head," which made Juliette snicker.

Roland threw up his hand. "You're right, I haven't. Sorry." He gestured toward his pals and said, "Brady . . . Elton . . . may I introduce the lovely Juliette Jinright. Juliette, these two low-lifes had the enormous privilege of rooming with me in college."

Brady looked like a linebacker, and Elton, on the other hand was so short and thin, he could've easily been a jockey. She bit her lip to hide her smile, when she pictured Roland as an extra if The Three Stooges should ever need to add another character. Eyeing his slicked down hair, parted in the middle, it was hard not to stare. Larry, Curly, Moe and Slick.

She said, "So nice to meet you guys. It's getting a bit chilly, so if you'll please excuse me, I think I shall go to my cabin. It'll soon be time for dinner." As she headed back to her room, she could only imagine how excited her mother would be if she discovered Roland was on the same boat. If Juliette could manage it, her mother would never find out.

CHAPTER 20

When Jericho walked into the hotel after work, the desk clerk called him over. "Jericho, I'm a bit confused. A letter came yesterday addressed to Mr. Jericho Rockwell, Room 212, Rawls Hotel."

"Thank you, ma'am." He reached for the letter that she held in her hand, but she jerked back.

"Not so fast. I'm confused. You registered under the name of Jericho Rhoades, not Rockwell."

"Yes ma'am, but the letter belongs to me."

"How can I be sure?"

"Well, ma'am, if it's not me, then I reckon there must be another Jericho in Room 212. I'd be happy to deliver it to his room for you."

"Are you saying you have more than one last name?"

"Ma'am, I have more last names than a dog's got fleas."

"You aren't wanted by the law, are you?" She grinned. "Don't be offended. I'm just picking at you. You're too sweet to be a criminal. Says in the corner it's from J. Jinright. I only know one J. Jinright, but it can't be her, because I happened to overhear Lois talking to Pansy on the phone and Juliette is practically engaged to the Governor's son. Or was it the Attorney General's son?"

Jericho tried not to show his impatience. "The letter, ma'am? Please?"

She held the envelope to her nose and sniffed. "She uses good perfume, whoever she is. I wonder if she's kin to Juliette." Slowly she eased the letter toward him and although he could tell she was wanting to know more, he didn't give her the answers she was looking for.

He rushed up the stairs, skipping every other one, and sailed across his bed with the letter. Why would Juliette be writing him when he'd be seeing her Saturday night?

He unfolded the stationary and attempted to read. There were some mighty big words in her letter, but he could make out enough to know that he wouldn't be seeing Juliette Saturday night, as planned. Naturally, he was disappointed, but he reckoned if things worked out the way he hoped, he'd have to get used to the fact that rich folks had ways of entertaining themselves that didn't include square dancing, peanut boilings or taffy pulls.

If she had a hankering to ride the high seas on a ship, he'd be obliged for her to do it before they married, since he'd had enough sailing to last a lifetime. He'd miss her for sure, but it would give him a chance to get some things done at work. He'd work overtime until Juliette returned, to prove to Mr. Granger that he wasn't wrong in putting his confidence in him. Jericho tried not to let his imagination run away with him, but he couldn't help believe that if Mr. Granger recommended him to Donald Matthews, the job would be his for sure. He had a year to prove himself worthy of such an important position. He stroked his forehead. *Me? Running a company?* Jericho wanted to believe it was possible. If only he could read and write better, since Mr. Granger wrote a heap of letters. With a year to learn, surely, he could do it. Sweet Juliette would be happy to help him with his reading and writing if she knew, but her mother would be sure to find out and he couldn't give her more reason to look down on him.

He stuck the letter back in the envelope and tucked it in his coat pocket before walking downstairs to the Dining Room. Finishing up a bowl of soup, he heard giggles, "Hello, sailor."

He jumped up. "Shelby. What are you doing here?"

"Don't look so shocked. This is a public restaurant. You might as well be a gentleman and pull out my chair while you're standing. There's no reason two good friends can't enjoy a meal together, is there? If we're gonna be friends, you need to get over thinking there's more to our relationship."

Jericho glanced around the room. "You know I don't think that."

"Then stop being so nervous." Shelby glanced up at the waiter. "I'll take what my friend had."

"Yes ma'am. A bowl of soup and cornbread."

"Excellent." She handed him her menu, then leaned over and whispered to Jericho. "See, how easy that was? Two friends, having soup together."

He wanted to believe she was right, but if there was nothing wrong with it, why did he feel as though everyone in the room was staring?

She was full of talk. In fifteen minutes, he'd already heard more about her than he knew about Juliette, even after hearing Octavious read a passel of letters. He knew where Shelby was born, about the time a snake bit her, how her grandpa squandered the family fortune, that her mama cooked the best chicken 'n dumplings and her younger brother died with smallpox. She hardly slowed down to take a breath.

He thought about how he and Juliette could sit in the swing for thirty minutes without saying a word, but words weren't necessary when they were together. Just feeling her beside him was enough. That was the difference in being with a friend and being with the girl who could make his heart pound like a jackhammer.

When Shelby stopped talking long enough to take a sip of water, Jericho put money on the table and stood. "Since we've both finished, I reckon I'll head on back to my room."

"Really? This early? I thought we could take a walk." She

smiled. "As friends, of course."

Jericho sucked in a heavy breath. Was he making too big a deal of this? What was wrong with him being friends with Shelby. If she happened to be ugly, would he worry as much about what people would say? But she wasn't ugly.

She called him paranoid and he reckoned she was right, if it meant what he thought it meant. Well, it was time he got over it. Shelby made it perfectly clear she understood how he felt, and she'd let him know that she was good with it. "A walk? Sure, friend. Why not?"

CHAPTER 21

Jericho and Shelby strolled down Watts Street, then circled back to Main Street and sat on the ledge of the wall around the Boll Weevil Monument.

She was full of talk, but Jericho didn't pay much attention until she hit on a subject that pricked his attention.

"I'll bet I know something you don't know about the girl you claim to be your girlfriend." She shrugged.

"She *is* my girlfriend. I don't care if you don't believe me."

"Don't you want to know?"

"Makes no difference to me."

"Well, my mama irons Mrs. Hawkins' clothes, and she heard Mrs. Hawkins talking on the telephone with Mrs. Clark and she told her that Mrs. Jinright and Juliette are on a month's cruise. Mrs. Jinright booked it because Juliette's rich boyfriend, Roland Roundtree is on the same boat and Mrs. Jinright can't wait for him to put a ring on Juliette's finger. If you ask me, those two deserve one another."

Jericho's throat was dry. "Gossip. That's all it is." Juliette had never even mentioned anyone by the name of Roland Roundtree, and he knew for a fact even if he did exist, she wasn't in love with him. She loved him and him only.

The more he thought about it, the angrier it made him that folks would waste their time by making up silly stories. "Shelby, you're wrong." He kicked a tin can down the road as they strode along. The further they walked, the harder he kicked that can.

"About what?"

"About ever'thing. Juliette wrote me a letter just before they left and plainly said she'd be gone two weeks—not a whole month. If she was planning on marrying somebody else, would she be writing me and telling me how much she loves me?"

"I don't know. Maybe she likes keeping a lot of fellows on a string. There are girls like that, you know."

"Not her."

"Jericho, what is about Juliette that made you fall in love with her? Was it because of her looks?"

It was a good question and one which he hadn't considered. Was it her picture that first drew her to him—because it was a fact he'd never seen anyone prettier. But would he have been so taken with her if she had written the kind of garbage that Pittsburg Party Girl wrote? The answer was no. He said, "Shelby, she's pretty all right, but it was her sweetness that made me know I was in love."

"I can be sweet."

He smiled. "Yes, you can. You're very sweet and whatever guy steals your heart will be a lucky fellow."

"I just wish it was you." After a long pause, she said, "If you had met me first, do you think you could've fallen for me?"

"Shelby, what difference does it make? I didn't meet you first."

Her head lowered. "I don't know. None, I don't reckon. But if I had the money to buy all those fancy clothes like she wears, instead of this old uniform, maybe you'd like me instead of her. If I tell you something, you promise not to laugh?"

"Promise!"

"Mama and Daddy pray every night for God to give me a good church-going husband. I'm beginning to wonder if their prayers are what's keeping us apart. Do you go to church?"

Jericho cupped his hands over his eyes and stared in the distance.

"What are you looking at?" Her lip poked out in a pout when he didn't respond. "Did you even hear what I said?"

"I heard you. Stay here, Shelby. I see someone I know." He jumped off the ledge and ran.

Thomas ran to meet him. After they embraced, Jericho said, "It's great to see you. What are you doing in Enterprise?"

"Looking for you."

"For me? Whatever for? You look great. I was afraid you'd

be—"

Thomas grinned. "Dead?"

Jericho avoided a response. "Let me look at you. You must've put on twenty-five pounds. I have so many questions it's hard to know where to begin."

"I'm sure you do."

"Come on over to the fountain. I have someone I'd like for you to meet."

As they headed toward the monument, Thomas said, "Man, this is great running into you fifteen minutes after stepping off the train. I figured I'd look for days before finding you. I can't believe it happened so quickly."

"Are you really saying you came here to find me?"

"I did."

"Why me?"

"Because you're the best friend I've ever had, and I wanted to see if you were as happy as I hoped you'd be. Did you find the girl called Alabama?"

"I did and she's swell. I can't wait for you to meet her."

As they approached the monument, Thomas took one look at Shelby and held his arms open. "Wowzer! You're even more beautiful than your pictures. Can I get a hug?"

She jumped down and glared over his shoulder at Buddy, with a quizzical look as Thomas embraced her. She giggled. "I appreciate the compliment, but have we ever met?"

Jericho interrupted. "Thomas, she's not who you think she is."

"You mean she's not—"

Shelby interrupted. "No, I'm not Juliette, if that's what you're thinking."

Jericho smiled. "Shelby, meet my good friend, Thomas Tippins. And Thomas, this is my good friend, Shelby. Shelby Sellers."

Shelby said, "So where did you two meet?"

Thomas said, "We were in the Naval Hospital at the same time. He was healing from burns and I had cancer."

Jericho said, "Did you say *had*?"

"That's right. A surgeon came down from Walter Reed and cut that sucker out. You know, the Bible says the fervent prayer of a righteous man availeth much, and when the doctor pronounced me cancer-free, I felt God answered your prayer, Buddy."

He swallowed hard. "*My* prayer? You really believe it?"

"Yep. I had lots of folks praying fancy words over me, but I can't help believe it was your humble, sincere prayer that got the Lord's attention."

Shelby said, "I can see you two have lots of catching up to do, and I need to get home and wash this uniform. It was a pleasure meeting you, Thomas."

"Likewise, ma'am. A real pleasure." He reached for her hand and kissed it.

She blushed.

After she left, Thomas said, "Before it gets any later, I suppose I need to find a place to lay my head tonight. Are there any good Boarding Houses in town?"

"I'm sure there are, but no way will I let you going to a Boarding House. You can stay with me."

"And where would that be?"

Jericho pointed across the street. "The Hotel Rawls. Grab your duffel bag and follow me."

Thomas's eyes widened as he glanced around the swanky hotel. "You must've robbed a bank. This place looks like it would cost a mint to stay here."

"Nope. I didn't have to resort to bank robbery. I found another way to make money. Got me a good job."

They took the elevator and Jericho led him to his room. Thomas said, "Geez, this is swell."

"I hope you don't mind sleeping on the sofa."

"Are you kidding? It'll be great."

"Thomas, I can't get over how great you look. When did you get out?"

"The Navy or the hospital?"

"Both."

"I was discharged from the hospital yesterday and from the Navy the day before."

"You're kidding? And you came straight here?"

"Yep."

"I would've thought you would've wanted to go home to see—"

He laughed. "Don't be afraid to say it. From the way the guys teased me, you thought I was a real mama's boy, didn't you?"

"I guess I did—not that I thought there was nothin' wrong with it. I wouldn't mind having a mama and a granny making over me. I ain't never known what that was like."

"Mama and Daddy taught me to be independent. I'm lucky to have a family who cares about me, and Mama never skipped a day writing to encourage me when I was so sick, but when I told her I wanted to look up my good friend who prayed for me, she was all for it. But enough about me. Tell me about Alabama."

"I looked her up as soon as I got into town."

"Well, how did it go?"

"It's a long story. I don't know where to begin."

"I've got all night. Why not start from the beginning?"

Jericho told him all about going to Montgomery and how Miz Lucy got him a job with her son at the Matthews Agency and the turn of events that led him to Enterprise. "If it hadn't been for finding the envelope with Juliette's name and address in the trash, I would never have known how to find her."

They talked for hours, then Thomas asked, "I still don't get it. You say she thinks you're the one she was writing letters to? She thinks you're Octavious?"

"Yeah, and things are going great. She's planning a Christmas wedding, and she thinks it was my idea."

Thomas threw his hands to the top of his head. "This is crazy man. What's she gonna think when she finds out you've been lying to her?"

"But it's not like that. I haven't lied."

"No? Are you saying your name is Octavious?"

"Of course not, but then I never told her it was."

"But you've never told her it wasn't. Buddy, I think you've allowed your infatuation with this girl to cloud your thinking."

"I ain't infatuated, I'm in love with her. And it wadn't my idea not to tell her, but Mr. Wilkerson is a good family friend and he's known Juliette all her life. He told me it would be better not to tell her right away but to wait until the time was right."

"Buddy, I hate to contradict your friend, but the time to tell her the truth was the day you met her."

"That's what I thought, but I trust Mr. Wilkerson."

"Well, I hope it all turns out for the best, but I don't mind telling you, this looks like a disaster about to happen."

"I thought the same thing when Mr. Wilkerson suggested waiting, but I'm thinking now that he knew what he was doing. When I first arrived, if I had told her I wasn't Octavious, she would've thanked me and sent me on my way. But by waiting, she's had a chance to fall in love with me, and when she does find out I'm Jericho Rhoades and not Octavious Rockwell, it won't make one iota of difference to her. Just like I wouldn't care if her name was Suzie Cupiedoll. I'm in love with her, not her name." His lip curled at the corner. "Besides, I have plans to change her name. She'll soon be the wife of Mr. Jericho Rhoades, CPA."

"CPA? Buddy, my friend . . . this has gone too far, already. It's bad enough she thinks you're someone else, but to lie about being a CPA? Granny always told me one little lie was like yeast. It keeps on getting bigger and bigger. Looks like she was right."

"You got me wrong. I didn't mean Juliette was my wife yet or that I was a CPA yet. I just meant that's my goal, and one day it'll happen. Wait and see."

"I hope you're right. Well, we've got lots more to talk about but I'm bushed. That train ride was rough, so if it's all the same to you, I'm ready to get a little shut-eye."

"Good idea." He took a pillow off the bed and threw to Thomas, then reached in a drawer and pulled out a blanket.

After lights were out, Thomas said, "You still awake?"

"Yeah. You need something?"

"Just an answer. Is there anything going on between you and Shelby?"

"No. Just friends. Why?"

"No reason. Just wondering. Good night."

CHAPTER 22

Juliette entered the cabin, jerked off her gloves and laid them on the night stand. Her mother was lying on the bed reading. Henrietta dropped her book, then grinning from ear to ear, she said, "Well, did you make any friends while sunning on the deck?"

"Friends? Not really. Well, I take that back. I met a nice elderly couple. They were holding hands. I thought that rather sweet. Mother, I tried to remember if I ever saw you and Daddy holding hands. I don't believe I did."

"Frankly, Juliette, I think it's rather silly for old people to walk around in public showing affection. I'll wager they only do it for attention. Probably never hold hands at home."

She shrugged. "You may be right. But it sure looked sincere to me. When Buddy and I are married, I hope we never stop holding hands and that I always feel chills running up my spine when he touches me."

"Juliette Jinright, I'm shocked that you would talk in such a vulgar manner."

"What did I say wrong, Mother?"

"I'm shocked that you have to ask. Talk of him touching you. It's not proper conversation for a young lady, and I hope I don't hear such filth come from you again."

"I simply meant I get all tingly when I hold hands with the man I'm going to marry. What's wrong with that? Aren't you supposed to feel something when you're in love?"

"Love, my foot. What do you know about love? Get your head out of the clouds, Juliette because you can forget about marrying that sailor. Not only is he crude, he's a liar."

"Mother, you have no right—"

"I beg your pardon? I have every right. I'll not stand by and watch my only child being taken advantage of by some ignorant gold-digger."

"You're wrong, Mother."

"Am I? Didn't you tell me that in those letters he wrote, he bragged about how rich he'was? Can you honestly believe he was telling the truth?"

"But we've talked about that, and I understand why he did it."

"Well, maybe you do, but I don't, so you may as well get it in your head that I won't ever stand by and let him take advantage of you. I brought you on this cruise with the hopes it would give you an opportunity to clear your head and see him for what he is."

Tears rolled down her cheeks. "I'm going back to sit on the deck, Mother. I can see you and I will never agree on the subject of Buddy. I love him and nothing you can say will change my mind. I'm just sorry that you are so close-minded that you can't see how wrong you are."

"Juliette, you've never talked to me in such a disrespectful manner. Are you really going to allow that nobody to come between us?"

"I have nothing more to say, Mother." She slammed the door as she ran out of the cabin.

Juliette was standing on the deck, looking out over the vast waters, when someone tapped her on the shoulder. She turned. *Not him. Not now.* Hiding her disappointment, she feigned a smile. "Oh! Hi, Roland."

"Hey, dollface." His brow creased. "Are you crying?"

She reached up and blotted her tear ducts. "Maybe I'm just overwhelmed by the beauty of the sun setting over the ocean. Beautiful, isn't it?"

"Very beautiful."

Juliette hoped they were both referring to the sunset, although his gaze had stayed fixed on her.

Standing beside her, he leaned against the rails. "I hope you're going to the dance tonight."

She shook her head. "I don't think so."

"I'd really appreciate it if you'd go. My two buddies have found girls to go with, and they're insisting I go with them, but I'd feel like a fifth wheel, if you know what I mean."

She feigned a smile. "I'm sure you'll have no trouble at all finding a girl."

"I'm afraid you're wrong. We both know I'm not the most handsome guy on the boat, and neither am I under a false impression that you have romantic feelings for me. You've already made that quite clear. I'm asking as a friend. Why should we both miss out on having a good time, when we could go together? If you say no, we'll probably both wind up here, wishing we could be at the dance."

This time, the smile was real. "I suppose you're right. But Roland, I don't want to hurt you."

"You're saying you'll allow me to escort you to the dance?"

"Yes, but you do understand I'm in love with a fellow back home, don't you?"

His face lit up. "I do understand. Thanks, Juliette. You're swell. What room are you in? I'll call for you at eight."

"Fine." Then, imagining her mother making a big deal of Roland Roundtree coming to their cabin, she shook her head. "No, don't call for me. Meet me just inside the door of the ballroom."

If he tried to hide the disappointment on his face, he failed, although he was very gracious. "Sure, whatever you think best. Eight o'clock, near the door."

Juliette went back to the cabin and was surprised to find her mother was not there. Reaching into her trunk, she pulled out the beautiful red formal Henrietta had bought her for the occasion, although Juliette never imagined wearing it. She held it up to her body and gazed at her image in the mirror. It might be fun to be dancing in the gorgeous ballroom, even if it wasn't with the one she loved.

The door opened and her mother froze in place, gaping at her daughter standing there wearing a hoop. Her jaw dropped when she eyed the red gown lying on the bed. "I do declare, miracles really do exist. Oh, honey, you're going to the dance. I am so pleased." Rushing over to help, she picked up the gown and lifted it over Juliette's head. "Suck in sweetie, while I zip it." Henrietta stepped back and with her hands folded under her chin, she oohed and ahhed. "You look beautiful, darling. I'm sure there will be many eligible bachelors there tonight, who will be lining up to dance with the most beautiful girl in the room."

Juliette could only imagine her mother's interference if she were to discover that Roland Roundtree was not only on the ship, but that he would be her escort for the evening. Glancing at her watch, Juliette groaned. *Fifteen 'til eight.* She hated to stand alone for fifteen minutes, waiting for Roland to show up, but wouldn't it be better than spending fifteen more minutes in the room with her mother, where her secret would likely leak out?

She picked up her evening bag from the bed. "I think I'll head that way, Mother."

With her hands planted on Juliette's shoulders, Henrietta kissed her on the cheek. "You look absolutely radiant. I have a really good feeling that this will be the beginning of a brand-new chapter in your life."

"Mother, I know you mean well, but I'm ready to write the last chapter in my life's book and it doesn't include the dance. I wish you could accept the fact that I'm in love with Buddy Rockwell and nothing or no one will ever come between us. I want to marry him so much it makes my heart ache."

"Fiddle-faddle. I think you delight in saying things you think might ruffle my feathers. I don't think you're in love with that sailor as much as you want me to believe you are. If you were, you'd be staying in tonight instead of wanting to look pretty to meet new suitors."

Her mother's senseless rant was almost enough to make Juliette jerk off the gown and forget all about meeting Roland. She wasn't sure why she agreed to it in the first place. It was too late to back out, now.

CHAPTER 23

Juliette ambled slowly down the long corridor and spotted Roland, standing outside the door, waiting for her. A sick feeling came over her, seeing the huge grin on his face. The way his hair was slicked down, she imagined he must've emptied an entire bottle of Vitalis on his head. She supposed he must've put on an extra twenty pounds since last wearing his tux, since his vest gaped open between the buttons and the rose-colored polka-dot bow tie couldn't have stood out more if he'd been wearing a Neon sign under his chin.

"Juliette, I was so afraid you wouldn't show."

"I told you I'd be here."

"I know, but Brady and Elton are both a lot better looking than I am and they get dates easily. After I introduced them to you, they went all ga-ga over how beautiful you are. They asked how I knew you and I told them we had dated. It seemed to make them angry and they accused me of making it up. Then I told them I was going to escort you to the dance and they called me a liar and said no way would you ever go out with me." He lowered his head. "It would've been a long swim home, if you hadn't come tonight, but there's no way I could've faced them if you had changed your mind about coming."

Juliette tried to make a joke out of it. "Well, I'm glad you didn't have to swim home, because I'm sure you would never have made it."

"I wouldn't have expected to, but I didn't care. It would be better than facing the guys."

Was he saying what she thought he was saying? The horrid thought that if she'd backed out of coming, it might've caused him to so something as crazy as jumping ship, brought shivers to her spine. "Roland, why don't we give them something to talk about?"

"You're leaving?"

"No, silly. I mean we'll act as if there really is something going on between us. When they get here, we'll pretend we're crazy about one another."

"It won't be pretense on my part, Juliette. I am crazy about you."

Maybe it wasn't such a good idea, but the thought of two bullies causing Roland so much anguish that he could want to take his life, burned her up. "Well, regardless of how I might act tonight, you do understand that I'm practically an engaged woman and it's all a game. Right?"

He smiled. "I got you. You're a real friend, Juliette. That soldier is one lucky guy to have a girl who's not only beautiful, but you're all heart." He was leading her onto the dance floor, when he looked around and saw Brady and Elton walking in. "There they are," he whispered in her ear. "I guess their dates are already in here, because they're alone."

She feigned a hearty laugh.

"Why are you laughing?"

"You just whispered in my ear, and they aren't taking their eyes off us. I wanted them to think you said something hilariously funny. I believe you told me you took drama. Well, the show is about to begin." She ran the back of her hand over his cheek. "Break a leg, Clark Gable. Show me what you've got." She put her head on his shoulder and closed her eyes, as they rocked back and forth in time with the music.

She raised her head. "I think it's working. They're walking over this way. You're doing great. Keep looking into my eyes, with that dreamy look on your face."

"Juliette, this is the easiest part I've ever had to play." He didn't take his eyes off her until he felt a tap on his shoulder. Brady said, "May I cut in?"

Juliette said, "Roland, I'll meet you at the punch table as soon as this dance is over."

"Sure, sweetheart."

Brady's brows meshed together. "You're with him? For real?"

"Didn't he tell you?"

"Well, yeah, he did. But—"

"But what?"

"What does a beautiful girl like you, see in a milksop like Roland Roundtree. The only thing he has going for him is his money. That must be it. You're after his money?"

Juliette had no time to think, before her hand burned on the side of his face. "For your information, he's a much better man than you'll ever be."

He rubbed his jaw. "Wow, you pack a punch. Can't you take a joke? Folks are gonna think I said something crude to you."

"You did."

She looked over his shoulder and saw Roland rush up behind him. He said, "Excuse me, friend, I think it's my turn."

Brady looked at Roland, then back at Juliette. "Sure. She's all yours."

"Yes, she is. All mine." Brady stormed off and Roland took her in his arms and winked. "All mine, for tonight, anyway." Then, he leaned over and whispered in her ear. "I don't know what he said to you, but it did me good to see you take care of it. I'll bet his jaw is still ringing."

"Roland, why are you hanging out with those bullies? Surely, you can find better friends."

"I didn't pick them. My mother did."

"My mother tries to pick my friends, too, but I refuse to let her control my life. We're both intelligent adults and capable of choosing our own friends."

"You're right. I didn't want to come on this trip, but Mother bought the tickets and paid them to come with me. Brady is a big football player, and Elton is President of the Student Government. She thought it would look good in the paper to have my name linked with theirs."

"The paper?"

"Yeah. I guess you didn't see it."

"No." She didn't see it, but she had a feeling she knew who had.

After the music stopped, they wandered over toward the punch table. Roland said, "You didn't tell me your mother was at the dance."

"I didn't know she was coming."

"Why don't we walk over that way?"

Juliette rolled her eyes. "No need. She's coming here."

Henrietta waved a handkerchief in the air. "Yoo-hoo. Wait up, kids." She threw her arms around Roland's neck. "Well, what a surprise to see you here, Roland. You look dashing. Doesn't he, darling?"

"Mother, you didn't mention you'd be coming to the dance."

"Well, after you left, I thought, why not? I was eager to see if there might be someone here that I might know."

"And I suppose you had no idea that Roland was on the ship."

"Well, now that you mention it, I do believe I read something about it on the social pages, but I declare, it simply slipped my mind. But you look as if you're having a wonderful time, so don't let me interfere."

Juliette looked over to see Elton and Brady watching. She eased over close to Roland and whispered, "Your buddies are still alone. I don't think they have dates. They probably only wanted you to think so."

"I figured as much. I suppose they thought if they told me they had dates, I'd stay in the room and not come with them."

Henrietta snickered. "You two look so cute, whispering sweet nothings to one another. I had a feeling this was going to work out."

Juliette looked at Roland and giggled. "Yes, Mother. You can't imagine how things are working out."

He curved his arm. "Would you like to take a stroll on the deck . . . dear?"

Sliding her hand through his arm, she tossed her head back. "I'd love it. You will excuse us, won't you Mother?"

"Of course, dear. I see someone across the room I'd like to speak to. You kids go enjoy the moonlight. It's beautiful tonight."

Leaving the ballroom, Roland said, "Your mother has friends on the ship?"

She shrugged. "She hasn't mentioned it. She seemed

surprised, so I assume she wasn't expecting to see them here."

Henrietta lifted the skirt to her gown and rushed across the room. "Garland, what a nice surprise to see you here."

The woman raised one brow. "Excuse me. Have we met?"

"Not officially, but I recognized you from your picture in the paper. I read Social Happenings every week. Wouldn't miss it. I thought you might like to know the Alabama State Attorney General's son and his date, the beautiful Juliette Jinright are on the ship. Since you're taking pictures, I thought I'd pass the information on to you."

"Jinright? Would she be the daughter of the late Steve Jinright, owner of the Cotton Mills?"

"Why, yes. That's Juliette. They've just headed out to the deck, and she's wearing a lovely red gown and carrying a pearl-studded evening bag. I'm sure you'll recognize her."

"I didn't get your name."

Henrietta shooed her away with her hand. "You'd better hurry if you want pictures."

"Thank you. Most of the pictures I've taken tonight are of older married couples without a story, so a picture of a young couple of interest romancing on the deck will be perfect."

CHAPTER 24

When Shelby Sellers asked for permission to switch her cleaning schedule, so she could clean the Matthews Building first, before going to clean the bank, Mr. Granger objected.

"I'm sorry if this schedule isn't working for you, Shelby, but there are times we stay later than five, and it would be disrupting to have you scurrying around in the room while we work."

"But I can wait outside the building until I see you leave, sir."

"Young lady, our agreement was that you'd come five nights a week after six o'clock, and either you continue that schedule, or we'll find someone who can accommodate us."

"I understand, sir. The bank closes at four, so I'll continue to go there first." Although she understood, she didn't like it. No longer would she be able to stand outside and watch for Mr. Granger to leave, so she could see Buddy. Alone.

Wednesday evening, after the floors dried, Shelby picked up

the wastepaper basket in Mr. Granger's office. When she turned it upside down to empty into the trash barrel, a twenty-dollar bill fell out of a brown paper lunch sack. Bending down, she grabbed the sack and opened it. Shelby's body charged with a nervous tension at the discovery of hundreds of dollars crammed in the small bag. Her heart raced. *Crazy!* Why would Mr. Granger throw away so much money? The only sane answer was it was unintentional. She'd probably get her picture in the paper for finding it. And a reward—surely, there'd be a reward if she returned it. *If?* The word "if" stuck in her throat. This was not a decision she needed to take lightly. She took the money from the bag, stuffed it into her pocketbook and hurried out of the building for fear Mr. Granger would realize he threw the bag into the trash and come back for it.

Shelby tossed and turned in her bed that night, unable to sleep. What if the police should come knocking on her door to ask if she found the bag? Wouldn't they want to look into her purse? She crawled out of bed at two a.m., took the money from her pocketbook and stuffed it under her mattress.

Thursday morning, she lifted the edge of the mattress to make sure it wasn't a dream. Guilt overwhelmed her. She'd never stolen anything in her life. Never. But she didn't steal the money. Did she? She found it. Someone threw it away. It's not against the law to take something that someone else has thrown into the trash, is it?

After convincing herself the money now belonged to her, a

little jingle came to mind. "Finders keepers, losers weepers." It wasn't her fault the money found its way into the trash can. She found it. Didn't that mean she could keep it? Never had she seen that much money in one place in her life. Mr. Granger lost it, but he could make plenty more, the same way he made the hundreds he so carelessly threw away. It would be no big deal to him. At least, that's what she wanted to believe.

****

Jericho arrived at the office earlier than usual Thursday morning. He'd work doubly hard to prove to Mr. Granger that he was responsible and could handle extra work.

Mr. Granger came in at seven. "Jericho, I hope you've thought about what we talked about."

"Sir, I've thought of little else. I know I don't talk like nobody who can run a business, but I'm gonna work on it. By the time you retire, I'll be talking like a college professor, you just wait and see. I ain't gonna disappoint you. No sirree, I plan to make you real proud you put confidence in me."

"I'm already proud of you, Jericho. And I admire you for wanting to better yourself for the good of the company. That's very admirable and I have no doubt that you can do anything you set your mind to do."

"Thank you, Mr. Granger. Ain't nobody never been as good to me as you and Mr. Donald. It was my lucky day when I stopped at Miz Lucy's Boarding House. Without her help, I wouldn't have met her son, and without his help, I wouldn't be here. He gave me two choices—Troy or Enterprise—and I've never regretted choosing this office."

"I'm a firm believer we make our own fortune."

"Well, I ain't looking for no fortune, but I do want to be able to provide a decent living for my family, after I'm married."

"I have no doubt that you'll do even better than that. Well, I need to take the money from the safe and get it to the bank."

Jericho watched as the old man limped over to the safe. His legs were bowed and though he didn't complain, it was evident his knees hurt with every step. He opened the safe and pulled out the bank bag.

"Mr. Granger, would you like for me to take yesterday's receipts to the bank?"

"Much obliged, but I plan to stop by the drugstore to have coffee and shoot the breeze with the fellows after I drop off the money. I don't have any appointments until after lunch, so I should be back in an hour or so."

At eleven o'clock, when Mr. Granger still wasn't back, Jericho became worried. What if he'd fallen and was in the hospital? It was a fact he was very shaky before he left for the bank. Or what if someone knocked him on the head and took the money? Jericho hadn't said anything, but he never had thought it was a good idea for the old man to be walking down the street, holding a bag with the name of the bank clearly stamped on it. He was an easy target for a thief.

He thought of calling the police, but there was always the possibility Mr. Granger spent longer than usual with his buddies at the drugstore and would be embarrassed if Jericho alerted the police.

The door to the office burst open and two policemen stood, glaring.

"What's wrong? It's Mr. Granger, isn't it?"

"Is your name Jericho Rhoades?"

"Yessir. I'm Jericho."

"Then you'd better come with us."

He stuck the ledger in the drawer. "How is he? Is he in the hospital?"

"We'll ask the questions when we get to the station."

"The station? You have him at the Police Station?"

CHAPTER 25

Juliette awoke with her eyes swollen from crying. "Mother, I don't know if I can ever forgive you."

"Stop being so dramatic, child. When you're a little older and have children of your own, you'll understand why mothers have to do things to protect their children."

"Protect me? Is that what you call this? I call it kidnapping."

"Kidnapping?" She gave a sarcastic chuckle. "Juliette, you are spoiled rotten. That's your problem. Most young ladies would give anything to have the opportunities you've had and yet you act as if I've committed a crime by giving you a chance of a lifetime to be on this fabulous cruise with some of the most influential people in the world. In spite of all my efforts to give you the world, you remain ungrateful. I don't get it."

"Mother, if you really thought you were doing something to please me, you would've been truthful. You said we'd be gone two weeks. Two weeks! That's exactly what you said, and now you're saying we'll be gone for a whole month? Unbelievable."

"Lower your voice, Juliette. These walls are thin. I'm sorry that you're so upset. I honestly thought that once we set sail, you'd be so excited, it wouldn't matter to you how long you'd be gone. Maybe I was wrong."

"Maybe? There's no maybe. You were very wrong."

"Well, there's nothing I can do about it now, except to apologize, but look on the bright side."

"There's a bright side? Then, please, tell me what it is, because I see no bright side."

"Isn't it fortunate that you have a friend to spend time with? You didn't seem to mind being away from that sailor friend of yours when you were dancing with Roland. You two made an adorable couple."

"Couple? You know how I feel about Roland, but you arranged this trip because you knew he would be on this cruise, didn't you? You never miss reading the Gossip Section in the newspaper and Roland told me it was in the paper."

"So, what if I did? I was only looking out after your best interests. Honey, you're still young and you were getting too attached to that sailor, whom you know absolutely nothing about. I know you think you're in love, but you're just in love with love. I'm sorry if you think I was being mean, but I love you too much to sit by and watch you destroy your life, without doing all I can to prevent it. If that makes me a bad mother, so be it."

****

Walt Wilkerson was walking out the door when his phone rang. Thinking it was probably Henrietta, he almost didn't answer it. Somehow, he had to distance himself from her but she'd become like a disease with no cure. When they were younger, she wasn't as controlling and the transformation had been so gradual over the years, he supposed he didn't see what a trap he'd fallen into until the situation with Buddy arose. Now, he realized what a snob she'd become.

It felt like déjà vu, all over again. He couldn't help thinking of how much he loved her when they were sixteen, and how he blamed her mother for years for pushing her toward Steve. Only in the last couple of years had he begun to believe that her mother had nothing to do with their break-up. Henrietta wasn't willing to give up the life to which she'd become accustomed, and now she expected her daughter to do as she did and marry for money, not love. But Juliette had nothing of Henrietta in her and if he could prevent it, he wouldn't sit by and watch Henrietta ruin Juliette's life the way she had ruined his.

After the fifth ring, he reached for the phone.

"Mr. Wilkerson? I'm . . . I'm in jail, sir, and I was told I could make one phone call." His voice broke. "I didn't know who else to call."

"Jericho? Is that you, Jericho?"

"Yessir. Mr. Wilkerson, I've been arrested, and I don't even know what I done."

"Okay. Calm down, son. I'm on my way. We'll get to the bottom of this."

"I'm scared, Mr. Wilkerson."

Walt heard the officer say, "Time's up."

"Jericho . . . Jericho?" Walt grabbed his coat and rushed out the door.

****

Shelby had thought of a dozen ways to spend her newfound fortune. She considered telling Jericho, but she knew she was only dreaming if she thought he'd encourage her to keep it. No, he was too honest for his own good. The words she spoke to him, just as Thomas arrived, came back to her: *"If I had the money to buy all those fancy clothes like Juliette wears, instead of this old uniform, maybe you'd like me instead of her."*

That would be the first thing she'd do with the money. She'd go to the beauty shop, get a permanent and buy her a few fancy outfits to wear for Jericho. Once he saw she could be as pretty as Juliette, he'd choose her. She knew it. She'd known it from the time he kissed her in the office. If she gave up her cleaning job, it might draw suspicion if Mr. Granger reported the money missing. Chances were, he wouldn't even mention it, since it would make him look incompetent for putting it in the trash. Not wanting to take a chance of getting caught, though, she'd continue working, as if nothing happened, until everything blew over.

After she and Jericho married, they could move to another town, and open up their own business. Probably something to do with ciphering, since he seemed to like it so much. He'd be his own boss and she'd stay home and raise their young'uns. Maybe three or four, but of course, she'd let him have a say-so about how many.

CHAPTER 26

The Police Chief held out his hand when Walt Wilkerson stormed into the station. "Walt, longtime no see. What brings you to the hoosegow, my good man?"

"Jerry, I got a phone call a few minutes ago from a friend of mine, saying you were holding him here. I'm here to see what this is all about."

The chief pulled off his cap and scratched his head. "A friend of yours? I think someone must be playing a joke on you."

"It's no joke. His name is Jericho Rhoades."

"You mean the kid? You're saying he's a friend of yours?"

"Yes. What's the charge?"

"Stealing."

"I don't believe it. I want to see him."

"Sure. Funny, though, Rhoades is not the name he's been going by." He led him down the hall and Walt saw Jericho gripping the bars to his cell.

"Mr. Wilkerson. Thank you for coming. I hated to bother you, but I didn't know what else to do. Mr. Wilkerson, they're saying I stole a bunch of money."

"Did you?"

"No sir. I don't have to idea what they're talking about. They emptied my pockets when I got here and I had three dollars and thirty-seven cents, but it was what I had left over from my last payday. I didn't steal none of it. I swear to you, I didn't."

"I believe you, Buddy. Try not to worry, and I'll get to the bottom of this."

"Juliette said in her letter she'd be gone two weeks and two weeks will be over tomorrow. What if they come home and her mother finds out I'm in jail for stealing? She don't like me now, but she won't never let Juliette marry me if she thinks I'm a thief."

Walt chewed on his lip. He didn't know if telling him the truth—that Juliette and Henrietta would be gone another two weeks—would ease Buddy's mind or cause him more grief. "Buddy, she won't be home tomorrow."

"Yessir, it'll be two weeks. I've been marking the days off on my calendar."

"Juliette was under the impression she'd only be gone two weeks, but her mother booked a month's cruise. So, see? We'll have all this nonsense about you stealing money cleared up before they get home. That'll be a good thing, won't it?"

"I don't know, Mr. Wilkerson. I can't seem to think straight anymore, I'm so scared. What if they send me to prison? Ain't no way for me to prove I didn't steal nothing."

"Buddy, do you trust me?"

"Yessir, I don't reckon there's nobody I trust more'n I do you."

"Then believe me when I tell you I won't quit until you're a free man."

After Mr. Wilkerson left, Buddy lay on the cot, staring at a roach on the ceiling. He wondered if the roach knew how lucky he was that there were no bars big enough to hold him—he could go and come at will. For the first time in his life Buddy was beginning to realize the true meaning of freedom.

****

Walt left the jail and went straight to The Matthews Agency. Gid Granger sat at his desk, eating.

"Gid, I can see I came at a bad time. Go ahead and finish your lunch. I'll come back a little later."

"Nonsense, I was just finishing up. Have a seat, Walt."

Walt pulled up a chair next to the desk, while Gid grabbed a napkin and wiped his hands. He picked up an apple core and bread crusts and stuffed them into a brown penny lunch sack. With a chuckle, he said, "I'm sorry, I don't have leftovers to offer you, but it's probably best. I'm afraid my lunches nowadays are rather boring." He crushed the top of the sack in his hands, and held his head back, as if he could see through the ceiling, straight up into the heavens. With a smile, he said, "Wilma used to delight in sending me to work with pork chops, potato salad, homemade bread and there'd always be a nice chunk of cake. I sure do miss her." His eyes widened. "I didn't mean just because she fixed good meals. She was an angel, but at least she's no longer suffering."

Walt nodded. "I'm sure you do miss her, Gid. Wilma was a fine Christian lady. Loved by all."

Gid's eyes welled with water as he opened his desk drawer and stuck the lunch bag inside. "Forgive me, Walt for being sentimental. I miss her every day, but some days are worse than others. So, to what do I owe this pleasure?"

"Gid, I need to hear the whole story from you, from beginning to end."

"What story?"

"About the missing money. I'll be frank. I consider Buddy Rhoades a special friend of mine, and I know you wouldn't have had him arrested if you didn't feel in your heart that he was guilty. But I have a gut-feeling there must be another explanation. I'll never be convinced that Buddy stole that money. I know you've told the police all you know, but would you mind too much going over the details with me?"

Walt was hoping he wouldn't be offended, and he didn't appear to be. After Gid went step by step over all the happenings in the office during the two days involved, he shook his head slightly.

Gid said, "Walt, I know how you're feeling. It hurt me, too. I didn't want to believe he could do such a thing, either, but after weighing the facts, it was plain to see there was no other possible explanation."

Walt stood and extended his hand. "Thanks, Gid. I appreciate you laying it all out for me."

"Are you saying it changed your mind?"

"No. I came in here believing Buddy didn't do it, and now I'm even more convinced."

After Walt left, Gid reached in his desk drawer to get a bottle of ink, but instead, pulled out a wadded lunch bag. "Where did this come—" His heart pounded when he peeked inside and realized he had mistakenly shoved it in the drawer instead of throwing it into the trash. He'd caught himself doing other thoughtless things lately. The more he concentrated on them, the more scatter-brained he seemed to become. What if he was losing his mind? If only Wilma were here, she'd know what to tell him to do.

Walt left the Agency and went across the street to the bank. He was glad there was no one in there at the time, other than the teller.

Pat greeted him with a smile. "Good afternoon, Mr. Wilkerson. How can I help you?"

"I've got a question for you, Pat, and I sure hope you can help me."

"You know I'll do my best."

"Do you remember the day Gid Granger came in here to make a deposit, but his bank bag was empty?"

She frowned. "I sure do. Poor fellow. I could tell it really rattled him."

"The paper said there was garbage in the bag. Would you happen to remember what kind of garbage?"

"As a matter of fact, I do. I could even smell it before I poured it out. There was an apple core and the edges off a bologna sandwich."

"Are you sure it was bologna? Did you see it?"

"Well, no, not the bologna, but I saw the red wrapping—you know, like the butcher puts around the bologna."

Walt popped his palm down on the shelf between them. "Thanks, Pat. You may have just saved a man's life."

****

He hurried back to the jail. "Jerry, is there somewhere we can talk?"

"Sure, come on back to my office."

The chief closed the door. "Walt, I know you don't want to believe he could've done it. Shucks, nothing hurts quite as bad as losing confidence in someone we trust, and I can tell you trusted the kid. But you weren't the only one he had fooled. Gid Granger was as shocked as you were to find out he was nothing but a low-down thief."

"That's where you're wrong, Jerry. I haven't found out he was a thief, because he's not. I'd trust Buddy Rhoades with everything I own. Just tell me why you booked him."

"You know why I booked him. For stealing."

"But I want to hear everything you were told that made you feel you had no choice but to lock him up."

"You're not gonna like it."

"I already don't like it, so tell me."

He rubbed his hand across his mouth. "Let me see . . . where do I begin?" He chewed the inside of his cheek. "Well, Mr. Gid said every night for the past thirty years, he's made out the night deposit at the end of the day and puts the money in a bank bag. It's a cloth bag with a drawstring on the—"

"I know what a bank bag looks like. Get on with it."

"Well, he said he then puts the bag in the safe, since the bank closes at four o'clock. Then, the first thing every morning after getting to the office, he takes the bag out of the safe and carries it to the bank to deposit."

A lieutenant knocked on the door. "Sir, you have a phone call on line three. It's the mayor. Says it's important."

"Thanks." He picked up the phone. "What can I do for you, mayor?"

Walt got up and paced the floor as he waited.

The chief said, "That sounds like a good idea, mayor. I'm sure I can send an officer over to talk to the assembly at the elementary school. Give me that date again."

Walt threw up his hands. "Important? That's what you people call important? A kid is in jail for something he didn't do, and he's scared to death. Yet, you feel a chat about a grammar school assembly program takes priority when his life is at stake?"

Jerry put his hand over the receiver. "Cool down, Walt. You act like we've executed him. I can only do one thing at the time." He removed his hand. "Sure, mayor. We'll make it happen." He hung up the phone. "Now. Where was I?"

"You said Gid Granger takes the bag from the safe every morning and deposits the contents in the bank."

"That's correct."

"So, if Gid is the one who puts the bag in the safe and he's the one who takes it out, why is Buddy being held?"

"Because he's the only one other than Gid who has the combination. Not only that, he was still working when Gid left to go home, last night."

Jerry pulled a pencil from behind his ear and thumped it on his desk. "Now, that you have the facts, do you still feel we have no reason to hold your friend?"

"I have even more reason to feel you're holding him without cause."

"Aww, Walt, give it up. The kid's guilty. It would take a slick lawyer to get him off and face it—you're no lawyer."

"It shouldn't take a lawyer. A little common sense would help.

I'm telling you, Buddy didn't take the money. I'd stake my life on it."

"I wouldn't be so quick to defend him if I were you. You might not know him as well as you think you do. They say the boy out of the Navy on a medical discharge and came here chasing after the Jinright girl. You know what the Good Book says, 'The love of money is the root of all evil.'"

"*They* say? You're ready to condemn him on hearsay?" He rubbed the back of his neck. "I'm telling you, you're wrong about the kid, Jerry, and one way or the other, I intend to prove it. I want to see him."

"No problem. You're free to pay his bail and get him out—unless you're not as confident in his good character as you pretend to believe."

"I have a very good reason for not wanting to post bail, but it has nothing to do with his character. It may be a long shot, but I think for the time being, it's best he stay right where he is." He followed Jerry and waited for him to unlock the cell door.

Buddy jumped up from the cot. "Mr. Wilkerson, I didn't do it."

Walt embraced him in a hug. "I know, kid. Don't lose the faith. The truth will come out. Be patient."

"Aww, Mr. Wilkerson, what faith? I might as well face it. I ain't got a prayer. Nobody has the combination to the safe except me and Mr. Granger and he don't even remember it half the time."

Walt whirled around. "What are you saying?"

"I'm saying I might as well grab my toothbrush. I'm as good as on my way to prison."

"No, I mean what did you mean by Gid Granger doesn't remember it half the time?"

"Oh, that. I wouldn't want it to get out, but he has his days."

"Can you be more specific, Buddy?"

He lowered his head. "Nah, forget it. He's a good man. I don't want to do or say anything that might make him look . . . uh, what's the word? Incompetent?"

"Buddy, if you know something that could help you stay out of prison, you need to come forward with it. You have your own neck to worry about."

"I know you want to help me, Mr. Wilkerson, and I appreciate it. Honest, I do. But Mr. Granger has been good to me and to shame his good name at this point in his life would be downright scandalous. I won't do it."

"Whoa! You aren't suggesting Gid plotted this whole thing, are you?"

"Of course not. Mr. Granger is a good and decent man. He'd never do that. He honestly believes I stole that money and that hurts worse than the fear of going to prison. I wish there was some way to prove to him that I didn't do it."

"Would you mind telling the nice lady at The Rawls that I won't need the room no longer? I've got a little money saved up, but I won't be able to afford to stay there long, now that I ain't got no job."

"Sure. I'll go by there after I leave here. Is there anything else I can do for you?"

"Can't think of nothing unless you're a praying man, and I got a feeling you are."

Mr. Wilkerson patted him on the back. "That's already taken care of."

"To tell the truth, I was already thinking about giving up that swanky room at The Rawls. I put my name on the list at the Brumble Boarding House, but I don't know how long that might take. I understand most of the folks there have been there for years."

"Mrs. Brumble is a fine woman and I understand she's a terrific cook. It's no wonder no one wants to leave there."

Walt Wilkerson attempted to keep Buddy talking about what he might want to do in the future and where he'd prefer to live, instead of focusing on the hopelessness of the situation. "Buddy, there's an elderly lady, Mrs. Cain, who lives in one side of her house and rents out the other. I can check and see if it's vacant, if you like."

"Mr. Wilkerson, you're a good man and I know what you're trying to do for me. But the way I see it, even if it is available, I couldn't ask her to hold it for me when we have no idea when or if

I'll ever get out of jail."

"Buddy, I may have something that might work for you, but I won't be offended if you turn it down. It'll take a lot of elbow grease to get it ready to live in and would be quite a step-down, after living at The Rawls. But the beauty of it is that it's rent free if you chose to move in. Before you agree, though, you'll want to wait until you're out of here so you can take a look at it."

"Mr. Wilkerson, you're about the best friend a fellow could have. I don't know why you believe in me, when nobody else seems to. I sure would like to think you're right and that by some miracle, the real thief would be found, and I could take you up on your generous offer. I don't mind hard work. In fact, I saw this empty cottage on the edge of town that I liked and it'd take a heap of work. Shelby—that's the girl who cleans our office—said a local man owns it. Before all this happened, I was hoping to find out who he was and see if he'd rent it to me."

"I know Shelby Sellers. A real nice girl. Comes from a good, God-fearing family, but they live hand-to-mouth." He shook his head, as if it pained him to finish. "Her dad is a cripple and her mother takes in ironing to put food on the table. Shelby has been a real blessing to them and cleans several office buildings around town to help out." He lifted a shoulder. "Sorry. I didn't mean to go on like that. What were you saying about finding a cottage that you liked?"

"Doesn't matter, now."

"I'd like to hear about it."

"Nothing much to tell. It's just an old deserted log cabin, on the edge of town."

Walt's eyes twinkled. "A log cabin, you say? And it hasn't been lived in? Did you happen to notice if there were Pecan Trees growing in the back?"

"Yessir. That's the one. Something just seemed to draw me to it. I picked up a pocket full of pecans while I was walking around the yard." His eyes widened. "I never thought about it at the time, but you reckon that would be considered stealing?"

"I happen to know the owner and he'd want you to have all the pecans you could pick up. I know, because I happen to own it. So that settles it. After we get you out of here and you start looking for a new job, I'll give you a good recommendation and you'll have a free place to live. This episode of your life will all be nothing more than a bad dream."

For the first time since being arrested, Buddy felt he had a reason to smile. "Mr. Wilkerson, I can't tell you how good it is to have somebody who believes in me. I sure thank you, sir."

"I've had several offers from people who wanted to buy it for the land, but I knew their first course of business would be to tear the place down. Call me sentimental, but it does me good, just to ride by the place and remember what life was like during the Depression. I don't ever want to forget how the Lord has blessed me. I'm sure it's been overtaken with all sorts of critters, so if you change your mind, I wouldn't blame you."

Buddy hung his head. "Critters are the least of my worries. For a minute, I almost forgot what I'm facing. How can I sit here and plan what I'll do when I get out, when we both know all the evidence is against me? Juliette will soon be back in town and although she'll know I'm not guilty, there ain't no way her mama would ever let her court me, even if I should get out. As far as the people in this town are concerned, I'll always be a jailbird."

"I think you underestimate the folks here, son. Have faith.."

CHAPTER 27

Two weeks later . . .

Henrietta and Juliette departed the ship in Mobile and waited almost an hour for a taxi to take them to The Battleship Hotel on Government Street. After checking in, Henrietta picked up a newspaper from off the counter.

The concierge said, "Excuse me, ma'am, but that's last Sunday's paper." He pointed a few feet over. "You'll find this morning's paper in the rack."

"This one's fine, thank you."

Juliette laid a dime on the counter and picked up the daily paper. Riding the elevator to their room, she said, "I know why you wanted Sunday's edition."

"Do you, dear?"

"Mother, you're addicted to gossip."

"That's a mean thing to say. Just because I enjoy reading

about the social events in Sunday's paper doesn't mean I'm looking for gossip. It's good to keep abreast of the happenings around us."

After arriving in their room, Juliette crashed on the bed. "I'm glad to be back on land. I've never been so ready to see home."

"Juliette, if you didn't enjoy our excursion, it's your own fault. I think you worked at trying to be miserable."

"It didn't take effort, Mother. I'm still upset that you would've kidnapped me for a whole month."

"For goodness sake, stop being so dramatic." She flipped through the pages of the newspaper, then squealed.

"Oh, Juliette, you've got to see this."

"If it's on the gossip page, I'll pass."

"No gossip. It's a picture of you and Roland. You didn't tell me a reporter took your picture."

She bounded from off the bed. "I do remember a woman snapping a picture when we were standing on the deck, but I had no idea she was a reporter. Let me see it."

The caption beneath the photo read, *Look who's about to tie the knot. The lovely Juliette Jinright, daughter of Mrs. Henrietta Jinright and the late Steven Jinright, founder of the Southeast Cotton Mills, was spotted on a cruise with. Roland Roundtree, son of the Honorable Alabama State Attorney General, Harlan Roundtree, and his wife, Hilda.. You read it here, first, folks.*

Tears flooded her eyes. "About to tie the knot? It's a lie. A big fat lie. We should sue the newspaper, Mother. They can't make up lies about us, can they? What if Buddy should see it?"

"Oh fiddle-faddle, you should be thankful for the exposure instead of worrying about prosecuting a reporter for doing you a favor. It's a beautiful picture of you."

Henrietta and Juliette took the elevator to the lobby after being notified that Walt Wilkerson was waiting for them downstairs.

He acknowledged Henrietta's presence with a blank expression and a cold nod. "I trust you had a good trip."

"It was everything I hoped it would be, Walt. Thank you for coming to get us."

He wrapped his arms around Juliette. "And how did the prettiest girl in the world enjoy her first cruise?"

Tears flooded her cheeks. "Don't ask."

As they drove through the Mobile tunnel on their way back to Enterprise, Juliette said, "Walt, have you had an occasion to see Buddy since I've been gone?"

"As a matter of fact, I've seen him often."

"Is he angry with me for not letting him know I'd be gone for a whole month?"

"No, he's not angry. He loves you, Juli, and he's missed you, terribly."

Henrietta eyes hardened. "For goodness sake, Walt, she doesn't need you encouraging her to continue the strange friendship with that . . . that illiterate sailor, so I'd appreciate it if you'd keep such opinions to yourself. Besides, while on the cruise, she and that nice young man, Roland Roundtree, renewed their courtship, so I'll thank you to stay out of her affairs."

Juliette glared out the car window from the back seat. "Strange friendship? That may be what you call it, Mother, but you're wrong. I'm in love with Buddy Rockwell and he's in love with me. I know you took me on the cruise, hoping I'd forget him and fall for Roland, but you could kidnap me for fifty years and I'd never forget Buddy." Her lips quivered. "Never."

Juliette recoiled when her mother gave a sarcastic chuckle, the way she always did when she wanted to downplay Juliette's opinion, as if it were too corny to be of any real value. "My stars, child, you are so dramatic. Will you never grow up?"

They were nearing Enterprise when Walt said, "I may as well prepare you both for what you're going to hear, once you get home." He pressed his lips together as if he were suddenly having second thoughts. Then, drawing a deep breath, he let the words tumble from his lips. "Buddy has been arrested."

The news seemed to please Henrietta more than it shocked her. She pulled out a compact and powdered her nose. "Well, I'm not surprised. I knew that boy was no good from the moment I laid eyes on him."

Juliette shrieked. "Arrested? What for? Mother, is there nothing you won't do to keep us apart? I know you had something to do with this. You hate him."

Walt said, "Juli, trust me, I understand why you feel as you do, but Henrietta had no way of knowing. I don't know what's going on, although I plan to get to the bottom of it because I don't believe for a minute the kid is guilty."

Henrietta pulled out a tube of lipstick, and gazing into the small mirror, she rubbed a bright streak of red across her lips. Until now, she'd seemed more concerned with her looks than with the news they'd been given. Blotting her lips on a tissue, she muttered, "Stop stalling, Walt. Go ahead and tell us why he was arrested."

He caught his bottom lip between his teeth, while staring straight ahead. "Stealing money from the company."

Henrietta threw up her hands. "Stealing? I'm not surprised. I was afraid he'd steal the silverware the night he had dinner with us. It's not hard to spot a crook. He has those beady eyes."

Juliette's voice was barely above a whisper. "He didn't do it. He wouldn't."

Walt glanced toward her in the back seat. "I agree, Juli. He wouldn't but it's up to us to find out who did. I have my suspicions, but if I'm correct, I need to give the guilty party a chance to come forward on their own."

Henrietta said, "For crying out loud, Walt. Just because you've taken a liking to the boy doesn't mean you have to defend him when the writing is on the wall."

CHAPTER 28

Octavious wadded the letter and threw it across the room. He paced the floor in his plush apartment on the beach. "He can't do this to me. It's crazy." Picking up the phone, he called his father. "I see you and Mother received a copy of the letter, too?"

There was a long silence on the other end.

"We did, Octavious, but you sound as if this caught you by surprise. Your grandfather told you years ago the stipulations to the trust fund. Your mother and I have been after you since you graduated from high school to settle down, but you wouldn't listen."

"I did listen. I joined the Navy like you wanted me too, didn't I?"

"Yes, you did—after you flunked out of three colleges, but you knew years ago that your grandfather was giving you ample time to marry and start a family. Now, you'll soon be approaching the cut-off year. Since you will be single when you turn twenty-five, the trust fund will go to your grandfather's college alma mater."

"That's not fair."

"Papa thought it was and it was his money. Your mother wants to speak to you."

She said, "Darling, how are you doing?"

"That's a silly question. I've just learned my own grandpa decided to cut me off without a cent. He never did like me, did he?"

"Oh, sweetheart, you can't blame Papa. He married at nineteen and was running a successful business by the time he was your age. He never dreamed you'd still be single at twenty-five. I know you were counting on the trust fund, but it isn't like you need the money. With what you get in the Navy and the allowance we send you, you should be getting by okay."

"Okay? I don't want to get by. I want what's mine."

"I'm sorry you're disappointed, Tavie. But I wanted to let you know the service will be held day after tomorrow at two o'clock at Weatherby Funeral Home. I've already been to Harvey's Mens' Store and bought you a nice suit to wear to the funeral."

"Funeral! You think I want to go to the old goat's funeral? I have no tears to shed, Mother. Sorry, I know he was your daddy, but I have no reason to want to go and pretend I'm in mourning, when I'm not."

When she began to bawl, his daddy took the phone. "Octavious, don't do this to your mother. She's going through enough, losing her father. The least you can do would be to come and go with her to the funeral."

"No way. I don't want to hurt Mother, but I couldn't sit through a service listening to some preacher who never knew Papa, standing up there telling what a fine upstanding, Godly man he was, when we all know better."

"I get that you're bitter, but you have no right to be. Papa made the will out while you were still in high school. If the trust fund meant that much to you, I would've thought you would've scouted around for a nice young woman to marry and share your good fortune, instead of squandering away the years with a bunch of floozies. Now it's too late to worry about what could've been."

"Maybe it's not too late. Does it say how long I have to be married before I turn twenty-five?"

"Well, no, but are you saying you're in a serious relationship?"

"That's exactly what I'm saying. Pops. Mark your calendar. I'll be getting married, come Christmas, and since I don't turn twenty-five until February 7th, the little wife and I will be in high cotton about the time we get back from our Hawaiian Honeymoon."

"That's good to hear, son. Do you think she'll agree to marry you?"

"Agree? She already has."

"Well, why didn't you say that in the beginning?"

"We weren't planning to marry until spring, which would be too late to receive the money from the trust fund, but now that I think about it, she mentioned a Christmas wedding would be grand. I'll see that she gets what she wanted."

"What's her name, and how did you meet her?"

"It's a beautiful story, dad. I'll save the details so we can share it with you and Mother in person."

Octavious hung up the phone and smiled. Of course, he was involved in a relationship, and of course they were going to have a Christmas wedding. He just wasn't sure who it was with, but since he'd proposed to at least four pen pals and none had refused his proposal, it was just a matter of choosing the right one. He laughed out loud. He was practically a married man and his grandpa's alma mater would need to find another donor.

He dug through a drawer full of letters, but after reading a few lines of each one and looking at the accompanying picture, he tossed it on the floor. Near the bottom of the pile, he found an old letter from the little gal in Alabama. He gazed at her picture and had forgotten just how beautiful she was. Not only beautiful, but she was as pure as the water coming from his Grandpa's flowing well and had already agreed to marry him. He'd look her up, get it over with, then shortly after his birthday, he'd file for divorce.

True, she hadn't written in a spell, but now he knew it wasn't because she fell for some other sucker. She assumed he was dead. He laughed out loud at the image of him showing up at her door, alive and well and ready to walk her to the altar.

She was too naïve to ever think the worst in people—unlike most of the girls he knew who could spot a scammer from the time he opened his mouth. He held the picture in front of him and grinned. "Maybe not 'til death do us part, honeybun, but at least 'til money from Gramps parts me not."

He had a furlough coming up and he knew where he needed to go. "Alabama, here I come."

****

Thomas hadn't planned to stay in Enterprise, but now there were two reasons not to leave. He wanted to get to know Shelby Sellers better and he had to find a way to help prove the innocence of his good friend, Buddy Rhoades.

After walking all over Enterprise looking for work, he finally found the perfect job as a salesman for Red Rock Cola, and even though it required travel three days a week, the pay was better than he had hoped for.

That afternoon, he went to the jail. "Buddy, keep your chin up. We're gonna get to the bottom of this. Mr. Walt seems to have a lot of influence in this town. Folks listen to him when he talks, and he's confident you didn't take that money."

"Thomas, I know you'll both do all you can to help me, but if

I didn't know better, I'd even think I was guilty. There's no other explanation. Face it, I'm sunk."

"No. I don't believe it, and I don't want you to believe it, either. I've talked to Mr. Walt and I'll be cleaning out the cabin, so it'll be ready for you to live in by the time you get out."

"Thomas, you're a real friend, but I know you're just passing through and I don't want you to feel you have to stay on my account. Where do you plan to go from here?"

"Not going anywhere. Didn't I tell you? I got me a job here in Enterprise."

"No kidding. Where?"

"Red Rock Cola Bottling Plant." He pulled a set of keys from his pocket. "They even gave me the keys to one of their trucks. I'll be traveling to stores, selling drinks but I'll be living here."

"That's great news."

"I was wondering if you'd mind having a housemate when you get out of here."

Jericho feigned a smile. He knew Thomas was trying hard to lift his spirits. "Having you for a housemate would be great. I just wish I could be as confident as you are that I'll ever get out. But even if I did, I'd be moving on."

"What do you mean? When they find the culprit who stole the money, your name will be cleared. There'll be no need to leave."

"That's where you're wrong, my friend. There'll be no need to stay."

"I don't get you."

"As you know, I only came to Enterprise to be near Juliette, but I've learned she's seeing someone else. Someone I can't compete with."

"Buddy, I think you're depressed and building something up in your mind. Things were good between you two when she left for the cruise. Right?"

"I thought so."

"And she hasn't returned, so things are still good."

"I'm guessing you didn't see her picture in the paper. The jailer gives me a paper every morning, although I mostly thumb through it. Sunday, I opened it up and saw Juliette's picture with some rich cat in a romantic scene on the ship. According to what I read, they're practically married, already."

"Gee, Buddy, I'm sorry. I didn't know."

The jailer entered and motioned for Thomas. "Time's up. The prisoner has another visitor, waiting."

Thomas threw up his hand. "I'll see you tomorrow."

Afraid the visitor could be Juliette, Jericho said, "No more visitors."

The jailer grinned. "You might like to see her first. She's a good-looking dame."

Buddy's jaw jutted forward, but he kept his mouth shut. He resented the galoot calling Juliette a dame. "I said I don't want visitors." Then he thought about Mr. Wilkerson. He didn't want to shut him out, since he was his only hope of getting free. "What I mean is, I don't want any female visitors."

"Fine. But if I were you, when the trial comes up, I'd plead guilty by insanity, because I think that would be a legitimate defense for you."

Thomas left the cell, walked down the hall and was surprised to see Shelby standing near the front door.

"Thomas? I didn't know you were still in town. I . . . I suppose you came to see Buddy?"

He nodded. "Yeah, I feel like he's being railroaded. He's not guilty, Shelby."

Her knees knocked. "Uh . . . how do you know?"

"Because I know him. I know he's not a thief."

Shelby's throat tightened. Thomas was right. Buddy wasn't a thief. She was. "They won't let me see him. Did you get to talk to him?"

"I did."

"How is he?"

"As well as can be expected, I guess. He's convinced he'll be convicted." He held the door open for her. "Say, would you like to go somewhere for a cup of coffee?"

"I wish I could, but I've just finished cleaning the bank and I still have to go clean the Matthews Agency."

"That's where Buddy worked. Right?"

She nodded. Was he beginning to suspect her? "I've gotta

go."

"How long will it take to clean the office?"

"An hour, maybe a little longer."

"Then would you meet me at the drugstore when you finish?"

"Okay."

Thomas escorted her to the Matthews Agency, then went across the street to the Café to buy a hamburger for supper. He didn't know if it was really the best hamburger he'd ever eaten or if it was because he hadn't had anything to eat since breakfast. He bought a Ledger and sat in the café, reading. His stomach knotted, as he read an article about the man being held for stealing hundreds of dollars from Mr. Gideon Granger at the Matthews Agency.

"Lies, it's all a bunch of lies." Anyone who didn't know Buddy would think there was no need for a trial. According to the biased write-up, a smooth talker by the name of Jericho Rhoades showed up in town, calling himself Buddy Rockwell, fooling the town's elect. It went on to say that only a crook would have reason to hide his identity. He proposed marriage to a young woman from a prominent Enterprise family, under the false name. In order to protect the wealthy young lady who was caught in the web of deceit, the paper refused to identify her. However, her mother stated she knew from the start the illiterate bum was up to no good. It stated further that Mr. Gideon Granger was fooled in to believing Jericho Rhoades was a decent young man, and entrusted him with the combination to the safe, which contained several hundred dollars. According to Mr. Granger, Jericho Rhoades is the only person other than himself, who knows the combination to the safe, and there was no sign of a break-in.

Thomas couldn't deny it looked bad, yet he refused to believe Buddy could do such a thing. One way or the other, he had to find the answer.

At eight o'clock the Cafe was beginning to close. He walked outside and noticed a group of fellows gathered around the boll weevil monument. Introducing himself, he kept his ears and eyes open, in the event one of them would slip up and say something that would help to free Buddy.

Someone in this town was a thief, and Thomas intended to find the guilty culprit.

CHAPTER 29

Monday, November 28th

Cold chills ran up Shelby's spine when she walked into the Matthews Agency. She felt as if someone was looking over her shoulder, shaming her for what she had done. Never in a hundred years would she have imagined things turning out the way they had, but then never would she have imagined that she could have done what she did.

In her mind, she had convinced herself that Mr. Granger was a wealthy man and wouldn't miss the money. It wasn't her fault he tossed it in the trash. Wouldn't anyone else who found it do the same thing she did? She had finished everything but taking out the trash. When she picked up the trash basket, she saw Mr. Granger's lunch bag thrown in there, just the way it looked the night the money fell out. Shelby ran to the bathroom and threw up. Why didn't Buddy want to see her when she went to the jail? Had he already figured out she was the thief? If only she could talk to him, maybe she'd have the courage to come clean. After emptying the trash, she locked up and left the building.

She gazed in the window of The Vogue, where all the rich women shopped and admired the dress she'd longed for since it was first placed on the mannikin. She'd pictured herself wearing the beautiful yellow sheath with a white bolero. She'd wanted to prove to Buddy that she could be just as pretty as Juliette if only she could go to the beauty shop to get her hair curled and wear expensive clothes like Juliette wore. Now, it didn't matter so much what he thought of her.

If she turned herself in, Buddy would never speak to her again for allowing him to be arrested and she wouldn't blame him.

"Hello, Shelby."

She turned quickly and saw Thomas standing there. When he invited her for a milkshake at the drugstore, she wanted to say yes, but her gut instinct told her to refuse. He was cute and she sensed he might be interested in her, but she couldn't allow him to get too close to her. It would only make things worse if the truth should come out. *If?* Her voice quaked. "Thank you, but I really should get home. How long will you be staying in Alabama?"

When he told her he planned to make Enterprise his home— that he had a good job and planned to move into a cabin with Buddy, her pulse raced. Had Mr. Granger dropped the charges? It was too good to be true, yet there was no other explanation.

"Are . . are they letting Buddy go free?"

"No. Not yet. But they will, as soon as I get to the bottom of this."

"You said you were moving into a cabin with Buddy? I don't understand. He has a room at The Rawls."

"Not anymore. He had to give it up. Couldn't afford it, now that he's lost his job."

"Where's the cabin?"

"Just out of town, where the pavement ends. It hasn't been lived in, in a long time, but I plan to have it livable by the time he gets out."

"I think I know the one. Buddy really took a liking to it. It belongs to Mr. Walt Wilkerson."

"Yeah, that's the one."

"Thomas, if you'd like help cleaning it out, I'm real good at cleaning. It's about all I'm good at."

"Thanks, but I'll be working during the day, and you work at night, but it's swell of you to volunteer. I'd like to buy you dinner at the Cafe sometimes, though, if you could work me into your schedule."

For the first time in her life, a really cute guy that she could fall for, appeared to be taking a liking to her—but that would all change if Thomas discovered she was the thief. She'd be sent to the Women's Prison in Tutwiler. The thought made her shiver. If

247

she *didn't* turn herself in, Buddy would wind up in prison. Neither scenario had a winning outcome.

She blinked back the tears. "Sure . . . yeah, we can do that. Dinner would be good."

His eyes squinted. "Are you crying? You are, aren't you?" He edged closer and wrapped her in his arms. "I know what you're feeling. I'm feeling it, too, but we can't give up, regardless of how hopeless it may seem. Buddy needs us to stay focused and keep the faith until he's on this side of those bars."

The words that were meant to comfort, only brought forth full-blown sobs. "Oh, Thomas. I don't know if I can do this." She knew he didn't understand what it was she couldn't do. As much as she didn't want to go to prison, how could she allow Buddy to go for something she did?

Thomas pulled a handkerchief from his back pocket and dried the tears streaming down her face. He didn't know what possessed him to do what he did next, when he lifted her chin with his thumb and kissed her. It happened before he knew what he was doing, standing there in the middle of Main Street. Was it pity or passion? How could he be sure? He wouldn't have blamed her if she would've slapped him—but she didn't. Perhaps he imagined what he wanted to believe, but her lips appeared as eager as his. He pushed away and turned his head. "I'm so sorry, Shelby. I don't know what possessed me . . . please, forgive me."

"Are you sorry you kissed me?"

"Sorry? No. Are you sorry?"

"No." Her lips quivered as she shook her head. "But I've got to go home."

"Do you mind if I walk you there?"

"If you want to."

"I do."

As they strode along, he pointed ahead. "This is the way to the log cabin."

"I know. I live just down the road from it."

When they arrived at her house, he reached for her hand. Their gaze locked. "Shelby Sellers, I can understand why Buddy considers you a very good friend. Lucky for me, he already has a girl. I don't want you to think I go around kissing all the girls. I don't. But I sure would like to kiss you goodnight, if you wouldn't mind."

"I reckon it'd be all right." She lifted her head slightly and closed her eyes.

With his hands planted on either side of her face, he kissed her, then stepping back, he took both her hands in his. "Shelby, would you mind if we had prayer together for Buddy? Some things are too big for man, but the Bible says nothing is too big for God. I'm a living example of the power of prayer."

The lump in her throat swelled until she thought she'd choke. "Okay."

Never had she heard such a sincere prayer for a miracle for Buddy. Shelby had no doubt God would answer such a heartfelt cry, but a miracle for Buddy would mean prison for her. If only she could turn back the clock and replay the day she picked up that lunch bag stuffed with cash. As soon as Thomas said "Amen," she rushed into the house.

Her mother was sitting by the fire darning socks. "Shelby, you look beat. I know you must be dog tired. If you'll pull off your uniform, I'll wash it for you. In case I don't tell you enough, me and your daddy are real proud of what a hard worker you are, but I wish things came easier for you."

She leaned down and kissed her mother. "You work hard, too. I can wash out my uniform. Goodnight, mama."

"Goodnight, shug. Me and your daddy prayed for you at supper that the Lord would put a good Christian man in your life. You're a good daughter and you deserve the best."

Shelby pulled the curtain that separated her bedroom from the front sitting room, fell on her cot and muffled her sobs in her pillow. She had a feeling God had already answered her mama's prayers. Though she'd known him for such a short time, it hadn't taken long to determine that Thomas Tippins was a fine, Christian man . . . too fine to fall in love with a thief.

CHAPTER 30

Thursday, shortly before lunch, Octavious Rockwell threw a bag in the back of his 1949 Packard convertible, then pulled out a map and discovered Enterprise was only about 200 miles from Pensacola. He could make it there before dark. He practiced his speech, all the way.

Driving through town, he spotted a florist, stopped and went in.

A friendly lady greeted him. "What can we help you with today, sir?"

"I want something very special for a very special young lady. What would you suggest?"

After showing him several floral arrangements, he shook his head. "Not what I had in mind." He promenaded around the two rooms as if he owned the place, then stopped and pointed at a large arrangement on a wire stand. "I want this one."

She smiled. "But sir, that's a funeral spray."

"I don't care what you call it. I like it. It's big and it's pretty."

"Are you sure? If it's the lilies you like, I can make up a nice bouquet of lilies that would be appropriate for a young fellow to take to his sweetheart."

"I don't want a nice bouquet." He picked up the spray. "Now, are you gonna sell it to me or do I have to find another florist?"

She sucked in a breath full of air. "Suit yourself." She seemed surprised when he didn't flinch when she told him the price for such a large arrangement. "How would you like the card signed, sir?"

He scratched his head. "To my beloved Juliette, from your loving fiancé, Buddy."

Her mouth dropped. "Did you say Juliette?"

"Yes. That's with one el and two tees."

"I know how to spell it. But I thought . . . never mind. Apparently, I was wrong."

He paid little attention to her rambling as he pulled an envelope from his pocket and checked the address. "Could you tell me where I can find W. Lee Street?"

She seemed flustered as she garbled out the directions.

****

On the way home from Mobile, Henrietta said, "Walt, please stop in the first Coffee County town we go through."

"We're coming into Opp. Would you like to stop here?"

"No. I said Coffee County. This is Covington."

Juliette muttered. "What difference does it make what county we're in? I could sure use a stop to stretch my legs. It's cramped back here."

Henrietta turned slightly. "You'll be fine, dear. It won't be much further."

Walt popped his neck. "I'm with you, Juli. I'm ready to get out of this car. Why does it have to be Coffee County, Henri?"

"I want a Ledger."

"My lands, Henri, is that all? You'll have one waiting for you when you get to the house."

"Walt, please, do as I ask you."

"I suppose you can't wait to see if there's a picture of you on the cruise so all your highfalutin friends can be impressed."

"Don't be absurd. I want to see if there's anything in here about that sailor's arrest."

He glanced in the rear-view mirror at Juliette. "Sorry, Henrietta. That can wait."

Walt pulled up in front of the Jinright home and was unloading the baggage when Juliette grabbed her new felt hat from over the back seat and slid out of the car. After buttoning her jacket, she ran her fingers through her curly hair, then plopped the hat on her head.

Henrietta stared. "Where do you think you're going?"

"To see Buddy."

"Have you lost your mind? Didn't you hear what Walt said?

He's a thief, Juliette and he's in jail where he needs to be, for crying out loud.."

"That's where I'm going. I can only imagine what he's going through, being jailed for something he didn't do. Mother, we've got to help him."

"*We*? Juliette, don't be naïve. He wouldn't be behind bars if he were innocent. I told you from the beginning there was something sinister about that boy, but I'm afraid you allowed his good looks to drain your senses. Now, go in the house and unpack."

"Mother, tell Greta to unpack my things. I don't have time to waste. I'm sorry you don't approve, but this is something I must do. Buddy needs to know I believe in him."

With her mother shouting, shaking her finger and insisting she give up such a foolish idea, Juliette struck off down the street and followed the railroad tracks until she reached the jail.

Then, pausing in front of the door, she froze. Never having been inside a jail, she envisioned prisoners beating on cell bars and screaming, the way she'd seen them do in a picture show. But she had to be brave—for Jericho's sake.

Walt drove away and Henrietta rushed into the house and yelled for Greta. "What did you do with the newspapers that came while we were gone? You did save them like I asked, I hope."

"Yes'm. I bundled them up and put them on the top shelf in the Butler's Pantry, like you told me to, Miz Jinright."

Greta handed her a bundle and Henrietta went into the Parlor and shuffled through each page until the following headline caught her eye.

MATTHEWS AGENCY SWINDLED BY IMPOSTER

The sailor who popped into town weeks ago claiming to be Jericho Rockwell has been arrested for swindling The Matthews Agency out of hundreds of dollars. Although there is much to be unraveled at this time, it has been determined that the name he's been using is an alias. His real name is Jericho Rhoades.

Rhoades was recently discharged from the Navy and as of this date, it is unknown whether it was honorable or dishonorable. According to reliable sources, he is purported to have come to our fair city for the sole purpose of bilking a young lady out of the family fortune. This imposter's trial should be swift and send a clear message to other would-be scam artists that Enterprise is a city of decent folks and we will not tolerate degenerates who think they can come here and hoodwink our residents.

Henrietta threw the paper on the divan and paced back and forth. "I knew it. My poor, sweet, naive Juliette. We're fortunate they didn't use her name. She'll be the laughingstock of Coffee County if it should get out that she was making plans to marry the thieving, lying rascal. I hope they'll send him off for life."

****

Juliette's heart beat so fast, she found it hard to speak as she opened the door to the jail and looked around. Surprised to find herself in an office with no jail cells in sight, and a family friend, Police Chief Jerry Sims smiling up at her from his desk, helped ease her fears.

Mr. Jerry reared back in his swivel desk chair. "Well, what do we owe this pleasure, Miss Juliette. You're looking mighty pretty these days. I declare seems like you grew up overnight."

"Thank you, Mr. Jerry." She lowered her head and twisted a handkerchief in her hands. "I'm here to see Buddy."

"I beg your pardon? Buddy who?"

"Uh, I'm sorry. His name is Jericho Rockwell. I understand you're holding him here."

A smirk snuck across his face. "So, what business would you have with the criminal, sweetheart."

She cringed. "Begging your pardon, Mr. Jerry, but Buddy is no criminal."

He swung around in his chair, then stood, leaning over with both hands planted on his desk. "You say his last name is Rockwell?"

"Yessir. I've been gone for a month and just found out today that he's in jail."

"Juliette, I heard talk that the prisoner was sweet on you, but sugar, you need to go home. I'm afraid there are things about this character that you aren't aware of, and I'd rather not be the one to break it to you." He swung his hand toward the door. "Go home, sugar. You'll find out the truth soon enough."

Bracing herself with her legs slightly apart and her hands crossed over her chest, she said, "May I see him, sir?"

"Now, if you refuse to take my advice, I reckon that'll be up to him. He turned away the last pretty young lady who came to see him. I'll have to ask him if he wants to see you."

"Fine." If Mr. Jerry was trying to make her jealous by mentioning another female had come to visit Buddy, he failed, since he admitted Buddy chose not to see her. Still, she wondered. She paced the floor, wrenching her hands as she waited for the Chief to return. *He called her pretty.*

The chief traipsed back in the room shaking his head. "Sorry, Miss Juliette. The prisoner has requested no female visitors. But you should thank your lucky stars. The best thing for you would be to distance yourself from this character."

"Did you tell him it was me . . . and not that other girl?"

"Yes ma'am. Seems he feels the same way I do. You don't need your good name tarnished by the likes of him."

Juliette cried all the way home. If only she could've been here maybe she could've done something to keep him from being falsely arrested. But she wasn't here, and it was all her mother's fault. As much as she didn't want to harbor such wicked thoughts, she couldn't help wondering if her mother could've had something to do with having him arrested.

CHAPTER 31

Octavious recognized Juliette's house from the picture she sent in one of her letters. After parking his car, he got out, straightened his tie and standing on one foot, wiped the dust off the top of his new brown and white wingtips onto the back of his pants legs. Then, reaching for the spray of flowers from the back seat, he sprinted up the steps and rang the doorbell.

Her mother came to the door and saw the funeral spray. "Young man, I'm afraid you're at the wrong address."

He pulled the envelope from his pocket. "No ma'am. I believe I'm at the right house. I'm here to call on my fiancé, Miss Juliette Jinright."

Henrietta looked past him at the fine new automobile parked in front of her house. "You say she's *your* . . . fiancé?"

"Yes ma'am. My name is Octavious J. Rockwell, III and Juliette has accepted my proposal of marriage. Is she here?"

Her jaw dropped. "No, she isn't." She opened the door and stepped aside. "She shouldn't be gone long. Why don't you come in and let's get better acquainted while you wait for Juliette, Octavious."

"Thank you, ma'am. I'd like that. It's a long drive from Pensacola and I'm ready to get out of that car."

"It's a very fine-looking automobile."

"I thank you ma'am."

Henrietta led him into the parlor. "You say you drove here from Pensacola? May I ask what you do there?"

"I'm stationed at the Naval Air Station, ma'am, but don't let that fool you. I can look around and see she's accustomed to a comfortable lifestyle, but I promise once we're married, she'll want for nothing. My grandfather has left me a generous trust."

Henrietta felt a blush heating her face. "Goodness, the thought of money didn't cross my mind. After all, if you love my daughter, that's all that matters to me. Could I get you something to drink, Octavious?"

"I'd like that. Sweet tea if you have it." He recalled signing his letters, Buddy. "Ma'am, my friends all call me Buddy, so I'd be much obliged if you would also."

She reached over by her chair and picked up a small silver bell and shook it.

"Greta, please bring our guest a glass of iced tea and a couple of your tea cakes."

It wasn't hard for Octavious to see that he'd won her mother over to his side. This was going to be even easier than he'd imagined.

"Buddy, it's nothing short of Providence that brought you here. However, it's too bad you couldn't have come a couple of months sooner."

"I don't understand."

"I'm afraid our Juliette has been hoodwinked."

"Hoodwinked? Who would be so evil as to deceive my sweet Juliette?"

"Well, I don't know where to start, or exactly what's going on but maybe we should start with how you and Juliette became acquainted and perhaps it will help the pieces fit together."

"That's easy, ma'am. I was in the Naval Hospital in Jacksonville with severe burns on my upper torso. I was reading the local news when I spotted a letter from Juliette, requesting the name of a service man who would be interested in being a pen pal. Now, normally I wouldn't have responded, but there was something about the way she worded the letter that let me know she was a kind and compassionate individual. Maybe I was feeling sorry for myself. The burns were very deep and painful, and since I normally sleep on my stomach, it was hard to get accustomed to sleeping on my back. I'm afraid I was sleep deprived. It was in the middle of the night, I took out pen and paper and responded. I fell in love with her through her sweet letters and I know she loves me, too." His brow furrowed. "You look worried. Did I say something wrong?"

"No. I don't think you did, but someone has said plenty of things that were wrong."

"I beg your pardon? I'm not following you."

"Buddy, I don't know how to tell you this, but I'm afraid there's an imposter pretending to be you. He's fooled Juliette and she is going to be crushed when she finds out that not only is he a thief, but he's made her think that he is Octavious J. Rockwell III."

His jaw dropped. "The dirty, rotten scoundrel. He won't get away with it. Is he still in town?"

"Yes. I'm afraid he's in jail."

He blew out a heavy puff of air. "Fantastic. So they caught him."

"Not for impersonation. He's locked up for stealing money for the firm he worked for."

It had to be Buddy although it didn't sound like the Buddy Octavious knew. But he knew for a fact that love—or the love of money— could drive a man to do crazy things.

Henrietta told Octavious about the letter Juliette received, saying he was dead. "My poor sweet girl was devastated. For weeks, she moped around the house, not wanting to eat or sleep. Then one day, a soldier showed up at our door, claiming to be you. Naturally, she was thrilled to think the man she fell in love with through his letters was alive and well."

"Ma'am, that breaks my heart. My poor Juliette." He shifted in his chair and glanced at his watch. "Where did you say she went?"

Henrietta looked down at the floor. "I'm embarrassed to admit it, but she went to the jail to see the imposter."

"What? If you'd be so kind as to point me in that direction. I'd like to confront this evil man in front of Juliette and have him admit he's a fraud."

Henrietta walked him to the porch when she saw Juliette coming down the sidewalk. "There she is. Maybe it would be best if you didn't spring the news on her quite so fast. I'm afraid my daughter is head-strong and if she feels she's being pushed in one direction, she's likely to take the opposite stand."

"Your advice is well noted, my good lady, but I've waited too long for this day to prolong our meeting."

Henrietta flinched when he ran with open arms and yelled, "Juliette, my darling."

She stopped in her tracks. When he threw his arms around her, she jerked back and swung her arm. Her hand smacked him across the side of his face, leaving her hand stinging, before she heard her mother scream, "Juliette, stop. He's your Buddy."

Juliette glared as he rubbed his hand across his cheek. Then looking past him at Henrietta, she said, "What are you talking about, Mother? I've never seen this character."

Octavious's lip curled in a rueful smile. "Please accept my

deepest apologies, dear Juliette. I should've listened to your mother. She advised me to take it slow. You certainly aren't the shrinking violet, are you?"

"Who are you and what gave you the right to put your hands on me?"

Henrietta stepped between them. "Suppose we go inside and sit down to discuss the situation like adults. Juliette, honey I'm afraid you're in for a shock."

Heading into the Parlor, Juliette eyed Octavious out of the corner of her eyes.

Henrietta said, "Juliette, I can explain."

She threw her palm in the air. "No, mother. I'd like to hear his explanation first."

CHAPTER 32

Octavious left his chair, walked over and kneeled in front of Juliette.

Henrietta groaned. "No, Buddy—not yet."

Juliette's brow furrowed. "What are you doing?"

He pulled a small ring box from his pocket and opened it.

Henrietta thrust her hand over her heart. "Buddy, it's too soon."

He glanced at her and smiled. "Begging your pardon, Mrs. Jinright. I've waited months for this day. It's not a minute too soon."

Juliette's eyes focused on the largest diamond she'd ever seen.

He said, "Juliette, I knew from the first kind, compassionate letter you sent to me when I was in the Naval Hospital that God had answered my prayers. I was so overcome with your sweetness, I read your letters aloud to the guys in the ward. I hope you won't hold it against me. Hearing your letters seemed to bring a sense of comfort to the suffering sailors. And although you've already accepted my proposal, I wanted to ask you in person. Juliette, will you marry me and let's have that Christmas wedding that we talked about?"

She burst into sobs. "I feel as if I'm in the midst of a bad dream. I don't know you."

"But darling, you know all there is to know about me. You know my name is Octavious J. Rockwell, III—known as Buddy, to you—and I met you through the Pen Pal section of the newspaper, while I recuperated from third degree burns in Jacksonville Naval Hospital. I proposed and after you accepted, I suggested a Christmas wedding. If I remember correctly, you wrote back that you'd always dreamed of a Christmas wedding."

Henrietta said, "Juliette, I can see this has upset you and that's understandable. That fellow in jail came here for no other reason than to swindle us, but he got stingy and swindled Gid Granger first. I feel like strangling him for toying with your heart."

"Mother, please. I'd like to be alone with . . . "

Octavious interrupted "Buddy. Surely, you remember why I prefer to be called by my nickname."

Her eyes squinted. "You . . . you don't like your given name?"

"Exactly."

When Henrietta stayed seated, Juliette glared. "Mother? Please?"

"Fine, darling. I only stayed to offer you my support. I have no doubt you two will work things out."

After she left the room, Juliette was full of questions, and to her obvious dismay, Octavious had a ready answer.

Her first question was, "What does the 'J' in your name stand for?"

Octavious chuckled. "You're not the first one to ask that same question. Would you believe it stands alone?"

"Meaning?"

"Meaning it doesn't stand for anything. My complete name is Octavious J. Rockwell, III."

By the time the inquisition ended, there was no doubt in Juliette's mind that Octavious was indeed who he said he was. But who was Buddy? The other Buddy? Her head pounded. Since his name wasn't Jericho Rockwell, he probably stole Octavious's nickname, also. What would she call him, now that she knew the truth? Reality set in. She'd have no need to call him anything. She wouldn't be seeing him again. The pain couldn't have been more severe if someone had stabbed her in the heart. Why did he make her fall in love with him? How could she have been such a fool?

Octavious's gaze stayed focused on her. "Darling, I don't mean to rush you, but my knees are beginning to get sore. I'll ask again . . . will you be my wife?"

She cocked her head to the side and swallowed hard. Then slowly shaking her head, she said, "I'm so sorry, Octavious—"

His brows scrunched together. "Buddy . . . please call me Buddy, the way you did in your letters."

"I can't."

Though he appeared hurt, his words were guarded. "I understand why it bothers you. You called *him* Buddy. No problem. As I mentioned in my letters, I don't like the name Octavious. It sounds so stuffed shirt, if you know what I mean. I'm just a down-to-earth guy who enjoys church picnics and that sort of thing. My mother calls me Tavie. Would that be easier for you?"

"No. What I mean is, I can't marry you."

He bounded to his feet. "You can't do this to me, Juliette. You promised."

"I'm so sorry if I've hurt you. Truly, I am. But I have a lot to work out before I ever agree to marry anyone again. It's not your fault, but I'm afraid I gave my heart away after I thought you were dead."

"But he doesn't own your heart. I do. You gave it to me, first. And, as you can see, I'm not dead."

"Why didn't you write to let me know?"

"I couldn't, sweetheart. The burns on my chest became infected and then I came down with a severe case of pneumonia. I was quarantined and it was touch and go for weeks. When I didn't return to the ward and my bed was assigned to another wounded sailor, the guys assumed I was dead."

"It seems they would've asked about you."

"Wouldn't have done any good. I'm sure you can understand why the staff at the hospital doesn't like to give out that information. It would be bad for the morale of the other patients. Therefore, when my good friends in the ward wrote you the letter, they did it because they honestly thought I was gone. They understood how much we loved one another and therefore felt you deserved to know the truth."

"Please, Juliette, please don't turn me away. Think of all the things we talked about in our letters . . . the things that made you fall in love with me. I need you, darling. I need you so much it hurts me."

Juliette buried her face in her hands and sobbed. "I don't even know what to call you."

He pulled her hands away and dried her face with his handkerchief.

"It's okay. I'd like it if you could call me Tavie, like my mother. It sounds endearing, don't you think?"

She snubbed and wiped her nose with his hanky. "Then Tavie, it is. I can see I'm not the only one who has been defrauded. We've both been terribly hurt."

"You're right, darling. And as eager as I am to talk about the wedding, we'll wait until you're over the shock to make our plans. I have a three-day leave since my dear grandfather, God rest his soul, passed away and his funeral is tomorrow."

"Oh, I'm so sorry for your loss."

"Thank you, but as close as I was to my Papa, I've suffered an even greater hurt today. I know for a surety that Papa is in a better place, but the place I've found myself in has left my vulnerable heart shattered into a thousand pieces. I thought you and I would be planning our Christmas wedding, and instead, I've learned some ruthless guy has stolen my identity and tried to steal my girl."

When tears streamed down his face, Juliette fought back her own tears. "Tavie, would you like to take a walk? I think the fresh air might do us both good."

His chin quivered. "Thank you. I'd like that very much."

As they strolled down Main Street, they passed a large brick church with beautiful stained-glass windows and giant pillars out front.

He said, "That's a beautiful church. Is it where you and your mother attend?"

She nodded. "It is."

"Then, I suppose that's where you and I shall recite our marriage vows. It looks as if it can accommodate a crowd."

She shook her head. "If I ever marry, I want a small wedding."

"Don't say, *if,* darling. Say *when.* You are too beautiful, too sweet to consider living out your life as an old maid and I intend to see that you won't."

Old maid? The alternative to not getting married hadn't really sunk in until now. Did she honestly want to live out her life, having people referring to her as an old maid? The thought caused her to shudder. "Tavie, when do you plan to leave for your granddaddy's funeral?"

"I've changed my mind and decided not to go."

"No, please don't let me be the cause of your not going. You wouldn't forgive yourself in the days to come."

"Juliette, that may be true, but I believe with all my heart Papa would understand why I now feel I can't possible attend his funeral. My heart can't withstand so much sadness. Losing the two of you has made me feel as if there's nothing left to live for." He turned away from her and pulled out his handkerchief.

Though he seemed to be attempting to muffle them, she could hear soft sobs.

Reaching for his hand, she said, "I know it hurts. I can tell you loved him very much. I lost my father several years ago, and I still miss him."

He squeezed her hand. "Thank you. I'm terribly embarrassed that you saw me shedding tears like a weak little milksop, but you're sweet to say you understand."

"I do understand, Tavie, and you should never be ashamed of your feelings. It proves you aren't a cold, hard individual without a heart, but you care deeply for others. That speaks a lot about your character." Her pulse raced as they trekked slowly down the sidewalk, hand-in-hand. Her instinct told her to pull away, but after witnessing his pain, her compassion wouldn't allow her to hurt the guy more than she'd already done. She'd already made it clear she had no intention of marrying him.

"Tavie, where are you staying?"

He pointed to the opposite side of the street. "There."

"The Hotel Rawls? It's a nice place and the dinners are great."

His face lit up. "Wonderful. Would you honor me by having dinner with me, tonight?"

"Thank you, but if that sounded as if I was hinting, I wasn't. I'm really tired. I don't know if my mother told you, but we've just returned from a month-long cruise, and drove home today from Mobile. After we got here, I went—" She stopped.

He lowered his head. "I know. Your mother told me. You went to see the fellow who came here to con you. I suppose he tried to make up more lies."

"No. He wouldn't see me."

Octavious laughed. "He knew he was cornered. I'm just glad I was released from the hospital before you married the galoot."

They turned around and headed back to Lee Street. "Tavie, I have another question. When you were released from the hospital, why didn't you find a phone and call to let me know you were still alive?"

"Didn't I tell you? I didn't know the guys had sent the letter until I was leaving to come here. I decided it would be better to show up in person. I imagined a happy reunion, but that didn't happen, did it?"

She muttered. "No, it didn't. I'm so sorry."

Standing at her door, he said, "Juliette, I loved you before I came here, but I love you even more, now that I've spent time with you. Would you mind if I kissed you?"

She bit her lip. "Tavie . . . please, try to understand."

He threw up his hands. "I'm trying, Juliette. Honest, I am, but how can I possibly understand? Tell me, truthfully. Do you understand? Do you understand how you could've fallen for a low-life who talks like a hick and can't put a decent sentence together?"

Her mouth gaped open. "How would you know? Do you know Buddy?"

"Of course, not. How could I?"

"I don't know. It just seemed odd—"

"You mean because I knew he sounds like a hayseed? Easy. Your mother and I had a long conversation before you got home."

She smiled. "I should've known. Goodnight, Tavie."

He reached for her hand and kissed it. "Goodnight, beautiful. May I call on you tomorrow?"

"I'm sorry, Tavie. I think we both need time to consider all that's happened. Please, go to your grandfather's funeral, and we'll correspond through letters, the way we began our relationship. If it's meant to be, we'll know it in time."

"In time? Time is the one thing I don't have, Juliette."

Her brow furrowed. "You sound angry."

He clenched his eyes shut. "Forgive me, darling. I'm not angry, just anxious. I'm so afraid that imposter will convince you that he's the man for you."

"Don't press me, Tavie."

"Sorry, darling. We'll do it your way, and if we find we've picked up where we left off, I'll still be hoping for a Christmas wedding."

"It's too early to discuss a wedding. We'll write and see where it goes."

"Fair enough, sweetheart. I won your heart once through letters. I have high expectations of doing it again. But don't give up on that Christmas wedding, because I haven't. We'll have a big blow-out—a wedding like this town has never seen before."

She rolled her eyes, then turned to go inside.

****

When Donald Matthews showed up unexpectedly at the Enterprise office, Gid Granger whirled around in his swivel desk chair. Then slowly rising to his feet, he lumbered over, with one hand extended and the other clenching tightly to his cane. "Well, what brings you here, Donald?"

"Good morning, Gid. I suppose I should've called you back to let you know I was coming, but it was a spur-of-the-moment decision. You didn't sound good on the phone. I decided to come see for myself if there's anything I could do to help out while you're short-handed."

"Donald, to tell the truth, I haven't been doing too good, lately. I should've retired six months ago."

"You'll be happy to know I've hired a young man, fresh out of college to come work with you. He comes highly recommended. He'll start tomorrow."

Gid bit his lip.

"I thought you'd be happy."

"I am."

"Then what's the problem?"

"Donald, what if Buddy isn't guilty and he goes off to prison because I turned him in."

"Maybe you should sit back down and let's talk about it."

Gid carefully went over all the details again. When he finished, Donald said, "I don't want to believe Buddy could've stolen the money, either, Gid, but desperate people do desperate things. We know very little about his background, other than he came here after being discharged from the Navy. I didn't vet him the way I usually vet employees, since I was desperate for help at the time and my mother, who has always been an excellent judge of character, thought he was not only brilliant but trustworthy. But looking back, I wish I'd dug into his background."

"But what if he didn't do it, Donald?"

"Then who did?"

"I don't know."

CHAPTER 33

Thursday, December 8th

Walt Wilkerson stomped into the jail and growled, "Jerry, I'm telling you, you've got the wrong person back there in the cell and I intend to prove it."

"Give it up, Walt. I told you earlier you could bail him out, but you chose not to. I reckon in spite of wanting to believe otherwise, deep down your gut tells you the boy's guilty as sin. It's bad to put your trust in someone and have them let you down, but we both know he did it."

"No, I still don't believe it, but I keep hoping that whoever stole the money will have a conscience and come forward after they realize their misdeed could jeopardize another man's life. If he appears to be walking around town, free, I have a feeling they won't be as plagued with guilt as they might be, knowing another man is locked up for something they did."

Jerry laughed. Out loud. As if it were the funniest thing he'd ever heard. "You're kidding, right? First of all, even if someone else did get the money, do you really think a thief would care who takes the rap? He'd simply be grateful to know he got by with it."

****

After weeks of waiting for Buddy to go to trial, and daily letters from Octavious, Juliette's resistance was worn to a frazzle. Everyone tried to convince her Buddy was not only a thief, but a liar. She didn't want to believe he set out to make a fool of her, but who was the girl who visited him in the jail? Maybe her mother was right, and love was nothing more than a fairytale. She could no longer think straight and eventually gave in to her mother's urging and Octavious's pleading for a Christmas wedding..

From the moment Juliette agreed, Henrietta had little time for Walt. And though her daughter took no interest in the planning, Henrietta didn't seem to mind. She had the church reserved and chose six of the town's most prominent young ladies to serve as bride's maids even though Juliette called them spoiled and spent as little time as possible with any of them. The flowers were ordered and a photographer from out of Montgomery was booked. The day the wedding dress arrived, Henrietta was more excited than the bride-to-be. In fact, she was the only one excited.

"I, Suwannee, Juliet, you act as if we're planning your funeral and not your wedding. You're about to embark on the most exciting day of your life when you'll be marrying the man of your dreams, and yet you sit around sulking all day."

"Mother, have you ever stopped to consider that maybe Tavie is the man of your dreams and not mine?"

Henrietta ended the conversation the way she'd done for the past month. She hugged Juliette and assured her what she was feeling was perfectly natural. It was wedding jitters, and she was a lucky girl to find someone like Octavious who was not only from a fine, wealthy family, but he loved her. Henrietta insisted that in time, Juliette would come to realize how lucky she was.

****

Shelby was cleaning the Bank building when she heard talk in the hall. A man said he heard Buddy's job had already been given to someone else, a sign that his employer knew which way his trial would go.

Then a woman responded that she saw no reason to waste money on a trial when everyone knew Buddy was guilty. The man agreed and said there was nothing lower than a thief and once Buddy was sent to prison, he hoped he'd never see the outside again.

Her heart felt as if it had split in two. She left the bank to clean The Matthews Agency and was surprised to see a stranger sitting behind Buddy's desk.

He jumped up, looking stunned. "Who are you? Do you work here?"

"I'm Shelby, the cleaning lady."

"Oh. Nice to meet you, Shelby. I'm Johnny Mack Jerkins. I've just been hired as the new bookkeeper. In a town this size, I suppose you already know the guy who worked here before me stole a pile of money and he's now in prison."

Her muscles tightened. "Jail, not prison."

He shrugged. "Yeah, that's what I meant, but from what I've heard, he's on his way to prison."

Shelby heard little of what he said after that, because she had an idea of a way she might save them both.

The man stood and took his coat from the hat rack. "Nice to meet you, Miss. I suppose we'll be seeing a lot of one another from here on out."

Leaving the building, she heard Thomas call her name. "Shelby, wait. Why are you in such a hurry?"

"I have something urgent to take care of, Thomas. Forgive me for rushing off."

"I'll walk you home."

"No. . . no thank you. I'm in a hurry."

Her mother was ironing, and her dad was sitting in his wheelchair by the fire. Shelby had a sick feeling when she opened the door and saw their eyes light up, the way they always did when she walked into a room. They had no clue the daughter they worshipped was not the girl they believed her to be. Going to prison was what she deserved, and she'd be willing to take her punishment—except it would break her parents' hearts. Imagining their disappointment was worse than imagining living the remainder of her life in prison.

Her daddy said, "The radio said it's gonna dip into the thirties tonight. I'll bet it was a cold walk home. Come sit by the fire and warm up."

She bent over and kissed him on top of his bald head. "I'm fine, daddy. Excuse me. I have something to take care of."

As she left the room, she heard her mother say, "I wonder what that's all about?"

Her pulse raced at the thought they might soon have the answer.

****

She grabbed a Blue Horse Notebook and a #2 pencil from her dresser, then sprawled across the bed and began to write:

Dr. Mr. Granger,

I have done a terrible thing and I don't expect you to forgive me. I can't forgive myself. But I was cleaning the office and about to empty the trash one night, when a twenty-dollar bill flew out of a bag in the trash can. I don't expect you to believe me because it don't sound possible, but it's the truth. I looked inside and there was more money in that bag than I've seen in my whole lifetime. What I shoulda done and what I did are not the same. I shoulda took it to you, but instead, I kept it. I ain't never done nothing like that in my life, but I stole it. You'll find every penny in this flour sack. I thought I could spend it, but after I got it, I didn't want it. I thought the right thing to do would be to put it back where I found it, but since I found it in the trash, I figured it best to put it in your desk. I'm so sorry. Please tell the Sheriff Buddy didn't do it and I'll be waiting for him to come arrest me.

Yours truly,

Shelby

CHAPTER 34

Gid Granger ambled over to the safe, opened it and pulled out the bank bag with the previous night's cash. He felt a sense of relief that he remembered the combination. For years, he never had to think twice, but lately he had to think twice about everything he did.

After making the deposit, he returned and gave instructions to the new bookkeeper, who seemed eager to work. Almost too eager. His constant questions made Gid nervous. Buddy had been quick to catch on and was able to work on his own. The thought that the kid could possibly be innocent still bothered him. The evidence was all there, yet the gnawing feeling that Buddy was incapable of such a dastardly deed caused him angst. What if?

He opened his desk drawer, then slammed it quickly, hoping Johnny Mack wasn't looking over his shoulder. It looked like a flour sack and no one had any reason to place a flour sack in his drawer. He must have put it in there, himself. But when? His suspicions had to be correct—he was losing his mind. He shuddered at the thought of being shuffled off to a home for old folks.

He waited for Johnny Mack to go to the water cooler, then eased the drawer open and peeked into the sack. His heart thumped so fast, he feared he was having a heart attack when he saw hundreds of dollars inside the bag. Then he saw the letter. Pulling it out, he read it three times before putting it into his pocket. He grabbed the flour sack and said, "Johnny Mack, I have somewhere I need to go. I don't have time to cancel my appointments, so please make my apologies. I have urgent business to take care of."

He headed straight to the Sheriff's office and laid the sack on his desk. "Dan, I have a confession to make."

Sheriff Dan Beckham laughed as if he'd told a joke. "I'm listening. What are you confessing to?"

"I had the wrong fellow arrested for taking the money. Buddy didn't do it."

The sheriff grimaced. "Aww, Gid, you're letting this get to you. Just let us take care of everything. He'll get a fair trial and if you're right and he didn't do it, it'll all come out at the trial."

"But there shouldn't be a trial. The money has been returned." He opened the flour sack. "See? It's all here."

"Gid have a seat." After he sat down, the sheriff said he knew what he was trying to do, but it wouldn't work. "If you let him get by this time, he'll do it again."

"But I'm telling you, it wasn't Buddy."

"Then who?"

"I don't wish to tell. The guilty party wrote a very repentant letter, put it in the sack with the money and expects to be charged with theft, but I'll go to jail myself before I'll give the name."

"Have you counted it?"

"I don't have to. I'm confident every penny that was taken has now been returned."

"Well, if you're dismissing the charges, I'll discuss it with the Prosecutor and get back with you."

Gid waited all afternoon, before the call came. "Gid, this is Dan. I wanted to call to let you know, we've notified the kid that he's free. I'm glad it all worked out."

Johnny Mack went home at five o'clock, but Gid told him he'd be staying later, since he had a late appointment.

When Shelby opened the door to clean the office, she turned on the light and gasped, seeing Mr. Granger sitting there. Her lip quivered. "Oh, Mr. Granger, I am so sorry. Are you waiting for the police to come arrest me?"

He stood and held out open arms. "Why would I want to do that? You were a brave girl to come forward to return the money. Thank you."

"If I'm not being arrested, does that mean Buddy is still in trouble?"

He shook his head. "No. There's nothing to arrest him for. Thanks to you for admitting what you did, I've dropped the charges. It's late, so I need to go, but I wanted to wait for you to get here to tell you the good news, myself."

"You're a good man, Mr. Gid. Thank you. I've been dreading Mama and Daddy finding out what I did. I'm afraid they think I can do no wrong. I knew they were going to be heartbroken."

"There's no need for anyone to know anything, except that Buddy didn't steal the money and that it's all been returned. Your name will never come up."

****

After a long day driving the truck for Red Rock Cola, Thomas was exhausted and went straight to the log cabin. Stumbling around in the dark, he knew there was something different, even before he lit the oil lamp. The room had a fresh, clean smell and a bouquet of Golden Rod was on the small porcelain table. A note was lying on the bed. "Congratulations on your new job. Love, Shelby."

He looked around at all the changes. The floor was swept clean, curtains on the window, and the cot was covered with a pretty chenille bedspread. The kitchen was stocked with two plates, two cups and saucers, utensils, an iron skillet and a coffee pot. The only thing lacking to make it into a real home was Shelby Sellers. He undressed for bed and crawled under the sheet. After tossing and turning, he jumped up, dressed, and ran toward town, hoping he could find her. He had something weighing on his mind, and it wouldn't wait until morning.

"Thomas? Is that you?" Shelby yelled as his image became clearer. "What a surprise. I thought you'd go straight to the cabin after driving all day."

"I did. But I had to see you, Shelby. We need to talk."

"Okay. I was on my way home. What do you want to do?"

He hadn't expected her to ask the question, and though he'd carefully rehearsed what he wanted to tell her, the unrehearsed version coming from his lips shocked him."Shelby Sellers, I'm in love with you, and I want to spend the rest of my life trying to make you happy. Will you marry me?"

Her mouth gaped open. "Thomas, are you drunk?"

He laughed until tears rolled down his face. "No, I don't drink. I love you, Shelby. I think I fell in love with you the night Buddy introduced us. I'll ask again, will you marry me?"

The longing in his eyes communicated what she was feeling. She'd been infatuated with Buddy's backwoodsy ways, but neither Buddy nor any other male had ever made her heart race the way it hammered against the walls of her chest, when she gazed into Thomas's baby blue orbs. Her voice quaked. "Thomas, I love you, too, but before I give you my answer, there's something you need to know about me, and it may change your mind."

"Nothing will ever make me change my mind."

As they headed toward the cabin, Thomas raved about what a

fine job she did, turning the cabin into a nice place to come home to. Shelby placed her hand across his lips. "Stop. I'm glad you liked it. But before I lose my nerve, I have to tell you something." For the next thirty minutes, she went through the whole rigamarole about how she found the money in the trash and a detailed description about everything that followed. She bit her lip. "So now that you know, if you want to change your mind, I'll understand."

"Are you kidding? I love you even more. Anyone in your situation could've been tempted, but you couldn't spend it because it wasn't yours. What about Buddy? Will he still go to trial?"

"No. I think there's red tape to go through before setting him free, but I'm expecting him to be out before morning. Now, if you still want to marry me, the answer is yes."

Thomas walked her home, and they went inside and told her parents the good news.

His feet barely touched the ground as he ran back to the log cabin. Funny, how tired and sleepy he was when he came home from work, yet now felt completely renewed and impossible to fall asleep.

"Shelby Sellers is going to marry me!"

CHAPTER 35

Thomas went to work early, got his assignment, then waited for the Coffee County Court House to open to apply for a marriage license. He clipped it to the visor on his truck, so he could see it as he traveled to Birmingham to make a delivery. It was a constant reminder that his prayers had been answered. Not only was he now going to live, he was going to marry the most wonderful girl in the world. They'd have children. Lots of children. He let out a loud "whoopee," as he headed north. He had a great job and Buddy would soon be free. How much better could it get?

The Sheriff called Walt at 7:00 A.M. to let him know the guilty party had confessed and the money was returned.

"Then he's free to go?"

"Not yet. I'll call you and let you know when the paperwork is complete."

Overwhelmed with gratitude, Walt wanted to tell someone the good news. In the past, that someone would've been Henrietta . . . or Juli. Now, they were the last two people he'd share the news with. If at all possible, Henrietta would find a way to keep Buddy incarcerated, long enough for Juli to walk the aisle with that Octavious fellow.

He called the sheriff's office three times during the day to find out the hold-up. Each time, he was given the run-around. Finally, at eight-fifteen that evening, the call came. Buddy was a free man.

The sheriff said, "I apologize for the long delay, Walt, but J.B. was out of town and we had to wait for him to—"

"I'm not interested in the details. Tell Buddy I'm on my way."

"But don't you want to know who the perpetrator is?"

"No, I don't." He didn't need to know, since he had already figured it out. It was good to find out she didn't disappoint him. Walt had known Shelby and her family before she was old enough to walk and he would've staked his life on her coming forward before she could allow an innocent man go to prison.

He drove to the jail and rushed into the office. Buddy sat on a bench, grinning as if he'd just won the lottery. "Mr. Wilkerson, I don't know what you done to get me outta here, but I'm mighty grateful."

"I didn't do anything, Buddy. You're out because the person who took the money has confessed and returned it."

"That was big of him, whoever he was, don't you think? I mean, he coulda kept the money and I don't reckon no one would ever have known the difference. I still can't believe I'm free. I thought I was on my way to prison and for a while there, I reckon I didn't care. After I saw the picture in the paper of Juliette with another man, I thought I didn't want to see her again, but I was fooling myself. I wanna hear it from her lips that she's sweet on that other fellow. If she tells me she is, then I'll leave her be, but I gotta know."

"Buddy, you and I need to have a long chat before you go see her. Why don't we sit down in the drugstore and discuss things over a milkshake?"

"What time is it? I hope they're still open, because a milkshake sounds mighty fine, Mr. Wilkerson. Thanks."

Buddy kept his elbows on the table, his face buried in his hands as Walt explained about Octavious Rockwell's appearing. He told him there was no truth to the article about Juliette and Roland planning a wedding, but the real problem was Octavious.

The bitter taste of bile rose up from Buddy's throat. "Mr. Wilkerson, I may never get another chance with Juliette, but you can't let her marry Octavious. He don't love her. I know he don't. I've gotta see her before she does something drastic—like marry the rascal. I don't know what his game is, but if he's pressing her to marry him, I guarantee you he's up to no good."

"Buddy, he's no longer pressing her. He doesn't have to. Juliette and Octavious have been corresponding daily and she's now agreed to marry him on Christmas Day, the way they'd previously planned in their letters."

He lifted his head and his lip quivered. "Then I might as well have gone to prison. I ain't got nothing to live for."

"Buddy, I know how much you love her, and I believe she loves you, but she's acting like a marionette with Octavious and Henrietta pulling her strings. Her mother has convinced her that you came to Enterprise for the sole purpose of marrying her for her money and that you never really loved her."

"But that ain't so. You know it ain't so, Mr. Walt."

"Yes, I do know. When I saw how you two looked at one another the night I took you to her house, I knew you two were meant to be together. I wasn't wrong about the sparks I saw, but I was wrong to convince you to hide your identity. I'm so sorry, Buddy. I feel I'm responsible for things turning out badly."

"Why you, Mr. Wilkerson? You've been nothing but good to me from the first day I got into town."

"No. I steered you wrong. You wanted to tell Juli you weren't the guy she'd been writing to, but I thought it best to wait. I kinda looked at it like when you're out fishing . . . there's the thrill of feeling a tug on the end of the pole, yet if you jerk too quickly, you'll lose the fish. Sometimes you need to let him run with it, but the mark of a good fisherman is in knowing when to pull it in. I thought you didn't need to be so quick in telling her she was wrong about you—that if she knew from the beginning you weren't the fellow she'd been writing to, you'd lose her. I thought more time was needed, but I was wrong. I should've told you to pull her in, sooner."

Buddy heard his voice crack. "Aww, Mr. Wilkerson, don't blame yourself. Shucks, I coulda told her at any point, but what you said made sense to me, too. I got enough on my plate without worrying about you feeling bad, so please don't blame yourself. I'm grown and make my own decisions."

"Thank you, Buddy."

"I drove by the cabin on the way to the jail, and Thomas has cleaned up around it. It looks good from the outside. I haven't seen the inside."

"It'll look good to me. I sure appreciate you letting me and Thomas live there. As soon as I can find me a job, I want to start paying you rent."

"I don't want your money. I haven't wanted to sell it to someone who only wants to tear it down, but I'm glad to have it occupied." He slurped the last drop of his milkshake. "Buddy, I know how much you enjoyed working for Gid Granger, but I suppose you've already heard you've been replaced."

"Yessir, and I don't blame Mr. Granger."

"Well, this would be temporary until you find another job you like, but I could use you stocking shelves at the grocery store from seven in the morning until noon, if you're interested. It doesn't pay much, but it could keep your stomach full until you locate something better."

"That's a real fine offer, Mr. Wilkerson. I'd like to take you up on it."

Leaving the drugstore, Buddy waved. "Thanks again."

"Hop in the truck and I'll drive you there."

"No thanks, I think I'll walk. I've been cooped up too long and can use a fresh breath of air."

As he neared the cottage, he saw a light burning. When he opened the door, Shelby squealed, and Thomas threw his arms around him. "Does this mean what I think it does?"

Jericho nodded. "I didn't expect to see you two here, but I'm glad you are. And yep, I'm free. Apparently, the thief had a change of heart and returned the money and the charges have been dropped." It was then he noticed all the changes.

Walt told him Thomas had cleared out the varmints, but he was shocked to find it looking so homey. "This place . . . it looks great."

Thomas draped his arm around Shelby. "You can thank my little wife, here. She did it all."

"Your wife? Your jousting."

"Nope. It's a fact. We tied the knot thirty minutes ago. I came by to pack a bag, and I've got to make a run to South Florida.

She's going with me. The Bank and Mr. Granger have given her the night off, and we'll be back tomorrow. You'll have the cabin to yourself, since we'll be living with her parents until we find our own place."

"Well, congratulations."

Whether it was the stress of facing an upcoming trial, losing Juliette, or the thought of having such fine friends as Thomas, Shelby and Mr. Wilkerson that caused him to slink down on the floor in full-blown sobs, he couldn't say.

CHAPTER 36

Friday, December 9th

Donald Matthews came into town after hearing the peculiar turn of events from Gid Granger.

The two men went to the City Café for a late breakfast.

"Gid, how's the new guy working out for you?"

"He's catching on, but I sure miss Buddy. He could work circles around Johnny Mack."

"Well, it wouldn't be fair to him to pull him, if he's doing his job, but I don't want to lose Buddy. I wonder if he'd be interested in going to Troy?"

"I think that's a great idea, Donald. Then when I retire, you could bring him back here to run this office."

"My thoughts, exactly. Do you know where he's staying?"

"I don't, but Walt Wilkerson has taken a real interest in the kid. I'm sure he can tell us."

After contacting Walt, Donald drove with him to the store, where Buddy was busy ripping open boxes and putting produce on the shelves. After hearing the proposition, tears filled his eyes. "Mr. Wilkerson, you've been good to me. I feel I owe you."

Walt placed his hand on his shoulder. "If you really want to do something for me, then take this job that Donald is offering. It's a great opportunity."

"Yessir, I agree."

Donald stuck out his hand. "Then it's a deal. I'll expect you to be at work Monday morning. That gives you a little break, which I'm sure you can use, after the ordeal you've been through."

Buddy didn't argue. He'd need a few days to try and convince Juliette to see him. If she refused, he'd rather be living in another town. The pain of running into her in Enterprise would be too great to bear.

After Buddy got off work, he stopped by the City Café for an egg sandwich and cup of coffee. He picked up a newspaper someone had left at a table. Thumbing through the pages, his heart pounded when he glimpsed a headline, "Jericho Rhoades is a Free Man." Feeling grateful that Mr. Matthews and his mother had taken time to teach him to read, a tear fell on the paper as he read the events that led him to jail and the event that set him free. He was glad the guilty party's name was withheld. After all, it took courage for them to admit their wrongdoing.

He turned another page and the grateful feeling suddenly turned to sadness, seeing a picture of his beautiful Juliette. His eyes skimmed the first line: "Mrs. Henrietta Jinright is pleased to announce the engagement of her daughter, Juliette Andrea Jinright to Seaman 2nd Class Octavious J. Rockwell, III."

He slammed his fist on the table. "No, no, no." Embarrassed that he'd said it aloud, he glanced around to see all eyes focused on him. The waitress said, "Is there something wrong with your sandwich?"

He lowered his head. "No. I'm sorry. The sandwich is great." He threw his money on the table and headed to 4014 W. Lee Street.

Marching up the steps to the house, he rang the doorbell. Mrs. Jinright opened the door and smirked. "I don't know who you are, but I do know you're a liar and I won't have my daughter associating with the likes of you, so I think you should leave."

"Ma'am I just need a few minutes to speak with Juliette, and then I'll go."

"Young man, if you don't want to find yourself behind bars again, you'll go now."

Juliette stood behind her mother. "Jericho Rhoades, I'd be obliged if you'd do what my mother said. I have nothing to say to you."

"Juliette, please. I only ask for a few minutes of your time."

"Shut the door, mother."

The knot in his throat swelled at the coldness in her voice. Had she turned into her mother? When the door slammed in his face, he ambled down the steps and headed to the log cabin. He didn't know how nor when, but one way or the other he had to talk to her.

Saturday, Jericho walked by a used car lot and spotted a 1940 Ford coupe. It was a beauty. Maroon with whitewall tires. He'd never really had a need for a car before, but it was a great deal. He clutched the steering wheel and feeling a new sense of pride, drove around town, thinking how much more fun it would be, if Juliette was by his side.

Sunday night, he drove over to a little country church near Shelby's house and sitting in the car with the windows down, he listened as the congregation sang a song about meeting Jesus alone in a garden. His throat tightened as they sang, *"He walks and talks with me and tells me I am his own."* Jericho knew how important it was to belong to someone. As a child he ached for a loving father who would call him his own. Next they sang *"He included me, yes, he included me, too."*

He swallowed hard, recalling how his heart broke when Gus chose to take Little Shug with him because she was his own. Jericho longed to be included, too. He wanted to be part of a family with a Father like the one these people sang about. A strange feeling came over him. He felt as if God were reading his mind, answering his non-verbalized questions, with each song that was sung. But it was when they sang, *"Draw me nearer. . .nearer, my God to Thee,"* that he knew for a certainty God had heard his cry, since he'd uttered those very words only moments before the music had even begun. The service ended with a woman singing, "Just as I am, I come." In his car, he bowed his head and though it was no garden, he knew in his heart he had a Father who truly loved him, just as he was.

People were filing out of the church, and hearing his name called, he quickly wiped his damp cheeks and saw Thomas and Shelby walking toward his car.

Thomas propped his arms on the window ledge and leaned in. "Why are you sitting out here in the dark? You should've come in. It was a great service."

"I knew I'd find you two here. I just came by to let you know I talked to Mr. Wilkerson and he's agreed to let y'all stay in the log cabin, since I won't be needing it anymore. I'm leaving in the morning for Troy, so if you're interested, it's yours to live in after tomorrow."

Though they were gracious enough to let him know they'd miss him, it was evident they were overjoyed at the idea of having a place of their own, instead of living with her parents.

Monday morning came too quickly. Jericho had not been able

to convince Juliette to see him. In twelve more days, she'd be married to that loathsome Octavious Rockwell and there seemed to be no way he could stop her.

Juliette marked off the days on her calendar and every passing day brought her closer to tears. Her mother entered her bedroom with a stack of cards in her hand and laid them on the bed. "Darling, I picked up our Christmas postcards from the photographer today. It's a terrible likeness of me, but it's a wonderful picture of you. I thought a simple wreath printed below the photo with a line, 'Christmas comes to West Lee Street, Merry Christmas from Henrietta and Juliette,' was sufficient. What do you think?"

When Juliette failed to pick one up, her mother said, "Aren't you even interested in looking at them?"

She nodded slightly. "If it's what you want, Mother, it suits me."

"Well, I was hoping it would be what you'd want to. I'll declare, I don't know why you've been so moody lately. With your wedding so close, you should be giddy with excitement."

What was the point in trying to have this conversation? Each time she questioned her decision, her mother would remind her of the lies Jericho Rhoades told her and how lucky she was to have found out before she married the wrong man.

On Friday, December 16th, Walt saw Juli walking into The Vogue, an exclusive ladies boutique on Main Street, and waited outside the door for her to come out.

When she emerged with two hat boxes and a garment bag he reached for them and walked her to her car.

"Juli, I haven't taken the opportunity to congratulate you on your upcoming marriage."

She forced a smile. "Thank you, Walt. I'm sorry that you and mother haven't been able to work out your problems. I feel it's partly my fault."

"Nonsense. It has nothing to do with you, sweetheart."

She rolled her eyes. "We both know better. It has everything to do with me. I hear you and Buddy . . . I mean Jericho have become quite close and you think I'm wrong to marry Octavious. Mother, on the other hand, hates Jericho and adores Octavious. Maybe once I'm married, you two can settle your differences. There'll be nothing left to argue over."

After placing her packages in the car, he took her by the hand. "Juli, before you leave, could I buy you coffee at the Café?"

"And a slice of pecan pie to go along with it?"

He winked. "Of course. I'd forgotten how much you like Theda's pecan pies."

As they strode down the sidewalk and viewed the men putting up decorations her voice quivered. "I've always loved Christmas. It's always made me happy to see the Christmas lights strung from one side of the street to the other and the beautiful window displays with giant Santas and wreaths everywhere."

"It's a beautiful time of year." He opened the door to the café, and they took a seat at the nearest booth. "But you don't seem happy, Juliette. Are you?"

Ignoring the question, she said, "I know you didn't bring me here for pie and coffee, so here's your chance to say whatever's on your mind."

He pushed back in his chair and stroked his chin. "You're right. And I thank you for giving me the opportunity to make my case." She had to know everything he knew, and he'd lay it all out in the hopes that she'd see things as clearly as he did.

Juliette listened intently as he began with how Octavious and Jericho were working together in the Engine Room when the explosion took place and they wound up in the Naval Hospital in the same ward.

She nodded, indicating she understood.

Walt told her how Octavious proposed to three other girls at the same time he was writing her. Juliette shook her head and muttered. "I know you want to believe it's true, Walt, but Jericho made it all up, hoping to sway you. I suppose he expected you to influence mother."

Walt talked faster. He told her how Octavious would read her letters aloud to the sailors in the hospital ward, and that while he was poking fun at her for believing his lies, Buddy was falling in love with her. Walt took the blame for the misunderstanding about Buddy's identity. "Juli, Buddy came to Enterprise because he thought Octavious had died, and he thought telling you was the right thing to do. When I met him in the drugstore, I honestly thought he was the sailor you'd been writing to, and I didn't give him an opportunity to explain. Obviously, you thought the same thing, the way you sailed into his arms."

"If what you are saying is true, then why didn't he tell me he was not Buddy?"

"Actually, he is Buddy."

"No. I'm sorry, Walt, but he's pulled the wool over your eyes. He's a real good liar."

"Listen to what I'm saying, Juli. Octavious was never called Buddy, but he began signing his letters to all the girls that way."

She shoved her chair back and stood. "I think I should go. I know you mean well, Walt, but you're trying to confuse me."

He walked her back to her car. "Juli. I'm trying to keep you from making a terrible mistake. You're not in love with Octavious. Admit it."

Her lower lip quivered. "I can't do this, Walt. I'm getting married in seven days. Please, try to be happy for me."

Walt hugged her. "You know how much I love you, kid. All I want is for you to be happy."

CHAPTER 37

Juliette went home and shut herself in her room. She knew Walt believed every word he said. She almost wished she could believe it, too, even if it wasn't true.

Walt was the only one who could see through her. He knew she didn't love Octavious. He also knew she was still in love with Buddy, regardless of how staunchly she denied it. *Buddy?* Her stomach knotted. It was hard to call him Jericho when she fell in love with him as "Buddy."

Burying her head in her pillow, all the times they spent together—times she tried to forget—came flooding back. The pillow absorbed the tears as she recalled their last date when she showed up at his door at The Rawls just before sunrise holding the picnic basket. The image of him coming to the door without a shirt, and the cute way he blushed when he saw her standing there and realized he was half-dressed, brought a smile. Then her pulse raced, recalling the scars on his chest. She wasn't shocked, since Octavious had written her about scars on his chest.

She popped her hand over her mouth. "Buddy isn't the liar. Octavious is."

Juliette called The Rawls and invited Octavious to come over.

"Now? I thought I wasn't to pick you up until seven."

"No. I'd really like to see you. Please?"

"Sure, I'll be right over."

When he arrived, Juliette suggested they sit in the porch swing. She recalled how romantic it was when she sat next to Buddy as they rocked back and forth, in sync with the beats of her heart. Yet, there was nothing even slightly romantic about being beside Octavious. All he could talk about was himself.

"Buddy?"

"Yes, dear."

"Would you think it dreadfully sinful if I asked you to unbutton your shirt for me?"

"Say what? Unbutton . . .my what?"

"Your shirt." She giggled and rubbed the back of her hand across his cheek.

His lip lifted as he leaned over to peek in the window to see if her mother was watching. "Really? Why?"

She feigned a pout and whispered in his ear. "Oh, dear, you do think I'm sinful, don't you?"

"No. No big deal. It's just . . . well, of all the girls I've ever known, you'd be the last one I'd expect to make such a request."

"What was I thinking? I can see I've shocked you. Since you're planning to become a preacher, I should've known better than to ask."

"Um . . .about that. I've changed my mind." His gaze locked with hers as his fingers fumbled from one button to the next. "I don't think I'd make a very good preacher."

"Maybe it's for the best. I'm not sure I'd make a good preacher's wife."

He stopped, then cleared his throat. "What if your mother should walk out here and see us?"

"She won't. Here, let me help you."

"Sure, doll. But maybe we should go sit in the car. Sitting out here in broad daylight makes me nervous."

By the time he finished his sentence, she clasped her hands around both sides of his shirt and jerked it open. Her lips pursed. "Just as I expected."

The porch swing lunged when she jumped out.

"Where are you going? What's wrong, doll face?"

"Where are the chest burns, Octavious?"

His eyes clenched shut. "Okay, okay. Maybe I fudged a little in my letters. But I really was burned. See?" He held up his left hand. "Frankly, you should be glad it wasn't my chest. I can tell you, the chest burns aren't pretty. I've seen them."

"So have I. Now, I'll thank you to leave." He jumped to catch

305

the ring when she slung it at him.

His face revealed his panic. "No, Juliette. You can't do this to me. We're too close."

"Who are you trying to fool. We aren't close at all. You don't love me, and I don't love you, Octavious."

"But sweetheart, what I mean is, we're too close to the wedding date to back out now. My parents will be coming down in a couple of days to meet you."

When he saw she couldn't be swayed, he lost his temper. "You owe me this, Juliette. I've wasted my time with you, and it's too late now to find another girl to marry before my birthday. I'll lose the trust fund my Grandpa left me."

"So, that's the reason you wanted to marry me?"

"I was falling in love. I really was. And I will, I promise. Don't you see? It isn't fair for all that money to go to his alma mater. Hey, let's go through with it, and I'll give you a hefty share. After we collect, we'll get an amicable divorce and be the richer for it. What do you think?"

She glared. "Unbelievable."

"Aww, doll face, don't you see, I need you? Please?"

"Octavious Rockwell, I wouldn't marry you if you were the last man on earth. Now, go." She picked up a broom that Greta left beside the front door.

He ran down the steps, buttoning his shirt.

She raced up the stairs and came down with her keys and her

pocketbook. Greta yelled, "Where are you going in such a hurry, Miss Juliette?"

"I have an errand to run. Tell Mother not to expect me for supper." She rushed over to the The Matthews Agency and was shocked to see another man sitting behind Buddy's desk. "Where's Buddy?"

"You mean the fellow who was in jail for stealing the money?"

"No. I mean the fellow who was wrongly accused of stealing the money. Where is he?"

"They hired him to work in the Troy office."

After quickly thanking him, she rushed out and headed for Troy. The Matthews Agency sign was easy to spot once she drove into town. She ran, opened the door to the office and saw Buddy sitting behind a desk. He jumped up. "Juliette? What are—"

He didn't have time to say anything else, because her lips were pressing against his.

He couldn't speak for laughing. "What just happened?"

"Buddy Rhoades, do you love me?"

"Do I? More than life itself, but . . ."

"There are no buts. You love me, right?"

"Yes. Yes, I love you, Juliette."

"Then will you marry me?"

"I don't have a clue what's going on, but yes, I will marry you. Today, if you like."

She laughed with him. "No. I want a Christmas wedding at the Lake, where we had our last date. Do you have any objections?"

He shook his head. "No. It sounds perfect. I suppose you want a Sunrise Wedding, same time, same place?"

She nodded. "Yes. A Sunrise Wedding. I love it."

In less than five minutes, they not only had the details to a perfect wedding planned, but the honeymoon, also. She kissed the tips of her fingers, then pressed them to his lips. "Well, handsome, I should go and let you finish your work."

"As if I could work after this." He glanced up at the office clock. "I get off in fifteen minutes."

"Fine. I'll wait for you out front."

When Buddy came out, she drove him over to a drive-in restaurant she passed on the way. They ordered hamburgers and cherry cokes and she told him all that had happened.

He said, "So let me get this straight. You broke up with Octavious because he didn't have scars on his chest?"

Giggling, she said, "That's about it."

"Well, if it's scars that you're attracted to, you'll be crazy about me."

After finishing their hamburgers, Buddy said, "I can't believe I'm going to run you off, but I don't want you being on the roads after dark. We passed the house I'm renting on the way here. If you don't mind, I'll let you drop me off there and you get started home."

The house was an old farmhouse, but at least it was a little bigger than Walt's log cabin in Enterprise that Buddy previously lived in. Juliette pointed to the car parked in the yard. "Looks like you have company."

"I forgot to tell you. I bought it just before leaving Enterprise. It's only a couple of miles to the office, and I like to run early in the mornings, so I didn't drive it to work. I've never owned a car before."

"I'm proud for you, Buddy. It's a real nice automobile."

He leaned across the seat and kissed her. "When will I see you?"

"At the wedding."

"What? Not until then?"

"We only have a few days, and since you're just starting out at your job and I have lots to do to get ready, we'll meet at the Lake at sunrise."

"I won't have a chance to see Thomas, but I'd like for him to be my best man. Since he doesn't have a phone, do you think you might see him before next Sunday?"

"Sure. Don't worry about a thing. I'll make sure to get in touch with him."

All the way home, Juliette practiced the speech she'd make to her mother. This was not going to be easy. Maybe she should run it by Walt first. No one knew Henrietta Jinright as well as he. When she rode by his house, she noticed his car was gone and drove straight home.

"Juliette, darling, is that you?"

"Yes, mother."

"Honey, Greta said you'd be late for dinner. I'm glad you're back. We'll put Perry Como's record, *White Christmas* on the Victrola tonight and decorate. Won't that be fun?"

"But we don't even have a—" She turned and looked out through the stained glass in the front door. "You won't believe this, Mother, but Walt just drove up and he has a huge Christmas tree in the back of his truck."

"Oh, didn't I mention that I invited him to eat with us and to help decorate? He promised to cut down the largest tree he could find. This is going to be a very special Christmas."

Juliette winced. Would she still think so after hearing the news of the upcoming wedding? "So, you two have made up?"

"Yes, we've been friends too long to let our differences pull us apart."

Feeling grateful for backup, Juliette let out a soft sigh. It would be much easier, convincing her mother she was doing the right thing with Walt's help.

He came inside and took his usual place at the dinner table. Out-of-the-blue, he blurted, "Well, Juliette, how was your trip to Troy?"

Her heart sank. This was not the blunt way she'd intended to bring up the subject, yet glancing at her mother, it didn't appear Henrietta was shocked at his question.

"Uh . . who told you I was going to Troy."

He looked at Henrietta and smiled. "No one. Right Henri?"

"That's right. We guessed."

"That's impossible. You couldn't have guessed, and I didn't tell anyone where I was going."

Henrietta said, "You didn't have to. Octavious paid me a visit this afternoon, pleading with me to convince you to marry him. I didn't understand what was happening, but I decided with all the turmoil, perhaps you two should hold off until spring to make sure you both were ready for marriage. Without realizing it, he put his foot in his mouth when he tried to explain why the wedding had to take place before he turned twenty-five. I ushered him out the door and called Walt to come over. I'm sorry, darling, for not trusting you to make the right decision. You were right and I was wrong."

"Mother, I'm still planning on a Christmas wedding, but with Buddy. I hope we have your approval."

Walt reached for Henrietta's hand. "Shall you tell her, or should I?"

"I will. Darling, since Walt has asked me to marry him, would you and Buddy object to a double wedding?"

Juliette stood and hugged them both. "I'd like that. I'd like it very much. But you may change your mind when you hear what we've planned. Since Christmas falls on Sunday this year, we plan to have a Country Sunrise Wedding at the Lake on Friday, December 23rd. The Matthews Agency will be closed on Friday before Christmas, and since Buddy has to be back at work Monday morning, we've decided by marrying on Friday, we'd have three days to enjoy a honeymoon."

Henrietta's jaw dropped. "Did you say sunrise? Gracious, child, do you know how early that will be?"

Walt glanced at Henrietta and grinned. "Yes, Juli. Your mother and I would love having a double Sunrise Wedding, wouldn't we, dear?"

"Yes. Yes, we would. It sounds perfect."

CHAPTER 38

Friday, December 23ʳᵈ

Friday morning, Buddy was up at 4:30 to give himself plenty of time to make it to Enterprise by sunrise at six-thirty-five. He put on the suit Miz Lucy gave him, packed enough clothes in his duffel bag to last him until Monday, then put the wedding ring in his pants pocket and stuck the marriage license in his billfold.

It was pitch-black dark as he stood on the porch of the old farmhouse. His heart sank, when he realized it was raining. Not a good day for an outdoor wedding. He reached into his pocket to make sure he remembered to put the ring in there. When he pulled it out, it slipped out of his fingers and fell between the cracks on the porch.

Frantic, Buddy ran and got a flashlight out of the car and crawled under the porch in search of the lost ring. Running his hand through the thick dust underneath the porch, he let out a yell when he felt it under his kneecap. He quickly crawled out and tried to brush the gray dust from his dark suit.

Driving down the dirt road, he could hardly see for the heavy downpour. The car slid, slamming him into a ditch in front of a farmhouse. Buddy knocked several times before a grumpy old farmer came to the door.

"Sir, I'm on my way to get married, but my car slid into the ditch. I see you have a tractor. Would you be so kind as to pull me out? I'm in much of a hurry."

"Do you know what time it is? Nah, I ain't gonna get out in this rain. Besides I'm eating breakfast. Now, shoo!"

"Please, sir. I'm supposed to get married at 6:30 in Enterprise."

"Ha! You'd be better off staying in the ditch." And with that, he slammed the door.

Buddy ran back down to the road at the sight of car lights approaching. Standing with his legs spraddled out and his arms flailing in the air, he yelled. "Help!"

Two men with fishing poles tied to the car, stopped and together they pushed the car back on the road.

Buddy thanked them and told them his story. The older gentlemen said, "Well, I reckon everything that could go wrong already has." Then he added, "You did think to get a marriage license, didn't you, son?"

"Yessir. I went to the Court House yesterday and got it."

"Do you mind if I take a look?"

"No sir." He pulled it from his wallet and the fellow looked at it and frowned. "But I thought you said you were marrying a little girl from Enterprise."

He smiled. "Yessir. I need to get there before sunrise."

"I hate to be the bearer of bad news, but you'll need a license from Coffee County. This one is from Pike County."

"Are you sure?"

The other fellow chuckled. "He should know. He's a judge."

Juliette chose not to wear the wedding dress her mother ordered for the previously planned wedding. Instead, she wore a beautiful two-piece white wool suit with a red satin blouse she purchased from The Vogue. Walt picked them up at six-fifteen and drove them to the Lake.

Although the radio predicted rain, the weather was clear, yet quite chilly. Walt parked, then with a bride on each arm, led them up the path leading to the Lake.

Seventy-five of their closest friends and relatives sat in folding chairs facing the decorated arch.

Henrietta glanced at her watch, then leaned over and whispered in Juliette's ear. "Dear, do you think Buddy knows what time the sun rises?"

She smiled and squeezed her mother's hand. "Oh, he knows,

for sure. He'll be here, any minute. We still have a few minutes yet."

Walt marched back and forth from the parking area along the edge of the pasture, to the Lake.

The sun began to peek over the horizon, yet there was no sign of Buddy.

Juliette could hear the oohs and ahhs as the sun cast its colors on the water.

Henrietta whispered something to Walt, then patted her daughter on the back. "I'm sure there's a good reason he's late, dear."

"Mother, I know there's a good reason. He'll be here."

"You don't have to pretend with me. I can see you're trembling, sweetheart and it's understandable why you'd be nervous."

"I'm not nervous, Mother. I'm cold."

Henrietta took the fur stole from around her shoulders and draped it around her daughter. By seven o'clock, Henrietta was antsy. Rubbing her hands together, she groaned. "Where in heaven's name is that boy?" Then leaning forward, she whispered, "Walt, I don't think he's coming. Maybe you should go see if you can locate him."

"Relax, dear. Something has come up to delay him. I'm sure he has a valid reason for being late."

"Well, if he's not in the hospital, I'd like to put him there. This is so humiliating. The people are beginning to talk. Poor Juliette, I can't imagine what she's thinking."

"Henri, she's thinking the same thing I'm thinking. Buddy is late, but he'll be here with a good explanation."

Henrietta's mouth gaped open, when Juliette stood, thrust her shoulders back and with her head held high, made her way to the arch. The crowd grew silent.

"May I have your attention, please? I've heard the whispers, and I know some of you feel I've been jilted, but you're wrong. I don't know where Buddy is or why he's been delayed, but I know he'll be here. I believe in him! I believe in us. But most of all, I believe in my Heavenly Father whom I trust even at this very moment is working all things together for our good. So, please feel free to leave if you must, but if you choose to stay, a glorious Christmas wedding will take place under this arch, as soon as my Groom arrives."

The crowd stood and applauded. Juliette wondered if they were applauding her speech, her courage or her dauntless faith. She turned when she felt her mother's hand on her shoulder.

With her other hand raised high in the air, Henrietta loudly declared, "I, too, believe, my darling. I do!" Then, Walt staunchly proclaimed his belief. Happy tears streamed down Juliette's cheeks when the crowd shouted in unison, "We believe!"

The accordion began to play "Joy to the World," followed by

other beautiful carols as the sun rose higher.

****

Buddy drove that coupe as fast as it would run and headed straight for the Court House in Enterprise. According to the Court House Clock, he was already an hour late. Since there were no phones at the Lake, there was no way to call Juliette to explain his delay.

When he learned the doors wouldn't open until eight o'clock, he drove to the log cabin. Surely, Thomas would have something to fit him. He pulled off his soiled clothes and found a beautiful pin-striped, double-breasted gray suit, much nicer than the wet one he took off. Perfect fit. After scrubbing the mud from his shoes, he hurried back to the Court House, and arrived just as the doors opened.

With the proper license in hand he drove to the Lake and heard cheering the moment he stepped from the car.

Juliette stood waiting on a red carpet leading to the arch, which was decorated with magnolia leaves, and giant Poinsettias. Walt and Henrietta stood arm-in-arm behind her. Buddy ran and stood beside Thomas.

Juliette's face lit up when Buddy winked and gave her a thumb's up as Mr. Gid played the Wedding March on the accordion. Her gaze lifted toward heaven as she whispered, "For this man, I prayed. Thank you, Lord."

318

When the preacher asked, "Who gives this woman," Walt stepped forward. "In the absence of her beloved father, it's my privilege to give Juliette to this man." Then, he stepped back and crooked his arm for Henrietta, his long-awaited bride.

Buddy blinked away a tear when his gaze met with Juliette's. Could this be real? He was marrying the girl called Alabama? If his heart beat any faster, it would beat out of his chest. Suddenly he understood what Miz Lucy meant when she advised him to bring God glory by making the most of his life. He would. How could he not? His heart overflowed with gratefulness. He still didn't know why Miz Lucy's son, who was so loved by his family, had to die or why he was allowed to live. But since he was, he'd use the years he had left, praising the Lord for the beautiful life that lay before him.

He had faced tribulations in his lifetime, but whatever obstacles came his way in the future, he could face with Juliette by his side.

At exactly 8:32 a.m., Friday, December 23, 1949, Juliette Jinright and her Buddy, Jericho Rhoades, were united in holy matrimony and began their happily ever after.

319

I've won numerous literary awards throughout the years, but the awesome friends I've met on this journey have been my true reward. Below is a listing of my novels:

SWITCHED SERIES: .

    Lunacy – Book 1
    Unwed – Book 2
    Mercy – Book 3

GRAVE ENCOUNTER SERIES

    When the Tide Ebbs – Book 1
    When the Tide Rushes In – Book 2
    When the Tide Turns – Book 3

THE KEEPER SERIES

    The Keeper – Book 1
    The Prey – Book 2
    The Destined – Book 3

HOMECOMING SERIES:

    Sweet Lavender – A Novel -Book 1
    Unforgettable – A novella - 2
    Gonna Sit Right Down – A novella- 3
    Hello Walls – A novella - 4

PLOW HAND – a stand-alone

A GIRL CALLED ALABAMA

Thank you for choosing my books. An Amazon review would be greatly appreciated. Reviews are even better than chocolate-covered cherries!

Kay